Honeysuckle Rose

An Inspirational Novel

Doris Gaines Rapp

Daniel's House Publishing
in cooperation with
Never Alone Publishing

Name: Doris Gaines Rapp
Title: Honeysuckle Rose: An Inspirational Novel
Identifiers: LCCN: 2023902768
ISBN: 978-1-7365-110-7-7 (paperback)
          978-1-7365-110-8-4 (eBook)

Cover design: Debi Lindhorst, The Type Galley
Cover photo: Photo 128603380 © Katarzyna Bialasiewicz | Dreamstime.com

Subjects: 1. Fiction/Christian Romance/Mystery & Suspense
2. Health & Fitness/Alternative Therapies (Creativity and Music)
3. Music/Musicals

Published by Daniel's House Publishing
Huntington, Indiana
in cooperation with
Never Alone Publishing
Fort Wayne, Indiana

DEDICATION

Honeysuckle Rose is dedicated to all who have suffered trauma: physical, emotional, professional, or relational. All those deep wounds can bring us down. We must find new ways to rise above our injuries in order to begin living again. Even though the pain may continue to exist, God will be with us. The Lord didn't say he would take away all of our discomfort. He said, "Take my hand and I will walk with you." With your hand in his, let him pull you up. Be positive, and find new, loving, and creative ways to live for him every day of your life.

CONTENTS

ACKNOWLEDGMENTS

I want to thank my beta readers, Vicki Borgman and Donna Nehring. Your interest and support of my writing, my characters, and my stories, are a real blessing.

I also thank Kim Autrey, my editor and publisher at Never Alone Publishing. Your energy is amazing, your talent abounding, and your encouragement always present. Thanks Kim.

CHAPTER ONE

Where am I? Why can't I move? Aden could think clearly, but she couldn't form the words out loud. *I am so stiff. What is going on?* Even more strange was her attitude about her circumstance. She didn't care. *Am I a spirit stuck between heaven and earth? I've heard of that sort of thing.*

Ravaging pain was everywhere, yet she seemed separated from her agony, like she was here, and her body was over there. *Did I bump my head? What happened? Where am I?*

Wait a minute. I was talking to Mom. Where's my cell phone? She looked around the dim, dirty space with walls and ground of red brick. What had Mama said? Had we talked today, or was our last talk long ago? If I could find my phone, I'd call her.

Aden thought for a minute. If I can't remember what the important conversation was about, was it really so special? From off in a murky distance, she heard chanting.

"Aden! Aden!" an entire audience in the huge theater chanted. Aden watched the cheering crowd, like a movie projected on the brick wall. Ear-piercing whistles, raucous applause, and shouts of "Brava!" filled the theater. And that all happened just twenty minutes before. Aden was so excited her mouth dried until her lips stuck to her teeth. She tried to swallow as she waited in the wings for her curtain call.

Beautiful, Aden cringed. *My first Broadway starring role, and I look like I brushed my teeth with Elmer's Glue.* Aden stood in the theater wings in her alternate reality, waiting for the most important moment in her life.

As she watched her image flicker on the makeshift screen, she started to remember what had happened that evening. A curtain call was in process, and Aden was waiting in the theater wings.

The gravelly voice behind Aden startled her. Standing in the shadows, suddenly, a firm, clammy hand grabbed her shoulder. "Enjoy your moment. The light burns out fast."

Aden spun around and stared at the man behind her. "Chandler? You're backstage. Who's watching the ticket booth?"

"My assistant." The ticket booth manager smiled, but his expression seemed empty.

Aden's skin crawled. *What is his problem?* "Brighten up, Chandler. Hailey will take her bow soon. I know she's your favorite."

Chandler agreed, embarrassed. "That's why I'm back here." He grabbed Aden's arm again, but it wasn't to congratulate her. He seemed nervous.

When it was time for Aden's curtain call, the odd conversation with Chandler dissolved. As Aden darted into the spotlight, the audience jumped to their feet as a roaring ovation filled the auditorium. The lights, applause, music, and the fragrance of roses surrounded her with praise. How could she know what waited for her that night?

The star of the new Broadway musical, *My Honeysuckle Rose,* curtsied with pomp and flair. She felt weak, and her insides rattled from excitement. Aden Malloy from Ohio, a transplanted rose to the most exciting place in the world, had arrived.

Erupting in laughter and smiles, the cast and the entire audience broke into joyous song.

Honeysuckle Rose

Aden watched the wonderful memory play like a video in her mind. *How did it all happen so fast?* She knew it could all come crashing down; it always did. But … when? Aden questioned silently. *Is it real?*

CHAPTER TWO

Aden walked around aimlessly in some dim, misty place, lost and alone. Her fuzzy mind continued viewing an out-of-focus video of joy and fun that had happened recently. It came to her in snatches of memory. A group of people was on a stage, taking a bow. The images began to clear, and the details expanded. Aden watched it all, a full-screen movie of the last half hour of her life.

Theatergoers slowly started up the aisle of the ornate theater, clattering happily about the fabulous performance.

After the curtain finally closed, the cast scrambled off the stage, sweaty bodies bumping into each other. The house lights went up, sending a glimmer across the theater as the audience continued with laughter and chatter.

Caleb Johansson, the male lead, threw his head back and roared. "We did it, Aden!" He swept her off her feet with powerful arms that reminded Aden of a football player, not a Tony Award winner.

"Caleb," Aden sang out, eagerly tossing her arms around his neck. "We did do it! Opening night, the second Friday in October, is over. We survived. And we brought the house down!" She let go of her exhaustion and converted Caleb's energy into her own as she filled with a second wind.

Aden's close friend, Cindy Streeter, the dancer in the musical's dream sequence, floated by, laughing. "Jeff and I will join everyone over at Floyd's place to wait for the reviews to come in. You two are coming, right?" She excitedly fanned her face with her hand.

"I cannot imagine missing the wrap party," Aden said breathlessly, her mind bouncing off the musical, her friends in the show, and Caleb. "My parents are coming too. But I thought we were going to Sardi's."

Cindy flapped her arms in after-encore super-charged energy. "Floyd Blackstone seems to think he has to block out everyone's steps, on stage or off, even when he's not the choreographer."

Caleb continued to massage up and down the back of Aden's red costume. His fingers were strong and aggressive. "Go change into your street clothes, Babe, and get your coat."

Aden reluctantly pulled out of Caleb's arms and backed away, still clinging to his hand. "I'll start changing, but I'm going to wait for my parents. They came from Ohio to see me on opening night, and I want them to come to the star's dressing room. I've asked them to join us for the party."

"Okay," Caleb said slowly, "but I need to go ahead. Floyd asked me to pick up some Danish from the new bakery north of the theater." Caleb bounced across the small hall to his dressing room.

"That's all right, Caleb," Aden waved her hand. "You go on, and we'll meet you at Floyd's."

Aden turned to the dressing room with the big star-shaped plaque on the door and ran her fingers over the shiny brass emblem. "The star's dressing room," she whispered as she opened the door and inhaled the aroma of stage makeup and false eyelash adhesive remover. All the theater smells, mingled with the fragrance of huge baskets of roses, greeted her senses. She had dreamed of this evening since her high school production of *Oklahoma* and her role as Laurey to Scotty Russell's Curly.

"You're still here?" A dark, husky voice whispered from the partially open door.

Aden startled and grabbed her chest. "Chandler? You're everywhere tonight." She laughed a little. "Are you stalking me?"

"Just looking for Hailey." Chandler turned, then stopped. "Better hurry. Everybody's leaving." He looked down the hall. "It gets pretty dark and lonely when you're the last one here. Take it from me; I know."

"Bye, Chandler," Aden said quietly as the man walked away. Aden stared at her tired reflection in the mirror. The sparkle in her blue eyes was there, but dark circles underneath required heavier makeup with each application. Rehearsals for *Honeysuckle* had been torturous—dancing until her feet bled and singing until she was too hoarse to speak. But it was all worth it. It had to be, or nothing made sense anymore.

Aden took a deep breath and studied her image in the mirror. Echoing in that doubting corner of her mind was the stern voice of her sixth-grade teacher. "Who do you think you are?"

That same old self-doubt darted through Aden's mind as she tried to focus on all of the evening. "Stop it," she whispered to herself firmly. "I'll choose to think of other things." Slowly, she generously slathered a magical cleansing compound over her face. The aroma of white flowers and rosewater floated around her. The delicate perfume brought back old memories of singing and dancing with Scotty. She smiled faintly and focused on other, sweeter memories.

"Skeeter," she remembered Scotty asking after one of their high school musicals, "you need some help?" Her childhood friend scooped out a huge glob of cream and smeared it on her nose.

"Scotty," she scolded him with a laugh, "you will get yourself into a world of trouble. You forget I know your mother." Her happy heart ached for what was.

Aden suddenly stopped viewing the video on the wall and searched the dusty space in which she found herself among the bricks and clatter of the road. *What is this all about? Am I dreaming or is this a nightmare? Whatever it was, it happened soon after I took my curtain call. I'm so confused. My mind is bouncing all over. And why do I think about Scott? Through all the rehearsals for Honeysuckle, thoughts of Scotty kept slipping through my line readings and chorus rehearsals.*

Aden searched her pockets. She didn't have her phone, but she had it earlier. Where had she put it? Her spirit wandered between heaven and life. The earthly Aden heard the

piercing ring of her cell phone, and then the
phone suddenly appeared in her hand. The
loud tone nearly shattered her dream.

"Hello?"

Floating mysteriously between two worlds, Aden sat
again in front of her mirror at her dressing table.

"Honey, where are you?" her mother asked. "None of
the cast is here at Sardi's."

"Momma, you and Daddy were supposed to stay in the
theater and meet me backstage," Aden said with a smile.

"Aden, we are so mixed up," her mother sighed
heavily into the phone. "I thought I heard you say you
would ride with Caleb to Sardi's. It's my fault."

Aden pulled a tissue from the box. "No, it's my error.
It doesn't matter, anyway. They changed the cast party to
Floyd Blackstone's apartment."

"The one we drove past yesterday when your dad and I
got here?" her mother asked.

"Right," Aden said slowly as she thought for a
moment. "You two go on over to Floyd's. I'll meet you
there. I'm still pulling myself together."

"Okay. See you in a while."

Aden put down her phone. Did Scotty even remember
it was my opening night? He sent no flowers and no text
messages. Nothing. She took a deep breath. Why do I think
about him? He's out of my life now. He didn't come to
New York with me. We aren't a couple anymore.

Suddenly, she was aware of the hollow emptiness of
everything around her. From the hallway, she heard the
sound of footsteps and called out, "Hello?" Lost in her

memories, she had paid no attention to what the rest of the cast was doing or not doing. *Did Mom and Dad turn around?* She stopped and listened. "Mom?" All was quiet. But she had just told her parents to go to Floyd Blackstone's apartment. Again … she heard a rustling sound. "Hello?" There was only silence.

Aden smoothed the front of her black slacks and pulled on a white turtleneck sweater. Looking in the mirror, she whispered with a sigh, "Black and white. That's a New York thing."

The October night air would demand a warm cover-up. When she finished dressing, she wrapped a pale blue cashmere shawl around her shoulders. The luxurious softness caressed her body. With her small, silver evening purse in hand, she flipped off the light in her dressing room and suddenly chilled in the darkness.

The hall was eerily quiet. The only light came from the stage, accompanied by the distant hum of a large floor polisher.

"Aden." A deep voice from behind breathed his hot breath on her neck.

"Oh … Charley." She tried to compose herself when she turned and saw the janitor's assistant close behind her. She looked toward the man who still used the polishing machine.

"Oh, that's Phil," Charley flustered a little. "Sorry to frighten you."

"I wasn't frightened. I just didn't know the two of you were still cleaning up. I thought you were sweeping. Brooms are silent."

"There's extra clean-up since it was opening night. The flower petals and all," Charley explained.

"Yes, the petals. I hate to give you more work, Charley. But I sure would like some of those rose petals."

"Sure." Charley's gritty smile exposed a few missing teeth. "We'll collect some. I'll save them for you. We have to hurry. The anti-bacterial fog will be released in a few minutes."

Aden chuckled lightly and waved. "I'll get out of here so you two can finish your work." She turned toward the door. "Thanks, my friend."

"I'll see you get the flower petals, Miss Malloy. They were beautiful," he called after her.

Reaching the door to the alley, her cell phone split the silence. Aden checked the caller ID and smiled. "Mother?" she asked into the phone. "Did you get to Floyd's apartment?"

"We're still in the cab." Pat Malloy took a deep breath. "I was just getting worried. I felt uneasy."

Aden reached for the dented brass doorknob that opened the stage door into the alley. The knob felt hard and cold, far different from the warmth and safety of the spotlight. "I was so excited I may have said almost anything, Mom. I could have told you to meet me in Central Park, at the Alice in Wonderland statue. I've been living in my Wonderland for months."

"Is Caleb with you?" her mother asked.

"No. No one's here but me, Charley, and Phil. Phil's buffing the floor." Aden pulled her delicate wrap around her more tightly. "I'm just leaving." She took a few steps and listened to the cold, empty shadows of the alley. The familiar crisp autumn air mixed with whatever was in the dumpster, creating an unusual aroma.

Where the alley opened onto Forty-Fifth Street, a cacophony of horns, foot traffic chatter, and the squealing tires of taxis and buses was a blaring contrast to the alley's silence. The spicy smell of BBQ brisket came from the restaurant next door. It reminded Aden she hadn't eaten anything since that morning.

"Oh, Honey…" Pat's voice continued to talk on through the cell phone.

Suddenly, a dark figure slammed into Aden and knocked her phone to the ground. Her mother could hear the frightening sounds of thuds and scuffles.

Before Aden could yell out, she felt another blow and a sharp sting in her throat and right leg. The attack happened in seconds. As Aden slumped to the ground, her whole body burned. The hottest fires blazed in her neck and leg. Blood, gushing from her throat and calf, soaked into the high collar of her white sweater, and oozed down her silk pants. With a mighty tackle, the evil presence flipped her backward over the galvanized pipe of an outdoor stair railing. Aden landed, broken and motionless, on the top three steps, where the blaze in her body consumed her.

"Honey?" her mother's voice called from the phone. With a tremor in her voice, Pat asked again, "Aden?"

Aden heard nothing. Broadway's brightest new star was falling from the darkened sky.

CHAPTER THREE

After that vicious attack, Aden was no
longer conscious, but a spirit divided
between earth and heaven. Near Glory's
gate, her spirit tried to talk to those still
firmly planted on earth. That is the point in
Aden's life when heaven and earth collided.

Aden shook her head in confusion, hoping to clear her
thinking. Where was she? What year was it? Was this that
late summer day she sat on the front porch at home with her
mother, or was that several years ago? She remembered a
sunny morning several years before.

"No, Mama, I can't wait," Aden had protested that day.
"Scotty and the rest of the kids left for college a week ago.
They've already been meeting with their professors for
three days. I can settle in with Karen and Steve this
weekend if I leave for New York tomorrow. I'll have a few
days to find my way around the city before my acting
classes begin on Wednesday. Tomorrow, Mama. My ticket
is for tomorrow." Aden remembered that late August
morning. She was calm but determined. "Mom, you already
called Karen and told her when my plane lands."

"I know," her mother relented as the porch glider
moved back and forth. "Karen was my best friend in
college. I know she will take good care of you. But—"

"She will. And … I can take care of myself," Aden whispered. Her long-haired calico cat jumped on her lap, fluffed her silky coat, and rubbed her head on Aden's arms. "I sure will miss you, Miss Fluff."

Pat reached over and nuzzled Fluffy's ears. "Your Grandma and Grandpa Malloy are coming tomorrow. They want to help send you to the big city."

Aden tossed her head. "What do you think, Miss Fluff?" Then she thought of another plan. "I know. Grandma and Grandpa can meet us at the airport food court. We can eat and visit at the round tables there."

"That sounds doable. I'll call your grandmother." Pat pulled a tissue from her pocket. "I'm just so afraid for you, Honey." She blotted her eyes.

"Mama," Aden hugged her mother. "I'm staying with friends you trust. When I get a good part, I'll find an apartment, above the fifth floor, in a building with a doorman. I promise. I'll be fine."

Then her mother's voice faded, and Aden returned to the now that followed the assault. Stumbling around the alley outside the theater stage door, Aden could hear other faraway noises, street sounds, horns, and people laughing. Maybe everyone beyond the alley was unaware she was there, just yards away.

"I'll take care of myself," echoed in Aden's ears.

That's odd. Listening, one of the voices Aden heard sounded like her father. Then she heard him speak again. His voice sounded anxious as his words pushed through the fog of her unconsciousness.

"Aden?" Miles Malloy sounded shrill, terrified. Aden watched from a faraway someplace as her father desperately searched the dark corners of the alley.

Miles was a beloved minister of a medium-sized church with staff under him. He was used to organizing people around important issues and coming to biblical solutions. He could not just stand still. He always had to do something. For Miles, searching was his choice of hope over hopelessness.

There was a loud bang. Aden thought she heard the sound of the dented green dumpster lid dropping into place. *Don't be silly, Daddy. I'm not in there. What is he looking for? Daddy, I'm over here.* Aden felt light and free as she swirled around, using the dance steps from scene two. *What did you think of the musical, Daddy? How did I do? Hey ... why don't you look at me? Don't you see me?* Aden could see her mother staring at the dumpster, wringing her hands.

"No, Miles. No." Pat's voice sounded panicked. "She's not in there. She can't be." Her brows were knit together in anguish.

Aden called out as if in a fog, *I'm here, Mama. Why can't you both see me? Did you like the play?* She bowed deeply and did a soft-shoe dance step over to the end of the alley: shuffle, ball, back cross, step.

Caleb Johansson came staggering aimlessly into the ghostly alley. Aden saw him searching frantically everywhere for something. Yet, Caleb seemed to see nothing.

Caleb, you came to get me. Thank you. Aden tried to take his arm and dance around the alley like their routine on stage. Her hand passed right through the crook of

Caleb's arm. *Why is everyone ignoring me? I'm right here.* Aden watched from a place beyond the reality of the alley, a place of haze and twinkle dust.

The light above the stage door sign gleamed in the night, casting eerie shadows all along the perimeter of the crusty red brick space. The alley dead-ended where the theater building connected to the after-hours diner to the south. No one came into the alley unless they were going somewhere backstage in the theater.

"Her phone," Pat whispered hoarsely as she slowly bent to pick up Aden's cellular telephone.

There it is. Aden tried to reach for the phone but couldn't connect. *I wondered where it was.*

Pat gasped. "The screen is broken. Oh, Miles …" she choked. "If she dropped her phone accidentally, she would have picked it up. She hasn't gone anywhere without her cell phone since she was twelve years old."

May I have my phone, please? Aden stomped her foot and wanted to yell, but no sound came. Mom, the last time you grounded me from my phone, I was fourteen, not nearly twenty-four.

Caleb stared at the cold brick-and-mortar that surrounded them. "But … where is she?"

If I could get my phone, I would call you. No one seems to hear me talking when I'm right here. Maybe Mom and Dad wouldn't hear me on the phone either.

Miles shook his head like he was trying to put the pieces together. "Caleb, Aden should be at Blackstone's apartment. Didn't she go with you?"

I already told you, Aden joined in, oblivious to her strange circumstances. Caleb and you guys were supposed to meet me at the cast party. If you don't listen to me, you will remain confused.

"No, we were to go separately. I had to stop for pastries." Caleb stopped with his hands on his hips and looked out toward the street. "I wasn't at Floyd's for very long. He asked me to run out for more Danish and doughnuts."

Pat's eyes snapped up sharply. "But … you didn't. When you came here, you were empty-handed."

Sputtering, Caleb tried to explain. "I just got to the bakery the second time when you called. You said something had happened to Aden, and I came right back to the theater." Tears pooled in the corners of his eyes.

Was the bakery Lotta Dough? Aden asked as she twirled around on the brick pavement. *I love that pastry shop.*

Pat looked away. "You should have stayed with her."

Caleb's shoulders slumped. "I went to Blackstone's apartment because Aden said she would follow me. Then I went back to the bakery. That's all I know."

That's right, Caleb. Aden raised her arms in triumph. You remembered. We were all meeting at Sardi's, where they'd have plenty of food. Then the plans changed to Floyd's apartment. She stopped. Then Mama called and … oh wow, my throat hurts. Trying to soothe her neck with her hand, she worried. I'd better get out of this night air. Laryngitis will be my next complaint.

"Baby!" her dad gasped as he stared into the black pit of the outside basement stairwell. "Oh, no, please God … no!"

What's happening? Aden tried to see where her father was looking.

Miles forced one foot onto the upper step of the stagnant stairwell and struggled to get to something on the stairs. "Patty, come and help me."

Aden stomped her foot again and crossed her arms. I'm not down there on the stairs, Daddy. I'm over here. What are you trying to do?

"Check her pulse," Caleb pleaded. His body hung over the railing as he anxiously watched. "Let me down there. I'll pick her up and carry her up here."

Aden's entire body shuddered. *Oh, no.* Moaning and weary, Aden moved over to the stairs. The closer she got to the steps, the weaker she felt and the greater her pain, especially in her throat.

"No!" Pat shouted. "Don't move her." She reached through the stair rails with trembling hands and lifted a limp wrist. "It's faint … but she has a pulse." She searched Caleb's face. "Caleb! Call 9-1-1."

Aden tried to get Caleb's attention. She frowned when she touched his shoulder. She didn't understand why she couldn't feel the tweed of his jacket or the strength of his arm beneath the cloth.

Caleb's hands trembled. He jerked his cell phone from his pocket and dialed. Pacing, he raked his fingers roughly through his hair. "Hello? Someone has been …" He looked toward the steps with frightened, hopeless eyes. "She's hurt. I don't know what happened. Come quick. She's unconscious … and," he gagged involuntarily, "there's blood everywhere. We're in the alley beside the Whiteway Theater, at the stage door entrance. Hurry!"

Aden's father stood up and studied the scene. Aden's head was lower than her feet as her body sprawled down the steps. "I agree. We shouldn't move her. We could hurt her more." Shaking his head, he whispered in desperation, "But this is awful. I have to do something."

"Miles." Pat knelt on the third step and slid her hand under Aden's blood-soaked hair. "I can't leave her like this—upside down. The blood is rushing out of her wounds."

Blood? Aden asked. What wounds? What are you talking about? You're scaring me.

Miles reached for the pink scarf Pat had around her neck. "Being upside-down might act as traction for her." He tugged on the corner of the fabric. "Quick, use your scarf to apply pressure to her neck. Maybe you can stop the bleeding."

Aden touched her neck. *Is it bad?* She was breathy and faltering. With her eyes fixed on Caleb, Aden listened and watched.

Caleb paced back and forth. "We don't know what's wrong with her." He slapped his hand to his mouth. "What if her neck is broken?" He seemed to choke on his words. "If she's moved, we could cripple her."

Cripple me? It all made no sense to Aden. No … I have to dance and perform tomorrow. I like to go shopping … and live my life. Don't hurt me.

"Caleb," Pat snapped, "don't say such a thing. Aden's neck cannot be broken." Pat pulled off the fine designer scarf she bought at a Fifth Avenue boutique that morning, wadded it into a ball, and applied it with pressure to the gash in Aden's throat.

That feels better, Mama, Aden whispered in silence. Your touch always makes my scrapes feel better.

"Caleb's right, Patty," Miles agreed reluctantly. "Be careful. If we move her—." His eyes searched the outer street.

At the clop, clop of a police horse, Miles hurried to the alley entrance. "Over here!" he shouted frantically.

A mounted officer squinted into the dim alley. "You need help?"

Pat called from the shadows. "She's hurt. Help us!"

"Yes, ma'am." The mounted officer rode into the alley. "How did it happen?"

Pat gritted her teeth. "How?" Shaking her head, she took a deep breath. "We just found her. We don't know anything. She needs an ambulance."

Miles ran over to the steps. "She was to meet us for a cast party but she didn't show up. Patty called her. She was okay at first. Then … a scuffle and her cell phone went dead."

Caleb's eyes seemed vacant. "We came looking for her."

The officer looked around. "Why was she in the alley?"

Caleb looked at him in disbelief. "She came out of the theater. It's opening night."

"Right," the police officer mumbled. "The ambulance will be here soon; the hospital isn't far. Detectives will have more questions for you. They'll meet you at the hospital."

At the wail of a siren, Miles ran back to the street. "They're coming!" he shouted.

Aden heard the moaning sound of the ambulance. I changed my mind. No, I don't want to move. I just want to go to sleep. That would be wonderful. The strain of hard work on the body can only be cured by a long sleep.

Miles waved frantically at the rescue team, directing them into the alley. "She's over here."

Aden heard the hurried movements. It came from somewhere outside herself.

Bright lights from the emergency vehicle's cabin flooded the alley. An EMT jumped out of the cab, hurried to the back of the rescue vehicle, and opened the double doors. "Excuse me," the medical worker said as he swung the gurney down to the pavement and followed Miles to the stairwell. "I'm Nick. You may need my name at the hospital."

Caleb stood motionless above the steps. His hands gripped the railing.

The officer dismounted. "Ma'am, please stand back."

A paramedic bent over Aden's body and lifted her hand. He nodded to Nick, his partner. "I've got a pulse. Get a large compression to stop the bleeding around her throat and a neck brace. I might need compression for her leg, too."

The policeman spread his arms. "Stand back a little more, folks. Let them work."

Nick's kind voice was to assure Pat and Miles. "We'll take real good care of your friend."

"She's …" Pat choked. "She is our daughter."

"Yes, ma'am."

The paramedic applied the compression to Aden's neck and held it there. After checking a few times, he grabbed the padded neck support, wrapped it around Aden's neck, and fastened it. With speed and expertise, the two attendants slid a backboard carefully under Aden's body.

Aden could feel the men moving around her, working on her like a lifeless rag doll. *Oh, no, what are they doing now?*

"On my count," the paramedic commanded. "One, two, three." They placed Aden's bleeding body on the gurney.

Oh ... Aden's head spun, and her stomach rolled with each movement, rotation, rattle, and bump of the gurney as they thrust her into the ambulance. *Be careful. It feels like my back is numb. I don't know why. Why do I hurt so much? Did I pull a muscle in my back when I was dancing? No ... I don't remember what happened to me.*

Nick pulled the key from his pocket. The paramedic climbed into the back with Aden. "Two of you are related to this woman, right?"

Pat nodded. "We are her parents."

Caleb said nothing. His labored, shallow breathing trapped words in his throat.

"Ma'am," the paramedic gestured toward Pat. "Jump in with your daughter." He helped her in, then motioned to Miles and Caleb. "You guys get a cab and follow us to Mount Sinai Hospital West, on Tenth Avenue."

They had to get to the hospital in time. Inside, Pat folded her hands over her bleeding daughter and prayed.

CHAPTER FOUR

Miles and Caleb were left standing, numbly watching the taillights of the ambulance pull away. Looking at Caleb, Miles stepped into action. "Let's go. You call Blackstone from the cab and let him know what's going on." Miles turned without looking back, hurried to the street, and tried to stop the first taxi that passed.

Miles saw the ambulance pull into the first lane of traffic and speed off, its siren blaring. Left standing in the street, alive with the hustle of nightlife traffic, Miles edged out farther, demanding his turn at a taxicab. All the vehicles were doing the possessive dance of the avenue, inching into their special lane of traffic. As drivers squabbled about their rite of passage, each bus and cab made their way forward. Finally, Miles stepped into the near traffic lane and waved his arms hysterically. If the other drivers weren't going to stop, they would have to run him down.

Caleb quickly grabbed his arm. "Miles, this is New York City. Get out of the street."

"No. I'm going to make one of those cabs stop." He jerked his arm out of Caleb's grasp.

The horseshoes clopping along the brick alley echoed back onto the street. The officer blew one short bleep on a whistle.

A Yellow cab slowed, and the driver leaned out of the window. "Hey Buddy, you tryin' to get yourself killed?"

He pounded the top of his cab with his left hand. "Officer, get him outta the street."

"Please … stop," Miles yelled. He raised both hands in front of him like a shield.

The cabbie gestured wildly for Miles to move out of the way. "What's goin' on?" the taxi driver asked when the officer motioned for him to pull over. The driver didn't wait for the answer. Miles' grief, written in smeared blood on his face, was enough to tell him everything. "Where to, officer?"

"Mount Sinai Hospital on Tenth."

Caleb grabbed the door handle. "We're following an ambulance. His daughter, my … friend, might have been attacked." Then he pointed to the huge sign mounted above the theater. "That's Aden Malloy, the star. She was … is … very beautiful." His voice trailed off to a whisper.

"Thanks, Buddy." The officer saluted the cabbie and turned his horse west toward Forty-Fifth Street.

"Stay safe," the cab driver called out the window in the officer's direction.

The mounted policeman touched his finger to his hat, pulled on his horse's reins, and directed the animal into the traffic.

Miles threw himself in the back of the cab and squared his shoulders, steeling himself for what might be ahead. Caleb quickly followed, slumping by the window. The two men sat at a distance in the back of the cab, saying nothing. Miles grabbed the strap by the door to steady himself as the driver swerved in and out of traffic. He watched the people hurry by on the sidewalk but saw very little.

It became uncomfortably silent in the back of the taxi. The unspoken words hung over them like a storm cloud. As the driver slowed at each traffic light, they could hear the conversations of strangers walking by on the sidewalk. Miles and Caleb continued in silence.

One man wearing a Mets cap pulled on a woman by the hand. Her high heels slowed her to a choppy clop. "Hurry up, Holly. I told Jason we'd meet them for a late dessert five minutes ago."

Miles thought of Aden. She was never late for anything. She danced her way through every activity, whether darting up to the corner to catch the bus, or running upstairs, two steps at a time. Miles wondered if his precious daughter would ever be able to walk again.

"Caleb," he began without turning in the man's direction. "I know it wasn't your fault. Someone…" Mile's voice cracked and caught in his throat. "Someone attacked my baby, and I wasn't there to protect her."

"Thank goodness I wasn't there," Caleb said as his breath escaped. "There would be nothing left of the show if we were both injured."

Miles clenched his fists. He had never hit anyone, but Caleb's self-centered attitude was more than he could take.

The two passengers rode on for several blocks in silence. There was nothing left to say … except to God.

CHAPTER FIVE

12 Midnight

The music of the street filtered into the cabin of the ambulance. The humming of the motor, the rise and rhythm of the cab, made a tempo that soothed Aden's pain-racked body. She thought she heard Scotty whisper in her ear for a brief moment and felt comforted. Memories of high school performances carried her out of her pain and into Scotty's arms.

Flashes of her high school prom floated through her traumatized mind. In her daze, she could still feel the soft fabric of her full red dress and the pinch of her high shoes. Aden and Scotty swirled into the center of the party with all their friends watching that memorial night. They practiced the music he had written just for them on the front porch of Aden's house. Their special music whirled softly while Aden smiled inside.

Let's Dance

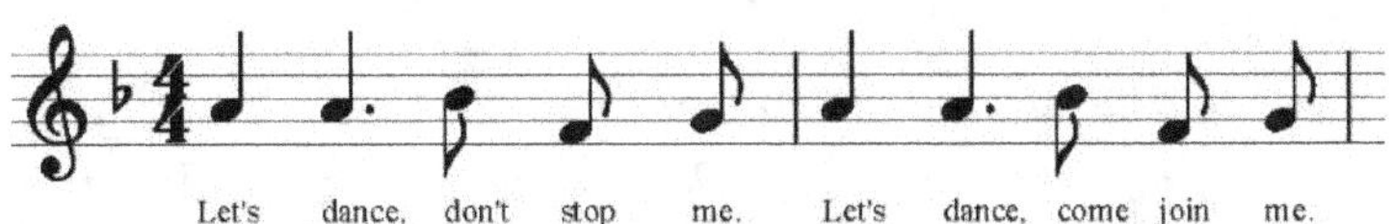
Let's dance, don't stop me. Let's dance, come join me.

Stay close while the mus - ic plays

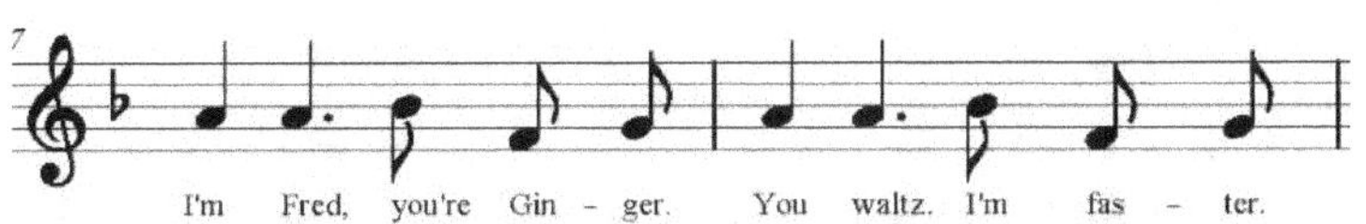
I'm Fred, you're Gin - ger. You waltz. I'm fas - ter.

Stay close while the mus ic plays. Dan cing shoes keep mov in.

Hap py feet keep twir - rling. Hold me close while dan - cing,

so I know you're near. Lis - ten to my new beat

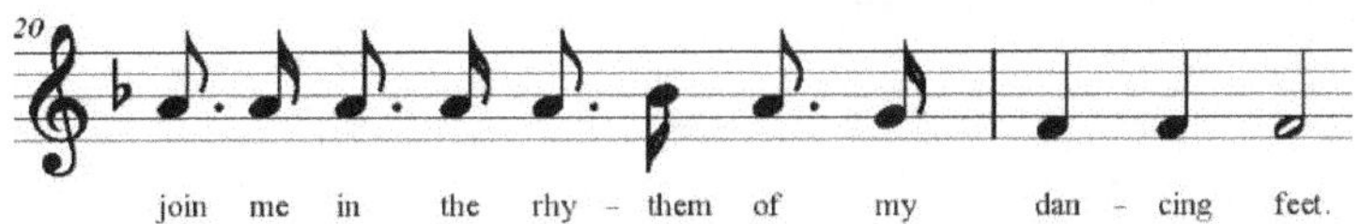
join me in the rhy - them of my dan - cing feet.

Then, the melody faded.

Is the ambulance stopping? Where are we? They'll move me again. I don't think I can stand the pain. What did the man say? Mount Sinai? The hospital? Maybe they'll give me some aspirin or something.

Aden couldn't see the sign. "The Crime Victims Treatment Center at Mount Sinai." But she could feel the hustle. *I don't want to go in. I'll just close my eyes and sleep. I am so tired.*

Suddenly, the hospital emergency room doors burst open. People in blue scrubs raced out, and their crisp white thick-soled shoes pounded on the entry pavement. Riding in the cabin with Aden, Pat frantically searched for medical workers at the ER entrance. Her eyes caught the wording over the door and was comforted when she saw the name of the hospital, Mount Sinai Hospital. Pat read about their special unit the Sunday before, before everything. Now, she was escorting her daughter into the trauma unit.

Pat jumped and grabbed her throbbing head when the back doors flew open. She tried to maneuver out of the way as Nick grabbed the handle on the side of the gurney.

"Hop out, ma'am," he said crisply as he started to move Aden. Pat's legs felt wobbly and weak. But she had to move. She took Nick's hand and slipped out of the ambulance with his help.

Aden was unconscious as the EMS raced her toward the door, but somehow, she knew her mother wasn't by her side anymore. *Mama, don't leave me*, Aden screamed helplessly in her head. *I don't know this place. I want to go home.*

The trauma team stormed through the double doors, one emergency worker on each side of Aden's wheeled stretcher. Time was vital, and Pat couldn't keep up. She ran frantically to match the pace of the gurney. Once Pat was by Aden's side again, she stayed near her as they rushed down the hall, trying to keep up, anxiously attempting to hold Aden's hand. Stained with her sweet daughter's blood, Pat's shirt and evening wrap were of no consequence. Her hair, scrambled from its fancy style, had fallen on her face, but she didn't notice. The only thing that mattered was Aden.

"In here." A nurse directed the medical team into a cold, sterile white exam area.

People Patty didn't know and had no choice but to trust, took her daughter away. The place was a swirl of activity, with personnel running in and out. Each pressed the antiseptic pump hanging on the wall before entering the exam cubical. Pat could smell the distinct deep cleansing of the hand sanitizer and wondered if her own hands were carrying disease. She shoved them into her pockets. A patient in the adjoining cubical moaned loudly, but nothing roused Aden.

"On my count. One, two, three," the paramedic called out as Nick helped him swing Aden onto the exam table.

Oh, be careful. I hurt. Mama, where are you? Aden silently called to her mother as the medical personnel took over, pushing Pat to the side. *No, wait. Come back, Mama.*

Pat gasped and held her breath. "She squeezed my hand. I know she did. She squeezed my hand."

"That's a good sign." The paramedic rattled off more information to an ER nurse. "Patient's name is Aden Malloy. ID and other information are in her purse."

The drawn curtains fluttered and snapped back and forth. Strangers, people moving Aden here and there at their whim, were busily darting in and out of the space. It almost made Pat dizzy. Something did.

A young doctor with a tattoo on his right forearm rushed in. Pat's mind darted to the ink art and wondered if the image would rub off on Aden's skin. Shaking her head to clear her silly thoughts, she watched as the doctor flashed a bright light into her daughter's eyes. A nurse on the other side of the examining table cut the high collar from around Aden's bloody neck. Pat could see that the bleeding had stopped, and clotting began. The flood of sticky red vital fluid down the front of her daughter's beautiful clothes bore evidence of the amount of blood she had already lost.

Why won't you listen to me? You're cutting my new shirt. I just bought this yesterday, Aden screamed in her head. She felt the bright light's heat above her as she drifted in and out of consciousness. There was a bustle of all those around her, but she couldn't make anyone hear her.

"Her breathing is shallow, doctor," the nurse announced, then looked closely at Aden's face. "Her face is tight and drawn down. I know she's in pain."

The spotlight's bright. Aden's unconscious mind swapped the glare of the intense medical light for the glory of the stage. *Look, Caleb, they're ready for our curtain call.*

In the whirling pain and confusion, Aden relived her time at center stage over the last … how many years? Several high school productions and then New York City. It was far more than six years. She was already twenty-three and a half.

I love you, Baby Girl. She remembered Caleb's confession, admitted that night of the dress rehearsal. *We make a great team,* he boasted. *You bring out my best in everything.*

A familiar song rang out in the distance. *Loving you, loving you, along the way, every day.* But it wasn't Caleb's face she saw in the scenes that played like her own life movie. In her unconscious, foggy dream, she took Scotty's hand as they danced to the music only Aden could hear.

I'm your Fred. You're my Ginger. Scotty laughed and twirled Aden around in a carefree spin. *Don't fall. We're moving.*

I could dance with you all night. Aden's heart was pounding. Odd, she'd never been short of breath while dancing.

Be careful. Aden heard Caleb caution as he twirled her around in her daze. *You'll trip me, Baby Girl.*

Aden's confusion mounted. *Caleb? But I thought I was dancing with Scotty. Where are you, Scotty?*

From somewhere came a presence. *Right here, Aden.* She felt her dance partner's hand in hers. *Stay with me,* she thought Scotty begged. *Stay with me.*

"Aden, Aden," she heard a strange voice call to her. It wasn't Caleb or Scotty. "Come on back, Aden. Stay with us." The doctor's words were strong and confident.

But the awake world was too real for Aden. *No, I want to stay here with Scotty. I want to run away from everything and yet stay right here. It hurts too much over there.*

CHAPTER SIX

12:45 a.m.

Pat followed Aden's gurney and more medical personnel as they ran into the examining cubical. Standing beside her daughter's blood-stained clothes, Pat's head started to swim as a wave of nausea flooded across her. Aden lay so still that her motionless body frightened her mother.

What's wrong, Mama? Aden asked from within the pain and fog.

Pat wrung her hands, not knowing yet the extent of Aden's injuries. Part of Aden's face and neck were covered in her own vital fluid. It looked to Pat like two black eyes were forming across Aden's beautiful face. Pat's eyes, rimmed with tears, swam in a sea of fear as she momentarily hurried out of the room and entered the hall near the nurses' station. Her head swirled, so she gripped the wide desk with both hands. Feeling faint, she rested her forehead on her arms.

A short, round lady in blue scrubs put her arm around Pat's waist. "Come on, honey. My name is Charlotte. Come with me. You can rest in the waiting room." Charlotte led the way into a large area with comfortable red chairs, racks of family-friendly magazines, and a gigantic television screen. "There's a coffee pot over there." She pointed to the hospitality center in the corner of the room. "There are candy bars and chips in the machines outside the door in a small vending space." Charlotte nodded in the direction of the machines as she hurried out. "I'll check on Aden and be right back."

Numb from worry, Pat looked blankly around the room. Why was it so hard to breathe? Short of breath, she couldn't stand any longer. She slipped down onto one of the club chairs, wringing her hands. Pulling the blood-drenched, cape-like wrap tightly around her with trembling hands, the fabric felt soft and warm against her skin. Pat called after Charlotte as the nurse started out of the waiting room, "You'll tell me as soon as you know something?"

"Patty?" Miles darted into the waiting room with Caleb close behind. Miles, mussed and crumpled, moved methodically, like a minister accustomed to dealing with a family crisis. Blood spots dotted his white shirt.

Pat jumped up. "Miles, you're here."

"How's she doing?" Miles and Caleb burst out in unison.

> Aden's out-of-body spirit sat on the back of a chair in the waiting room and listened. *Hi, Caleb,* she sang out, but no one seemed to listen.

Pat sat down quickly. Her head felt light and woozy. "I don't know yet. A nurse, Charlotte, said she'd let me know as soon as they have something to tell us. I think they lost her a few times."

Caleb paced back and forth on the gray, figured floor tile. "I can't believe this is happening to me … to Aden."

Aden shook her head. *What happened to Caleb? Funny, I never noticed before. You make everything about yourself.*

Charlotte walked crisply back into the waiting area with a man in green scrubs. "Mr. and Mrs. Malloy, I see Caleb Johansson is here." She nodded, then smiled at Caleb. "My husband and I were at the opening tonight performance before coming in for the late shift."

Pat rubbed her aching forehead. "Was that tonight?"

Aden stopped drifting from person to person, her eyes wide in surprise. *Opening night was tonight?*

"Yes, honey." Charlotte patted Pat's shoulder. "Mr. and Mrs. Malloy, this is Dr. Meyers."

The doctor was tall and muscular. His scrub shirt rippled across his arms and chest. Pat saw strength in his physique, which quickly translated to hope.

"Doctor," Pat began as she grabbed Miles' arm for comfort and support. "How is Aden doing?"

"Let's sit down." The doctor led them back to a small conversation area. In the center of a cluster of chairs, a circular wooden coffee table supported stuff people could no longer hold. Dr. Meyers rested his forearms on his knees, removed his scrub cap, and raked his fingers through his hair. "We lost her a few times, but she's doing much better. She's not conscious yet, but you can go in shortly."

Aden rose and drifted out of the waiting room.

Worried, Pat threw her hand to her mouth and moaned slightly. Her heart pounded as she grabbed her chest. The doctor's words were more than she could absorb. Pat said nothing but fixed her eyes on the medical man who held Aden's life in his hands.

Dr. Meyers looked at Pat and spoke gently. "She won't be able to talk. She shouldn't even try. I've called in an otolaryngology surgeon who will repair any damage to her vocal cords and close the wound. There won't be much of a scar. The wound appears clean, not jagged or missing any skin or tissue."

"Will she be able to sing?" Caleb fidgeted with his phone, then shoved it back into his pocket.

"Sing?" Dr. Meyers asked with raised eyebrows. "I don't know. We'll have to see how she heals."

Caleb rolled his eyes. "That's what she does, doctor. She sings." Caleb's voice was stiff and uncompromising.

"Oh, I didn't know," Dr. Meyers added. "She sings?"

"Yes." Pat looked away from Caleb and pulled up straighter. "She's the star of a new Broadway musical. It opened tonight." She cleared her throat, almost in sympathy with Aden's pain. "My question is, will she be able to talk?"

"We won't know that yet either." Dr. Meyers leaned back and folded his arms across his chest. He looked up at the wall clock. "It'll be hours before we can pull all the answers together."

Pat hadn't even noticed a clock or much else around her. It was after midnight. How was that possible? Her insides rattled and churned.

"And her leg, doctor?" Miles questioned. "What about walking? My mother used a wheelchair for a while. We still have it in storage."

Caleb paced back and forth. "A wheelchair?" he snapped. "What about dancing?"

"Dancing?" Dr. Meyers' tossed his scrub cap lightly around in his hands. "I can tell you the slash in her leg isn't deep, and the bone is intact. We've stopped the bleeding and repaired the muscle. A cosmetic plastic surgeon is on her way to put in the final stitches. You shouldn't even be able to see where it happened."

"So," Caleb sighed in relief, "we will be able to dance."

"After physical therapy, her leg will hopefully heal enough to put her tap shoes back on. We'll have to see how she does." Dr. Meyers rubbed his arms. "The other, greater concern is her back."

"Her back?" Pat blurted out. "She was stabbed in the back, too?" A distant siren broke into Pat's world, adding an aura of dread. Clutching Miles' arm, she clung to her rock of twenty-six years.

"No … no," the doctor assured her with a softening in his voice and a touch of his hand. "I'm sorry, Mrs. Malloy, no."

"Dr. Meyers. Please answer the call," the loudspeaker interrupted.

"Excuse me," he stepped to the door. "I'll be right back."

"No, please …" Pat begged as the doctor walked out of the room.

Charlotte immediately filled in the information Pat and Miles desperately needed. "No, Mrs. Malloy, Aden wasn't stabbed in the back. But remember, she was flipped over that stair railing."

"Oh, yes, yes." Pat pushed her hair back from her forehead and held her bangs down with her fingers as if forcing them to stay in place.

"Remember, they have already taken an x-ray," Charlotte explained. "The computerized results will be sent very soon."

"Good," Dr. Meyers announced as he burst into the waiting room. "An orthopedic surgeon has read Aden's back x-ray."

"And…?" Caleb asked as he scooted to the edge of his chair. His body was rigid; the heel of his right foot bounced up and down frantically.

"Her spine appears to be intact," Dr. Meyers began again. "It wasn't severed … and the vertebrae don't appear to be fractured. But …"

Pat held her breath. "But?"

"While most of her spinal column is okay, it looks like a disc, probably two, in the lumbar area is ruptured. That will require immediate repair."

"Will that keep her from walking or dancing?" Caleb asked again.

Dr. Meyers smiled. "Ortho surgeons do disc repair and replacement every day with immense success. They may decide to inject some surgical cement to repair it."

"Oh my," Pat breathed out slowly. "Surgery to fix the discs and another operation to fix her throat. And … she still hasn't regained consciousness."

"I checked after that phone call. Your daughter is coming around." Dr. Meyers offered a broad smile. "You can see her for a minute before she's prepped for surgery. She won't be able to talk and may not be awake enough to understand why she can't say anything. I don't want her upset or frustrated just minutes before a procedure. Kiss her and tell her you will see her later."

"All right." Pat tried to stand on weak legs.

Cindy hurried into the waiting room, followed by Jeff Brukowski, her eager, on-again-off-again dancer/boyfriend. "Mrs. Malloy, I'm Cindy Streeter, and this is Jeff. We're dancers in the show. I just heard about Aden's accident. I'm a friend of hers and had to rush over and see how she is doing."

Trembling in exhaustion and fear, Pat touched Cindy's hand. "Yes, Aden told me about you. The attacker slashed her leg and throat and threw her over a railing, breaking some vertebrae. She's ready to go into surgery right now." Pat started to follow Charlotte. "Cindy, leave your number at the nurses' station, and I'll call you when we know more."

"Great." Cindy seemed to exhale all the air inside her. "Jeff and I will go back to Floyd's and let everyone know what happened." She reached up and gave Pat a light kiss on the cheek. "I'll wait to hear from you."

Dr. Meyers looked at Caleb. "Just family, please."

Miles jumped up and grabbed Pat's waist. "Are you okay?"

"Yes, I think." Her shoulders felt heavy, but she squared them as best she could and put her hand on her husband's arm to steady her balance. "Come, Caleb. Tonight, you're family, too. Perhaps … a brother."

CHAPTER SEVEN

Late Friday night – 1:30 a.m.

Charlotte crisply led the way to the examination area where Aden lay. "She is still pretty beat up, don't worry. She's unconscious again but is improving. Aden is right down here."

The outer hub in the wide hall encircling the nurses' station was a buzzing beehive of activity. An aide helped an elderly man into a wheelchair as blood dripped from a gash on his forehead. Two large brown eyes peered fearfully from behind a woman's leg as she carried another child, limp and asleep in her arms. The youngest boy's cheeks were bright red. One lonely man, rubbing his eyes, sat alone on a bench sobbing. He buried his head in his trembling hands as his body sagged into a crumpled state. The smell of a janitor's disinfectant caused Pat to grab her nose and mouth as they passed a team of cleaning people. The strong, clean smell penetrated Pat's sinuses like a knife blade. Those who were hurting, broken, and bleeding flooded the area. Patty began to stagger as she touched the wall to steady herself.

"Are you okay?" Miles asked as he looked back at his wife, slowing down to match her pace.

"I feel strange," Pat admitted, whispering. "The room is closing in, and my chest feels tight."

Miles stopped immediately and put his arm around her waist. "Do you need a doctor?"

"I'll get a nurse," Caleb offered.

"No, Caleb, no," Pat protested. "We have to get to Aden. I was overcome when I saw all those sick people when Aden was hurt so badly. Hurry."

"Right in here," Charlotte directed, following a doctor.

Aden lay limp and still on the white sheets, now stained red. Barely drifting in and out of consciousness, she tried to understand what had happened. Someone outside the tiny exam room said, "If she were my daughter, I'd thank the Lord she was still alive."

Aden's overwhelmed family followed the medical staff into the exam area. The doctor patted the sheet that covered Aden's feet. "Hi, Aden. I'm Dr. Meyers." He spoke out with energy and strength. "I know you may be confused. You can't talk now, and … I don't want you to try."

Aden wanted to force her eyes open. Was that Scotty who spoke to her a few minutes ago? Or was Caleb there? *I want to talk;* she demanded inside herself. *You have to listen to me. I'm in pain. Where's Caleb?*

Pat balanced herself on Miles' steady arm as the three stood behind the medical personnel, out of the way. She glimpsed at Aden through flying elbows and shoulders as they bent to attend to her daughter. Patty was in full view of the monitor machines that clung to Aden's arms and beeped indifferently. It all seemed so cold and sterile.

Aden opened her mouth, but no sound came out. *I'm confused? Of course, I am. Why can't I talk?* Her eyes filled with fear, and tears flooded down her cheeks.

"It's okay, Aden," Dr. Meyers said as he smiled, massaging her foot. "We don't want you to talk … so good … I'm glad you're not trying." He picked up Aden's foot an inch or two and patted it lightly with the tip of his finger. "Are you awake enough to feel me touch your foot?"

Yes, I can feel you touching my foot. Well … sorta. She nodded slightly. But it feels like all of my skin has gone to sleep.

Pat gulped and held her breath. She suspected Dr. Meyers was assessing Aden's reflexes. Could Aden still feel her graceful, dancing feet? When Pat saw Aden bat her eyes, she exhaled deeply.

"Great!" The doctor smiled broadly. "I take the eye blinks to mean *yes*. You can blink once for yes and twice for no." He feather-touched Aden's foot again. "Okay, make sure I understand Bambi's eye blinks." He laughed lightly. "Are you able to feel this?" He rubbed the top of Aden's right foot.

Aden blinked once. Yes, I can feel that, even with the dead-skin feeling.

"And this?" he questioned as he softly stroked her left foot.

Aden's lips turned up slightly as she paused in silence and blinked once. *I can feel that better than the other one.*

Miles and Pat threw their arms in the air triumphantly. "Praise the Lord," Miles shouted.

The corners of Aden's mouth turned up slightly. *Daddy, I can hear you.* She started to slowly reach for her throat.

Dr. Meyers quickly took both of her hands in his. "Aden, do you remember what happened to you?"

Remember? Did something happen? Yes, someone ... Aden's eyes grew large with terror. Pulling her hands from the doctor's grip, she tried to grab the compresses at her throat. *Get him off me. Help! Someone, get him off me.*

Dr. Meyers quickly reached for her hands again while talking calmly. "Yes, Aden. There was damage to your throat after opening night. After your mom and dad give you a kiss, we'll fix that for you."

Aden jerked her right hand free and put her thumb and first two fingers together, creating a talking gesture. Her eyes searched for her mother's face, knowing she could interpret for her. *Mama, tell them what I'm asking. Will I be able to talk? Can I sing?*

"Will you be able to talk?" Dr. Meyers asked the question for her. He responded, "Not the first day or two. But, yes, your neck will heal."

Aden relaxed and blinked rapidly, seeming to be relieved. *Good, good.*

"Now, Mom, Dad, kiss her on the forehead, and we'll whisk her off for repairs. We'll check under the hood and tighten down anything that's loose."

I'm not an old Chevy. Aden wished she could tell him.

Pat moved closer, leaned over, and lightly kissed Aden's brow. "I don't want to get too close. I'm afraid I'll hurt you more if I touch you. We don't want another screw coming loose." Pat kissed her again. "I love you, Sweetie. We'll wait for you in the waiting room."

I love you, Mama.

Miles took Aden's hand in his and bowed for a second. "The Lord will be with you, Baby. Your mom and I will be here when you wake up." Kissing her cheek, he squeezed her hand.

Thanks, Daddy.

"I'm sorry to interrupt," a woman with dark hair and large glasses stepped inside the tiny room. "I'm Detective Angela Alverez."

"Detective," Dr. Meyers spoke up. "Miss Malloy can't talk right now."

Alverez removed a small notepad from her pocket. "I just have a few questions."

"Sorry. It's not that our patient doesn't want to talk," Dr. Meyers explained bristly. "She cannot." The doctor gestured with his hand across his neck.

The detective looked over the doctor's shoulder at Aden, still stained, clotted, and beaten. Alverez was strong yet gentle. "Aden, I'm Detective Angela Alverez. I know your injury won't let you speak. As you remember what happened, please write it down." She reached around Dr. Meyers and patted Aden's blood-caked hand. "The department will check back with you soon. I'll do everything I can to find who did this."

Aden blinked frantically. Alverez? Okay. Write down what? What happened to me?

"I'll let you rest." Alverez took a business card from her jacket pocket. "Here's my card. If you, or your family, need to contact me, don't hesitate to call."

Aden's eyes searched the room for safety. She felt alone among those in medical garb. When she saw Caleb, her mouth opened in surprise and excitement. *Caleb, I didn't see you. You came.*

"Don't try to say anything, Aden," Caleb echoed the warning. "I'll be here, too." He smoothed her hair and kissed her forehead. Then he whispered, "The first reviews are already in."

Already? I don't know if I want to hear this. Is it good?

Caleb smiled warmly. "My favorite lines from George Graham's column are: 'Caleb Johansson knows how to enjoy the roses. Now the whole world has a new star to love, in the fresh and sparkling Aden Malloy. Tonight, she was everyone's *Honeysuckle Rose.*'"

Aden closed her eyes while the strains of her beloved show's overture sang in her head. Although no one could hear her, she sang every word in her woozy, semiconscious state.

CHAPTER EIGHT

After 3 a.m.

Blurry shadows moved around the well-lit recovery room, but Aden could hardly see or make out who was there. A voice from far off was saying something to her. In and out of a deep and helpless sleep, she couldn't understand what the dim figures were saying. Her body felt heavy, like she had sunk down into the bed and couldn't climb out. A silhouette floated out of the room, saying, "Now, don't forget to breathe, Aden. In and out. Breathe deeply."

Inside, she thought that was a silly command. *Breathe? Everyone breathes.* What was the apparition talking about? But Aden was still coming out of the anesthetic and didn't care. She wanted to stay asleep a little longer, where there was no pain or fear.

Like a feather touching her cheek, the warm breath of a deep baritone whispered in Aden's ear. "Skeeter? I'm here. I won't be able to stay for very long. But I can stay until I get caught and tossed out. They said family only."

Aden recognized that voice. Scotty Russell was the only person in the world who called her Skeeter. Drifting in and out of awareness, the faint presence of Scotty seemed like a vapor. Was he really there? How could he be? He would have told her he was coming for opening night. The first night's performance is a huge event in the life of the entire cast. Scotty certainly understood that. They had talked about it often enough while sitting on her front porch at home during the rain.

A warm hand smoothed across her forehead and then gently touched the tip of her nose. That was one of Scotty's signature moves of endearment.

From the smooth, deep voice beside her, she heard a familiar jingle. "Skeeter, ever sweeter. My sweet, Skeeter." Then the voice added, "I wrote a song for you, Skeeter. If You Were Mine."

If You Were Mine

Aden smiled through the fog of anesthetic and pain medication. It felt like Scotty was right there in the recovery room beside her.

"Rest and heal, Skeeter," he soothed as he gently kissed her hand. "I don't have much time. That nurse will be back in a few minutes. I just had to see you."

Aden's eyes fluttered a little, but her eyelids were too heavy to force open. She wanted to see if Scotty was really there. Was he just a dream, or wishful thinking?

The dream-like essence of Scotty drew even closer. "I see you in there, Skeeter. Wake up." He sat on the bedside chair and caressed her arm. "I was thinking, do you remember the opening night from our senior year musical? We did two performances, Friday night and Saturday night. The cast party after the final performance lasted until the wee hours of Sunday morning. It was the height of my life, and I shared it with you. We danced for hours around the swimming pool in Ashley Bowman's backyard. Our shoes clicked like we were tap dancing on the cement apron that surrounded the water. The music director, drama coach, and parents who wanted to share the fun were there." Scotty took her hand and caressed her fingers in the soft dip of her thumb. "Skeeter, ever sweeter, wake up."

Footsteps and talking sounds from the hallway forced their way through the muddle of Aden's attempts to awaken. She heard Scotty say, "She'll be in here in a minute."

The Scotty-presence sat quietly, his gentle hand in hers. The smokey fragrance of leather, like the jacket Scotty always wore, tried to draw her out of her fogginess. Aden longed to hear the sound of his voice again.

A feathery kiss on her brow told her he was still there. His voice was low, almost broken. "I should have been there in the empty theater with you. I should have told you I was coming. I should have put my bruised ego aside and been there for you." His voice drifted away for a moment. "Our drama coach teased, 'You coulda, shoulda, woulda, but didn't. Don't should on yourself.'"

Aden remembered everyone's beloved Miss Maynard, coaching from the sixth row of the auditorium. Visions of Aden standing center stage at a rehearsal caused her to smile inside. *I know, Miss M. It's not what I shoulda done, but what I willa do.* In the depth of her daze, Aden wanted Scotty to know she didn't blame him for anything. If he had really been there, she *coulda* told him. Maybe someday, she would be able to soothe his feelings of guilt.

Aden felt her Scotty phantom continue to caress her fingertips. "I just want you to know you can do anything, Skeeter," the sweet, dear voice told her. "You've proven that already. You wanted to go into musical comedy on the big stages of New York City, and you did. What happened to you last night was not the end of that dream. It was only the beginning. I promise you, Skeeter, you will sing and dance again and act circles around those who have ever dared to walk onto a stage. Just remember …"

> If you were mine,
> I'd spend my time…
> Loving you.
> If you were mine,
> You'd find that I am
> Close to you.

A shrill female voice broke Aden's sweet daze. "I'm sorry, mister. This is the recovery room. Miss Malloy won't be ready to receive visitors until she gets to her room. She's not even fully conscious yet." She eagerly patted Aden on the arm. "But you are coming around, real fast, Aden."

Scotty's shadowy presence squeezed Aden's hand. She felt the tender strength in his fingers. "You know I'm here, Skeeter. Sorry, I can't stay around until tomorrow when we can talk and catch up. I have to get back to Ohio. I had to see you were coming out of it before I left."

Aden thought she felt Scotty's fingers reluctantly slip away. Inside, she set her mind on what she knew. *Regardless of what anyone tells me in the next few days, I know Scotty was here. I felt him near me.* But would she remember that moment when she finally woke up?

CHAPTER NINE

Aden awakened in the hospital on Monday morning to the musical notes of her own solo singing softly in the background. She wanted to stretch, but her body felt heavy, and the brace around her neck was stiff. Her head throbbed with a beyond-words kind of ache. She tried to make sense of the injuries she didn't even remember. Aden just couldn't understand it. She decided not to dwell on it anymore.

The production techs at the theater had burned all the music from opening night onto a disc. The day before, after finishing the matinee performance, Caleb brought in an old portable CD player. The deep, mellow notes of Caleb's baritone, paired with Aden's lilting soprano, filled the hospital room. Aden's heart healed a little each time she heard the musical score.

Honeysuckle Rose Interlude

A multitude of clear cut-glass vases crowded every flat surface in Aden's room. Blossoms in red, pink, and autumn orange opened their soft petals, bursting with the heart-melting aroma of the beautiful rose. Standing out from the fancy glass containers, a quart-size Ball canning jar held sweet-smelling red rose petals. Aden smiled, thinking of Charley sweeping them up.

Miles charged energetically into Aden's hospital room, flung the drapes open, and greeted the day. "I see you're awake," he chattered as he looked out the window at the bustling city. "Let's get some light in here. Remember, Baby: light heals, darkness steals."

Aden squinted in the bright lights of the sterile room. She was awake enough to realize she was not at home but in the hospital. Still, nothing looked familiar. A strange man in a New York Mets baseball jacket stood at the open door, smiling deviously at her.

"Aden? How are you feeling?" The man's question was sympathetic, but his stare was unnerving.

No sound came from Aden's lips, no matter how hard she tried to scream. Regardless of her heavy brain fog, she knew she didn't know the man. That frightened her. *Who is he? I don't know what's going on. What happened?*

Aden's father turned around just as the Mets man started to speak again. "Who are you?" Miles barked. "What are you doing here?"

The man fixed his eyes on Aden, but his hands fumbled in his jacket, then dug into his pants pockets. "Sorry," he kept searching for something. "I can't seem to find my Press Pass."

"The press?" Miles snapped and started for the man. "You get out of here."

The Mets man immediately backed away from the door. "I just wanted an exclusive interview about Aden's condition and her reaction to what happened to her." Beyond the door, the man called over Miles' shoulder. "Miss Malloy, did you know your attacker?"

"She was nearly killed," her protective father seethed. Miles backed away from Aden's door and blocked the man's approach. "What do you think her reaction would be?"

Aden heard the man shuffle and stumble as her father chased him down the hall. She couldn't process what she heard. While she didn't remember the attack, since she came out of the coma, she seemed afraid of every strange face that came into view. Her father and the reporter used words Aden never believed would apply to her. *Attacked? Almost killed? What is he talking about?*

Unable to turn her head with the rigid plastic cervical collar around her neck, she couldn't see what was happening. But she heard her dad yelling at someone, and it frightened her. From what Aden could hear, it didn't seem to be the same person. There was someone else in the hall. Her father's tone was different but still anxiously angry.

"Hope you enjoy your coffee," Miles barked. His voice became louder as he returned to Aden's door. "Someone is supposed to guard my daughter's room at all times. You might get burned on that precious cup if you have to chase someone down the hall." It was strange for Aden to hear her dad yell. She never heard her dear, sweet father get angry or raise his voice at anyone.

"I'm sorry," the other male voice apologized defensively. Aden decided the man must have been a policeman guarding her door. She heard the officer respond in a low voice. "I didn't think the few seconds it took me to get to the coffee pot would be a problem."

"You're just lucky she wasn't hurt." Miles barked as he stood in the hall and closed Aden's door.

Muffled or not, Aden still made out some of the jumbled words and sounds from the hall. But most of what she heard; she didn't understand.

Mild-mannered Miles lashed out at the guard. "That man said he was with some news service. He wanted to exploit Aden's pain and injuries from her attack to better his own career. That guy had no press credentials and was visibly nervous. Maybe someone recognized him. Get as much information as you can. Ask all the medical staff as they walk past Aden's door if they knew him."

"I am so sorry," the guard blubbered again. "I'll report it to the station. They can get a sketch artist down here. Maybe we can ID the man through some facial recognition software. If we can find which media outlet issued the Press Pass, the picture on it will also be in the credential file. He'd be in the system."

"I'll be here," Miles said as his voice calmed a little. "Let me know when the artist gets here. I'll call Detective Alverez." Miles went back into Aden's room.

Aden pounded her fist on her tray table and shook her head insistently. Her arms flailed around in disgust, causing her to bump into a large vase of roses on the side table. The bouquet teetered a little. The sweet Demask aroma from the arrangement reminded her of the two dozen blooms that filled her arms during the curtain call on opening night. Searching her mind, trying to comprehend what happened, she filled again with questions. *When was opening night?*

Miles whipped around with his hands on his hips and a wry smile. "Are you mad because it's morning, because I let the sun in, I interrupted your music, or because you were afraid of that man who stared at you?"

Aden smiled sheepishly and covered her face with her hands. She opened her mouth and screwed up her face as though she were screaming in the highest octave, but not a single sound escaped. Inside, however, she yelled, *I don't know. I'm just mad. Maybe at all of it.*

"Don't get too worried," Miles assured her. "The guy was probably a newsman. I actually got upset with the guard." Her father looked down and swallowed hard. "I couldn't protect you Friday night." He stopped quickly and changed the subject. "Your throat specialist will be here this morning. Try not to talk until the doctor lets us know what's happening." Miles was calm as he poured out the water into Aden's pitcher. He refilled her covered tumbler with the bottled water from a small frig below the wall cabinet.

Aden sipped a little from the cup and thumped it briskly on the table. With an over-stretched shrugging motion, she frantically pointed to the wall's white staff board and clock.

Miles walked over to Aden's bed, sat down on the edge, and took her hand. "It's Monday, Honey."

Aden's eyes filled with panic. Her trembling lips formed a single word. "How?"

Miles looked away for a minute. "A man attacked you in the alley outside the theater Friday night after the opening. You've had two surgeries and been unconscious for a long time." He patted her hand as tears began to roll down Aden's cheeks. He didn't say how she was found or what evil happened to her. He simply said, "Your neck was injured. Don't talk."

She only nodded, then imitated someone writing on a pad of paper. When her dad gave her a pen, she wrote, "Was Scotty here?"

Miles' eyebrows furrowed. "Scott Russell? I haven't seen him."

She scrawled across the paper, "I could feel him. He was here."

Miles explained as he patted Aden's hand. "He had a lot of important work to finish at the University. I'm sure he was in Ohio."

Aden couldn't talk. Arguing with her father was an impossible nuisance if she used only some pen scratches on paper. She looked away as tears filled her eyes. Maybe Scotty wasn't there after all.

"The specialist should be here soon. Mom will be back in a minute." Miles got up and busied himself around Aden's room. He fluffed and smoothed her bedding and opened and closed the closet door … just busy stuff. "I know today is Monday, and … they talked about your being transferred to a rehabilitation center this afternoon." The words came out of his mouth, but he didn't look at Aden. Her tight expression was too painful for both of them.

Rehab center? Aden slammed the flat of her hand on her tray table, made two fists, and waved them in the air while hissing through her front teeth. She shook her head back and forth. Anyone could see she opposed the plan.

"Dr. Rumple," Miles sighed in relief when the orthopedic doctor entered Aden's room. "We have a bit of a situation here."

"We do?" Rumple questioned as he went to Aden's bedside. "Are you any part of this kerfuffle?" He glanced at the CD player and added, "Can we turn the music off?"

Aden gasped just as another physician came into the room. Her expression formed a question for the entire room to interpret.

"This is Dr. Abigale Hammerstein," Dr. Rumple introduced. "She did the surgery on your throat and vocal cords sometime on Friday night or early Saturday morning. You were unconscious." He nodded again at the CD player.

"I'll turn it down," Miles offered but then saw the fallen expression on Aden's face. "First, you must listen to a few bars of the soprano's solo."

Both doctors paused a moment and listened respectfully. As the music swelled, their expression melted in pleasure.

Honeysuckle Rose

"Beautiful," Dr. Hammerstein whispered with wide-eyed astonishment.

Dr. Rumple smiled, then finally said in appreciation. "That singer is amazing."

Miles' voice cracked as he explained. "That is Aden's voice," he boasted. "That is the voice we have to save."

CHAPTER TEN

"I will do everything I can to save your beautiful voice, Aden." Dr. Hammerstein patted Aden's hand as Miles turned down the music.

"Hammerstein?" Aden's mouth formed the name in surprise.

"Yes," Dr. Hammerstein said with an upward lilt to her voice. "And … no … I do not sing or write music." She feigned a pout. "Oscar Hammerstein was a distant relative, but any musical talent got lost on its way through the cousins once and twice removed." She took Aden's hand in greeting. "I have treated many professional singers from the Broadway stage to the Metropolitan Opera."

Tears filled Aden's eyes. She put her first two fingers to her lips and blew a salty kiss at Dr. Hammerstein.

"First," the doctor began, "open up so I can see your throat." She pulled a small flashlight from her pocket and shined the beam into Aden's mouth. Humming and mumbling, she turned the light off, stood back, and folded her hands. "Now … I want you to try to answer a few questions."

Aden nodded in agreement.

"Okay, the obvious question is, does your throat hurt?

Miles stood off to the side and smiled when Pat entered the room. With his finger to his lips, he cautioned his wife to remain silent. Together, they moved to the small sofa in front of the window and anxiously sat on the cushion's edge.

"A little," Aden whispered hoarsely, her eyes large. "Like, I have a sore throat with laryngitis. Dr. Hammerstein—"

"Call me Abby," the doctor offered. "Great, Aden." She gently touched Aden's lips. "That's a good start. Now, I don't want you to talk very much. Let your voice rest. The knife cut your throat but only bruised your vocal cords. There was a tiny nick. It will take some time for your voice to return."

"The knife?" Aden asked. "Someone cut me? When?"

Miles reminded her, "You were attacked as you came out of the theater on opening night."

"Who would do that?" Aden whispered hoarsely in disbelief.

"Detective Alverez is still chasing down some leads." Pat's voice was calm and strong. "We don't know anything yet."

"When can I go back to the theater?" Aden squeaked out in a voice two octaves lower than her usual tone.

"It's not just your voice, Aden," Dr. Rumple patted her arm. "Your leg and back have to heal."

"My back? Did he cut my back?" Aden grabbed the cool sheet, knotting it in her fists.

"No. You injured your back when you fell. Evidently, the assailant flipped you over the outside railing to the cellar and pushed you down the steps." Rumple filled in the details Aden hadn't remembered. "I repaired the discs in your back, but your spinal cord got bruised pretty badly. You'll need physical therapy, usually at a rehab center."

"I'm bruised everywhere," Aden whispered and rolled her eyes. "I'll never wear black and blue again."

"Now, that's funny," Dr. Rumple said as he chuckled.

"What isn't funny is the possibility I won't be able to walk. Doctor, can I?" Aden pleaded, her weak voice broken and strained.

"Let's try," Rumple announced. "I want you to get up and take a few steps." He turned and spoke to Aden's mother. "Does she have a robe?"

"Yes." Pat's hands trembled. She opened the tiny closet in the corner of the room and removed a lightweight, silky, duster-length robe. "I brought it in for her yesterday." Pat positioned the robe until Aden was ready to wear it.

Dr. Rumple held the covers. "Now, roll over on your side; keep your legs together; swing your feet over the side of the bed; and push yourself up using your elbow."

Charlotte waved a two-finger "hi" at Aden's parents. She brought a plate of freshly baked doughnuts that smelled like cinnamon and sugar and placed them on the over-bed table. "This will give you something to enjoy while waiting for your lunch to arrive."

Aden got up as Dr. Rumple instructed.

"That's right," Charlotte said. "Stand up leaning forward, then straighten—nose-over-toes," she coached. "Put those dancing feet on the floor."

"Thank you," Aden said softly and grabbed Charlotte's strong arm. "Oh," Aden moaned. "It's hard." She tried to straighten her back as best she could. "I'm wilting."

"It will take time and work, but you can do it," Dr. Rumble assured her. "From what I hear, you are a hard worker on floor routines. Physical therapy will help strengthen your back to keep up with your legs. Dancing will be a great second workout, a little at a time."

Aden's face strained and contorted as she tried to use her strength to unfold her back and stand up straight. She tried to stand tall and demand that everyone listen, even if only in a whisper, "No rehab center. My condo. A therapist can come there."

Miles jumped in to explain. "Aden has a small dance studio in the second bedroom of her condominium. It has a ballet barre. She can get anything else the therapist says she might need."

"But, Miles," Pat warned with a tightened brow. "She lives alone. What if she falls?"

"I can fall in a rehab unit, too," Aden insisted.

Her mother's brow gripped into a deep channel. "What if whoever attacked you comes back to finish the job?"

"Medic alert button," Aden whispered. "Like I'm ninety-five."

Abby waved her hand. "You're already talking too much, Aden."

"It's my decision," Aden insisted. "I know. My body feels like I'm a hundred. I live on the fifteenth floor. No one can come through the window. Ralph, the doorman, won't let anyone in through the door. He says, 'I'll toss the interloper out.' I've seen him do it." She muffled a painful laugh, then tried to clear her throat.

"But," Pat began again.

"You two," Aden pointed to her parents, "please, bring in microwave meals for my freezer." To Dr. Abby, she pantomimed a zipped mouth, "A quiet condo, except for music."

Dr. Hammerstein jumped in. "No singing. Little or no talking. Come to my office for your follow-up visit one week after complete rest. We'll evaluate your progress at that time and try to project your future."

"No singing," Aden mouthed. She knew her condo would be full of song. Strains of music would fill her room and heal every broken bone and jagged knife cut in her body. Then she remembered one of her dad's favorite phrases. He preached on it often. "Healing takes belief, belief takes trust, trust takes looking at life with hope."

CHAPTER ELEVEN

Monday Afternoon

"You're awake," Pat sang as she walked back into Aden's room after lunch. A nurse had drawn the institution drapes again so Aden could sleep. But that made the mood gloomy and dreary. "I see someone pulled your drapes while you napped. Were you able to eat your lunch?"

"A little," Aden admitted, her voice weak and broken. "I'm not hungry. I hurt. Don't want food."

"The doctor said, if you want to go home, Honey, you'll have to build up your energy," Pat stated, like any mother taking care of her child. "And you'll need tons of energy to heal. It takes a lot to repair all of that damage."

"Damage? Awful." Aden used few words. Her expression fell as she closed her eyes. "What will people say? There goes Aden Malloy—singer with no voice— dancer who can't stand."

Pat didn't correct her. "The Good Lord made our bodies repairable. Don't worry about that now." Sitting on the sofa by the window, she leaned toward her daughter. "Dr. Rumble said, since you don't want to go to a rehab center, you can probably go home Friday. First, you'll have to go over some things with a physical therapist. The therapist will make sure you are safe at home."

"Really? What? A dance routine?" Aden sighed, remembering all the hard work she had put into the show.

Now, it felt like she would have to climb out of a well just to get to level ground.

Pressing on, Pat seemed to tick off a list, evaluating the safety of Aden's condo. "I already answered some questions. I told them you have no stairs in your condo. You have a walk-in shower, an exercise room, a doorman, and friends nearby. The physical therapist will ensure you can walk without stumbling and know how to use a cane properly, perhaps a walker first."

"A cane?" Aden could barely squeak out a sound and did her best not to shriek.

"A cane," Pat repeated. "You won't use it for long … and possibly a walker at first."

"Neither," Aden stated flatly through gritted teeth.

"You decide," her mother said without arguing. "The doctor won't release you until you at least know *how* to use the cane. You can rest some more here at the hospital, rather than at home, until you're ready to learn."

"Knock it off, Mother. I'm not twelve," Aden spit out in a painful, gravelly voice.

"I know you're not a child, Aden Rose. You are twenty-three years old and have been living on your own for nearly five years. You're an adult. Now, act like one." Pat lowered her voice and added without waiting for a response, "I also told them your dance studio has a Murphy bed. Your dad and I can stay there for a few days while you adjust."

"Mother … no. I'll do this myself." Aden's expression was hard and determined.

Miles spoke up as he breezed in, full of positive energy, "Hi, you two."

"Don't get too chipper, Miles," Pat warned him. "She says she's on her own."

"Really?" He kissed Aden on the cheek. "How about this? I brought someone to help you plan a home-bound activity between rest and physical therapy." He paused and waited for Aden to look at him.

"Daddy, please," she sighed. "Stop."

"Sorry … no, I will not. You will need things to do to keep your spirits up or to build them up. Mom and I will call you every day and check on you." He watched as Aden rolled her eyes like she did when she was fifteen. "That's for our mental health, not yours." He smiled, put his hand softly on Patty's shoulder, and gave her a sideways hug. "We are staying at your place right now—"

"What?" Aden snapped to attention.

"We're helping get your condo ready for you. We'll change the sheets, wash the towels, do the dishes, and run the sweeper before we leave. Don't worry," he assured her. "We'll leave it spotless."

Aden lifted her hands and let them drop in surrender as she grinned sheepishly. "Oh, Daddy."

"Today, I brought someone with me. Please make your grandmother welcome," he announced with a flare.

"Mimi?" Aden whispered through the stones and gravel in her throat.

"Aden, your blinds are closed again," her father reminded her as he smoothed the sheets on her hospital bed. "Light heals. Darkness steals." He turned and opened the drapes.

"No," Aden gasped as she shielded her eyes from the bright light.

"The hot sun will burn off all the depression and disappointment in your life," Miles spoke softly. "And remember, your grandmother always says, 'Get your head out of the dirt and your hands in the soil. Plant love and harvest with God.'"

"Good morning, Precious." A seventy-five-year-old woman with the spirit of someone thirty years younger called out as she entered room 222. She fanned her hand toward Miles and Pat and smiled. "You two run along. Aden and I have some visiting to do."

"Mimi, why did they make you come?" Aden protested as she grabbed her throat in pain. "You hate New York."

"Yes, but I love *you*, Aden Rose." Aden's grandmother put a small package on the over-bed tray and pulled a chair closer. "Now, you are not supposed to talk too much, so I'll do all the talking. You do all the listening." She smiled and folded her arms across her lap.

Aden nodded and looked out the window at the autumn sky. Dry, golden leaves blew past the window, reminding Aden that it was the beginning of New York's theater season. It occurred to her that rehearsing for the show had left little time to see the glorious pageantry of fall. It was supposed to launch her big break as a musical comedy actress. Now, all of that was as crippled as her body.

"I brought you two gifts, Sweetheart," her grandmother began. The wrapping paper, bursting with colorful flowers, seemed to smile from the bed tray.

Aden didn't reach for the package but continued her restful gaze out the window.

"Here, I'll help you." Rosemary smiled as she pulled on the ends of the pale-yellow ribbon. "I thought you'd like the color, given the name of your musical, *My Honeysuckle Rose.*"

Aden didn't respond or look at the gift but lifted her finger a little. A light rain began outside like her world was shedding tears. Aden didn't realize it, but all her crying that day was a blessing. She had not been able to cry since she regained consciousness. How was it possible that she could have lost everything in one random act of violence?

"It's a prayer journal." Mimi quietly placed the notebook in Aden's hand. "I've attached a wonderfully slim silver pen to the inside and started some headings you might like to use."

Aden smiled faintly and opened the journal. It crackled a little and smelled new.

Rosemary had multiple tabs with titles such as Family, Friends, and Healing. Then Aden stopped and slammed the book closed.

"What's wrong?" Mimi asked but seemed to know.

Aden pulled the journal open and thumped her finger on the next topic. "Attacker?" She growled with her damaged vocal cords.

"Now, Aden." Mimi looked at her squarely. "That man slit your throat. Your ability to speak again will depend on your willingness not to talk too much now."

Aden turned and glared at her dear grandmother with a heart so full of anger and self-pity that she didn't have room for kindness, forgiveness, or prayers for the offender. "I can't walk because of the slashes that evil man inflicted on the calf of my leg. I could barely hold my back up straight after he flipped me over, and I landed on my back on the stair railing. So … I can't dance. I can't talk, and I may never sing again."

"Aden Rose," her grandmother whispered, "there were a lot of I's in that statement. If you want to heal completely, you'll have to work harder in physical therapy than in dance rehearsals. And you'll have to focus on others if you want to heal your soul. Aden, forgiving the man who assaulted you doesn't excuse what he did or shield him from the consequences of his crime. Pray that your assailant receives all good things from God and finds peace in the punishment he will surely receive for his actions. Aden, it will set *you* free."

"Grandma…"

"No, don't talk. But remember, like your daddy said, only with new words—*good thoughts heal; bad thoughts steal.*" Mimi smiled. "I know I'm speaking in jingles. Sorry, but your dad and I are poets." She waved her hand in front of her, erasing an imaginary blackboard. "Your mama and daddy took me to your condominium." Aden's eyes grew large. "You have a lovely wide terrace that receives a lot of sun and laps up the rain. I will start a large-pot garden for you tomorrow that will bud in beautiful, aroma-filled fall flowers."

Aden shook her head and scowled. "I don't garden."

"You *didn't* garden, my dear," her grandmother corrected her. "Now—you will. Gardening is therapy for the heart. You will dig your hands in the sweet soil God has given us, the very foundation for our roots." She closed her eyes. "I can see myself working my hands into the soil. And you will press the tiny seeds into the clean, fresh dirt. They are the new beginnings of every possibility." Into the phantom dirt, Mimi pretended to drop a speck. "As you and God walk through your Garden of Aden, you'll water the plants with the holy water of clean, forgiving thoughts." With her hands, she poured from an imaginary watering can. "Then, you'll sit on a bench your daddy will build for you and pray over your lovelies, all those you have bound within your prayer journal. You will unbind them, lifting them up to God's life-giving light."

CHAPTER TWELVE

October 15

It was Tuesday afternoon. Lunch had been chicken noodle soup, applesauce, and a small dish of ice cream, a usual hospital meal. Aden's throat was painful, and she couldn't talk. Soft foods allowed her to swallow. Aden's gaze snapped back to her open door as an aide took her tray away. The police guard had been dismissed. Since all the medical staff had gotten to know Aden, they acted as her guard or watch-out. But who caught her eye earlier that day before the door completely closed?

There, there he is again. Aden's heart began to pound a little harder as panic crept in. She waited before whoever stood in the hall appeared a second time.

"Miss Malloy," the man in a scruffy, tan raincoat opened the door a few inches. "Sorry I didn't knock. I know you can't call out to let me come in."

"Who?" was her only question as she pointed firmly at him.

"I'm a fan, Aden," he explained as he opened the door wider.

"No, I can't talk," Aden stated flatly.

"You listen here, Miss Uppity. You are a public figure. If you think you're going to get anywhere, it will be because your fans have supported you—"

"Who are you?" A woman in black scrubs demanded.

"Who are you?" the man spit back.

The woman in black checked the hall. "Greg," she called to a male nurse. "Get this man out of here." She turned to the strange intruder. "Or do I have to call security?"

Greg was tall, with well-developed muscles under his scrub shirt. "Mister," he addressed the man in tan, "you are in the wrong place. I'll help you find the front door." Greg got behind the man and herded him off the floor.

"Miss Malloy?" The new woman in Aden's room stood beside her bed. "The man is gone. A male nurse helped him find his way home. You're safe." She patted Aden's arm. "My name is Nicole. I'm your physical therapist while you're here in the hospital. I understand you want to return to your own home rather than go to a rehab unit."

Aden nodded and checked the hall behind Nicole again. The therapist closed the door.

"My job is to help you find ways to perform the daily living tasks you will have to handle on your own."

"How will you do that?" Aden asked in a raspy whisper.

"We'll tackle your voice first." Nicole looked around Aden's over-bed table and picked up her phone. "Since you aren't supposed to talk much, I can record a message for you."

Aden didn't try to answer verbally. She nodded her head in agreement.

Nicole smiled. "I'll record, and if you don't like the message, we can change it. Before I begin, is anyone at home most of the time who can take your messages?"

"Home?" Aden mouthed and shook her head no. Then she formed the words, "It's New York. Everyone is busy."

"That's okay. I know of a great answering service with reasonable charges. I can hook you up with them if that's all right?"

Aden nodded again. But deep inside, anger was beginning to rise. She had been a strong, independent person all her life. The thought of all those people intruding on her daily activities made her cringe. She thought of all the people she would need to help her.

Nicole put the phone to her ear. "You have reached Aden Malloy. I'm not taking calls at this time. Leave a message, and my answering service will pass it along. Have a great day." She looked at Aden and raised her eyebrows. "Do you approve? It is still personal, but we'll leave the talking to the service."

Aden opened her mouth, then simply nodded her head slowly, with only a modicum of enthusiasm. She needed to keep others out of her business. This could be the beginning of a difficult time.

"You can eliminate your phone answering the calls and have the entire connection routed to an answering service if you'd rather. Let the service answer the phone and take messages." Nicole placed the phone on the table. "Now, I want you to get up and walk across the floor. I need to see what issues we're dealing with." Looking around, Nicole added, "Let me help you with your robe."

Standing on her feet was far more painful than anything Aden had imagined. Her leg was numb where the man's knife viciously sliced into a muscle and nerve. Pain oozed through the numbness to add reality to the injury.

With her spine glued together like Humpty Dumpty, she could not force her back to hold her up straight as much as she stretched. She was bent and struggling. All she wanted to do was sit down or go back to bed.

Nicole watched Aden walk a few steps and sized up her walking gait. "You're doing great, Aden. Your limp could throw you off balance, and your back is still weak. You'll need a cane for balance and support."

"A cane?" Aden growled. "Mother and I talked about the wicked stick."

"Try not to talk," Nicole reminded her. "Hopefully, you won't use the cane for very long. Carry the staff on the side opposite your leg injury."

"Opposite?" Aden considered the possibility of cane use, but … on the opposite side? "What good will that do?"

Her therapist looked intently at Aden and cautioned, "I know you want to live alone, Aden. With the attack, you have several injuries. Any of them could cause you to fall and require using a cane. You cannot lay on the floor of your condo for days until someone comes by."

Visions raced through Aden's head of languishing on the cold hard tile of the kitchen, unable to lift herself off the floor. She blinked away what she saw and changed the image to what she could handle. Gruffly, she said to Nicole, "I'll have my neighbor check on me every day. A prearranged signal from me would tell them I'm okay without hollering through the door." She fought back the tears that threatened to take over her determination to show strength in the face of body weakness. "Okay, okay," she whispered.

"It's now Tuesday afternoon. Let's go over this week's five goals. You might be released Friday after lunch if:

- your incisions close successfully,

- we've established an exercise routine for you,

- you have been weaned off some of your stronger medications,

- and you can get around safely in your home and take care of yourself."

"Wow," Aden sighed. "Give me that cane."

Nicole came twice a day for the rest of the week. They worked on leg strengthening exercises and core building. Steps were conquered with the use of a cane. Training with a grabber helped Aden get clothes out of her dryer without bending.

Aden felt herself grow stronger physically and more fearful emotionally. She was angry with herself for not being in control of her fears. Still, she would have to return to the world where anything could happen. It already had.

CHAPTER THIRTEEN

Early on Friday

Miles and Pat had three days to prepare Aden's condo before she came home. They knew their daughter was well organized, but with her use of a walker and cane, the layout of her living space may have to change. A quick stop at a corner hardware store and a convenient grocery provided some needed supplies.

"What are you doing, Dear?" Pat asked when she saw her husband drilling a hole in Aden's front door.

"I am installing a peephole. Aden can check the hallway before she opens the door." Miles blew sawdust specks from the opening.

"Just like the Hilton," Pat said with a smile. "I just hope Aden wants a hole in her door."

"She's getting more than a peephole," Miles said with a huge smile as he pulled out another piece of hardware. "She already has a chain lock on the door. I imagine that was on the door when she moved in." He showed his wife the additional shiny new lock. "This is a deadbolt. I had the tumblers keyed to use the same entry key as the door lock." Miles was creative with his hands and good with small home repair projects. He quickly installed the deadbolt and finished setting the peephole.

Miles gathered up his tools and stood back, admiring his handiwork. "She will be glad the new hardware is here.

You know Aden, she'll balk at first. *I can do it myself,* has been her theme song since elementary school. Aden has no idea who attacked her, and she can recognize her friends. With the doorman's help, she can filter those who can get near her door. To those she lets in, she can visually select even fewer."

"I've walked all over the condo," Pat said as she studied the floor Miles worked on. "I don't see any trip hazards except the small red throw rug at the entrance. I rolled it up and put it in the back of Aden's hallway closet."

"Good. Now go into the bathroom with me and help me find the best placement for a couple of grab bars. I want them positioned so no matter which way Aden turns, she'll have something on which to grab."

"That won't take long." Pat agreed. "Your mother is coming soon to put together a surprise on the terrace."

A few well-placed screws in some brackets and two grab bars were quickly installed in the bathroom. One in the shower and one near the toilet. "That job's done," Miles said with a grin of satisfaction.

The kitchen was a greater challenge for Pat. She wiggled and pushed the frozen food she and Miles purchased into the apartment-size freezer. Closing the freezer door, she checked to make sure its overstuffed state wouldn't cause it to pop open again. "The freezer is as small as the kitchen. I guess that's appropriate," Pat said with a laugh. "But then, Aden didn't come to New York to become a chef."

"There are restaurants all over Manhattan that deliver," Miles said as he poured two mugs of coffee and took them into the living room. "Let's enjoy our last day in New York."

"A little coffee before your mother gets here would be wonderful, Miles. I hoped finding time to relax would provide an opportunity to worry less." Pat sank down on the sofa. "Worry less, plan more," she stated with determination. "We'll spend some time with Aden, and then—"

"I know," Miles agreed and added a tone of calm and comfort. "It will be hard to leave Aden here alone and go back to Ohio. But that's what she wants. We'll respect that."

Pat stared out the windows into the city Aden loved and sighed. "I hope her strong sense of self-reliance helps her now when she needs extra strength and bravery."

####

Later that day, Miles and Pat caught a cab to return to the hospital. As the cabbie stopped in traffic, the burning cedar ash from a trash barrel wafted over from an alley. Winter was coming. It was hard to believe it was nearly Thanksgiving, but the blaze of falling leaves in the park showed that time was passing.

As they walked into the familiar hospital room, their daughter was dressed and ready for the day. And hopefully, ready to go home. They found her working with her physical therapist.

"Aden, one last goal," Nicole was saying. "We'll go down the hall and practice getting in and out of a car." She paused, "Hi, Pastor and Mrs. Malloy. I'm glad you're here. Come with us to the car model we have in the therapy room, and you can see how Aden needs to conquer getting in a car." Nicole turned. "Get the cane, Aden."

Aden stared at the loathsome walking stick and cringed. But she did not retreat from the cane's power to set her free from isolation, from the limitations that kept her from her dreams. In surrender, she whispered a prayer. *God, I hate that cane, but I give its use to you as a gift. You will find a reason for me to use it.*

Following her successful training session on the therapy car, Aden was released from the hospital. Late in the afternoon, she went home to an orderly condominium where an assailant could wait behind any door.

CHAPTER FOURTEEN

Monday—October 24

Aden loved New York City and found it easy to get around. The avenues in the city run north and south, and the streets flow east and west. Her condominium was on West 53rd Street. High on the fifteenth floor, her terrace caught the warm, rising sun.

Angry over the injuries to her painful body, Aden didn't even step out onto the balcony in the three days she had been home from the hospital. Before her life stopped that night in the alley, she loved sitting in the fresh air and sunlight on the terrace, listening to the cacophony from the street far below. Back home, when she started the arduous task of putting the many pieces of her life back together, she found herself avoiding the garden. The huge planters and raised garden beds filled with the flowers her grandmother found at a greenhouse in the city blew gently in the breeze, alone and unseen. Mimi managed to find soil, pots, and blossoms among the concrete and buildings on Park Avenue. One pot was full of joyous, blooming flowers Mimi had brought with her from her own backyard garden. In Aden's current emotional state, she anticipated what would come. When the cold season blew in, and the flowers lay dormant for the winter, it would remind her each winter day of everything she had lost.

Soothing music filled the living room as Aden sat in front of the blackened flat-screen TV and slowly sipped her first cup of coffee of the day. Aden was in her home, but her home was not yet in her. She saw but didn't absorb the carefully chosen paint colors of cream with pale blue accents. The furniture had touches of the same shade of blue on a field of beige. When the painters transformed the bright red and navy-blue walls into the colors that spoke to her, Aden felt the peace that only color can bring to calm the mind. The ring of her cell phone startled her. It didn't matter. She hadn't started answering the ring yet. Looking at the phone screen, her eyebrows raised. She recognized the number. The very thought of hearing from the one on the other end of the line made her hands begin to tremble and her heart pound. Holding her breath, she slid the green icon up and put the phone on speaker to free her hands. "Hi, Scotty."

"You knew it was me," Scotty Russell said sheepishly.

"Um-hum, it's on the screen," she said in a gravelly whisper.

"Right. Aden …. Your voice, it sounds like it hurts. How are you doing? Your attack is all over social media."

"I'm home now."

Scotty leaped on her answer. "Home? In Ohio?"

"No … in my condo in New York." The next moment of silence screamed louder than words. "I can't talk long, but I was wondering why… I thought you were going to come to the opening."

"I did," he said lowly.

Suddenly, Aden was excited and surprised by the anger that also surfaced. "You were here? Why didn't I see you?"

Aden heard nothing for a second but the sound of Scotty's breathing.

His soothing voice sounded sullen. "You were all caught up in that Johansson guy. I figured you didn't need me."

"You didn't come to the hospital either." Aden could hear her own disappointment betray her feelings.

"I did go to the hospital," he tried to explain. "You were still in recovery."

Aden's eyes brightened, and her heart quickened. "I knew I felt you there, Scotty."

"I thought only family members were allowed to see you." Scotty's voice turned hard. "Aden, I'm not family."

Tears threatened her eyes and tightened her throat. "You've been part of my family since elementary school. You were the brother I never had." She paused, but Scotty said nothing in return. "It sounds like someone is at the door. I better go."

"Wait, before you hang up," Scotty shot back. "Can I come to see you?"

"Will you?" Aden wondered if she could place any hope in Scotty's coming when he hadn't before, regardless of the number of plans and promises he made. And yet, he was there on opening night. "When, Scotty?"

"Soon," he stumbled.

Aden's heart sank again. Her words sounded flat. "Sure, Scotty … soon. Let me know. Gotta go. Bye." She sank into the old disappointment that always followed Scotty's failed promises. *There's rain behind every silver lining.*

The doorbell rang over Scotty's words that still spun around in her head. The buzzer didn't sound like any other doorbell. With Aden's love of music, the doorbell tones were notes from the first bar of The Sound of Music—*The hills are alive.* But her reaction to the four upbeat notes was not melodic to Aden. She jumped at the intrusion. Would she ever feel safe again?

Leaning heavily on the armrest of her chair, she slowly raised herself to a nearly full standing position. Almost dragging her leg, she struggled toward the door. It frustrated her when it took extra time to get across the room. She railed against her cane and stomped it on the floor. Everything seemed to make her angry and embarrassingly frightened. *I have a right to be angry.* But it was fear that she couldn't handle. She had never been afraid of anything.

The opening song to the second act of *Honeysuckle Rose* was still playing on the CD in the background. Aden tried to use the melody to set her pace, but she couldn't force herself to be joyful about it.

Mornin' Mr. Sun

Everyone is not dancing and singing, she grumbled. I can scarcely walk.

It was too early for Caleb. When she looked through the door peephole, she didn't recognize the woman who stood there. She had been waiting for the physical therapist. Could this be she? Peering through the door's tiny safety opening, she felt silly. She didn't live in a hotel room. Before her dad and mother returned to Ohio, Miles installed the peephole without discussing it with Aden or asking her permission. He said he wanted to ensure she could see who she was letting in. The truth was, she was very glad the silent sentry was there. She didn't intend to admit most people into her condo, but opening the door to anyone frightened her now. The authorities hadn't identified or caught her assailant. During the short time she had been home, no one had come to see her. Caleb said he would stop in between the matinee and the evening performance. Now, she was at the door, not knowing who or what waited on the other side. Despite Scotty's call and the joyous background music, fear gripped her and would not let go.

Her heart filled to the point it felt like she was going to suffocate. She was not able to get her breath. *Now what? Am I hyperventilating? Why?*

The hills are alive … her doorbell rang again. Oh no, she gasped without speaking. Am I having a panic attack? Or did I take in too much air when I panted toward the door? The doorbell rang a third time.

Aden leaned heavily on her cane and tried to take a few steps. Her chest burned with pain. *Why this violent reaction?* She paused, leaned on the back of the living room chair, and tried to catch her breath. *The hills …* the bell was impatient. Aden stumbled to the door and peeped through the viewer.

"Do you have identification?" she asked hoarsely through the closed door.

"Sure do," a male voice announced but stood to the side of the peephole.

"I'm sorry, I can't see you," Aden murmured, feeling trapped with fear.

"May I help you?" she heard an unfamiliar female voice ask as the woman joined the man in the hall.

The man's voice lost some of its assertiveness. "No … this is Carol and Chris Foy's apartment, isn't it?"

"No, I'm sorry, it is not." Aden heard the woman say. The man's footsteps in the hall brought a small measure of relief.

The woman spoke toward the door. "I'm Heather Boston, Miss Malloy. Your physical therapist."

Aden's hands trembled as she tried to steady herself on the door handle. "May I see some identification?"

"Of course." Heather held up her driver's license and business card.

Aden searched the woman's identification for every detail, not just her name or the therapy center she represented.

Watching the door, the woman in the hall seemed aware that Aden was scrutinizing her. She smiled as she looked up at the peephole. "I'm Heather Boston," she announced again. "Orthopedics New York sent me."

"Okay." Aden sighed in relief. She twisted the lock on the door and threw the deadbolt her dad had installed. Holding her breath, she unhooked the chain and opened the door.

CHAPTER FIFTEEN

When Aden opened the door, a young woman in black workout clothes stepped into the small entry foyer and looked around. "Nice place," she admired. Checking out the flooring, she continued without stopping. "I love the honey-colored parquet floors. The varying shades of hardwood add life to the rooms."

"Thank you," Aden whispered lowly. "Come in. As you can see, this is the living room."

"Oh, wow! Your terrace is magnificent," Heather exclaimed as she bounced over to the sliding doors that led outside.

Aden ignored Heather's comment and started toward the smaller of the two bedrooms. "My dance studio is in here. It's just 10.2 x 11.5, but it has a workout barre. I think it will be okay."

"Aden, come out here first." Heather didn't follow Aden but opened the door and stepped onto the balcony. With her arms spread out to greet the morning sun, she closed her eyes and inhaled deeply.

Aden walked into the large living space and stopped in the middle of the room. "I prefer not. Let's just go into the studio."

Heather turned and blinked a disbelieving glance in Aden's direction. "No. We'll start out here."

"No, indeed," Aden sighed and sat on the edge of the comfortable French-designed couch shaped in a gentle curve. "I don't want to go out there." Her voice sounded raspy and raw.

Heather stepped back into the room. "Why? The terrace is beautiful. It's like a garden in the sky."

"I don't like the balcony," Aden gritted through a dismissive whisper and tried to wave Heather off. As she turned, she studied the terrace from a distance.

"It is wonderful." Heather looked beyond the balcony to the office buildings across the street. The lights on thousands of desks were turning on, like jewels dropped into a mounting. "Aden, if we're going to be able to work together, you will have to be willing to do things you don't want to do."

Aden didn't respond but carefully tried to raise herself off the couch. She gently fell back onto the deep seat and put her hands over her face. "I can't even get up."

"I know," Heather said, both encouragingly and insistently. "That couch is a little low for you. Put a pillow on it to make the seat higher. Then, lean forward and remember … nose over toes."

"Nose over toes?" Aden grumbled, her face screwed up like she had eaten an unripe, bitter persimmon. "Just like Charlotte said," she mumbled.

"Yep. If you look at your toes when you rise from a seated position, you will already be halfway up. Then, just straighten up."

"Heather," Aden spit out in anger, "I can't stand up straight. Either no one told you of my condition, or you can't see."

"They told me, and I can see." The physical therapist smiled and spoke softly. "Now, for today, since you are having trouble, it's nose over toes."

Aden glared at her therapist, looked at the floor, and kept her eyes on the tips of her shoes. Slowly, she stood up, then straightened into an upright position as best she could. "Does that make you happy?" she sneered.

Heather shrugged and went back out on the balcony. "It's only important if it makes you happy."

Aden stole a frightening glance toward the sliding doors that led outside. "I'll be a target out there," she whispered.

"You can hide the rest of your life or strengthen your body and take charge again."

Aden said nothing while she limped out onto the terrace with her cane in her hand. Only the sound of heavy breathing from the effort it took just to put one foot in front of the other was heard, like an off-key harmony to the background music. "I hate this thing," she said as she waved her cane around. "I've been here alone for three days with this ugly stick."

"Perhaps a walker would be better," Heather said and winked.

"That isn't funny," Aden said gruffly. "My own grandmother isn't old enough for a walker."

"It has nothing to do with age, Aden," Heather said softly. "It has everything to do with need."

"Okay, okay. My cane is my new best friend," she said sarcastically. Looking out toward the avenue to the east, she allowed herself the luxury of inhaling the sweetness of the warm autumn morning.

"This garden will help in your therapy, Aden," Heather studied the terrace layout. "These raised bed planters look like they're made of two-by-ten boards of red cedar stacked into thirty-inch tall beds. They should withstand the rain and snow." She stooped down and stretched her arm across one of the planting beds. "They appear to be a good width, about four feet. You will be able to reach across them comfortably." She smiled as she looked from the beds to Aden. "Someone has already filled the raised beds with potting soil and plants."

Against the building was a shelf of colorful ceramic pots with hand-painted symbols of love and serenity. "These small pots appear to be planted with herbs," Heather observed as she broke off a snippet of one of the plants and sniffed the aroma.

"The larger pots," Aden added in a gruff whisper, "are planted with more of Mimi's favorite flowers."

"Favorite?" Heather asked. "That's nice. And, it's twice as nice that they are all fall flowers."

"Yes," Aden answered weakly as she struggled to walk around her newly gifted garden. The pain in her back increased, and she stiffened even more rigidly. It felt like someone had laced a corset too tight around her middle.

"The potting beds are planted with Japanese windflowers." The words rolled off Aden's tongue softly, like a beloved, well-rehearsed script. "Those pink-flushed blossoms look like dogwood, don't they? The small lavender-blue flowers are asters, and the pink blossoms with the succulent bluish-green leaves are called Autumn Joy." She smiled to herself. "I like that name. Also, the Sweet Kate, with the purplish-blue blossoms and yellow foliage, is wonderful. But the golden color won't develop as well without direct sun. The overhang from the floor above will block that." Turning to some huge, individual pots, she added, "Like I said, the large pots are overflowing with fall chrysanthemums, Grandma's favorite. She just planted the garden the other day."

"The other day?" Heather questioned in disbelief.

"Well, actually." Aden relaxed and smiled." Well, like I said, she brought some of the bedding plants from her home the other day and transplanted them into the large, individual pots that were already here." She reached down and touched the petals of the golden Mums. "The other flowers she found at a nursery right here in Manhattan. Isn't that amazing?"

"Your grandmother is quite a gardener," Heather admired.

"She's the president of her garden club in Greenville, Ohio." Aden finally smiled broadly while filled with pride. "In the summers, I used to go to my grandparents' house and help her in her garden while Grandpa mowed the lawn."

"I can see a master gardener has trained you well." Heather clapped her hands together as she moved from plant to plant. "Now watch," she said as she sat on the edge of one of the potting boxes. "Sit down with a small weeding fork. Be careful not to twist. The bruised and partially torn muscles in the lumbar area of your back need rest and healing. Remember, your spine is repaired with glue. You can reach gently, always tightening your abdominal muscles. We'll practice some core-building exercises in a while."

Heather paused and focused on another of Aden's injuries. "Be careful to keep your leg straight for now. The gash in your right calf is where his knife cut the muscle. Luckily, he didn't stab you deep enough to break a bone. The doctor repaired the damage, but the wound hasn't closed yet. It's too soon. You don't want to pull the stitches apart before the slash can knit completely."

"Right," Aden agreed. "I don't want the laceration to start bleeding again." She sat on the opposite end of the wooden flower bed.

"Also," Heather added, "don't move your head. Right now, the neck brace is keeping your head rigid. As your neck heals, twisting your head may seem easier, but remember, your vocal cords are healing, too."

Aden stood up and tried to square her shoulders. "Let's go in."

"Yes, but first, I want you to practice a few deep breathing exercises on the terrace. With the roof from the upper floor, you'll be able to be out here even in light rain."

"I sing, Heather. I know how to breathe. And remember, rain isn't good for vocal cords."

"I know you sing. Humor me. I want you to practice tightening your lower abdomen to the point it remains tightened without thinking about it."

"Heather, I—"

The therapist reached down and picked up a pillow to fluff. "If you want to get off this terrace, Aden, let's begin. Stretch out on the lounge chair."

Aden finally closed her eyes as her shoulders slumped in surrender. She slowly lowered herself onto the white, wicker, thickly padded terrace couch. She placed her fingertips on her lower abdomen pulled the muscle group toward her backbone.

"If you are touching your back to the lounge, you're working too hard," Heather reminded her.

"Oh, okay," Aden agreed. She had finally learned something she didn't already know and felt a tiny wisp of positive energy.

"Aden, I know you're talking too much. Once I've asked my initial questions, you'll talk less. I'll be back tomorrow morning. I want you to practice tightening your core and doing light stretches across the flower beds without twisting," Heather announced. "Tomorrow, I'll bring some directions for Pilates exercises you need to do at least twice a day out here on the lounge. I'll train you in them first."

Aden thought for a minute. "Twice a day? I can do four a day and speed up my recovery."

Heather smiled as she watched Aden's expression. "Twice a day will be fine. More would be okay, too. Now, let's go into your studio and check that out."

Aden led the way back through the living room. There was a little hope in her step.

Heather observed the living space and commented, "The area rug looks large enough that it won't move or kick up."

"Good," Aden whispered and added under her breath, "because I like it, and it isn't going anywhere." She laughed a little. "There was a small rug in the hall that Mother put into the closet. That was good."

Heather smiled. "It sounds like your parents made a thorough safety check of the house before you came home from the hospital."

The spare bedroom was small, about ten by nine. The door was at an angle, off the tiny hall that led to the kitchen. A closet to the left of the door inside the room provided additional space for her clothes. Floor-to-ceiling mirrors covered the closet doors. Along the long wall facing the windows, there was another closet-like door behind which the Murphy bed waited to be pulled down into place. The dance barre, positioned at Aden's waist level, stood away, parallel to the windows, and stretched across the room's length.

"This will be perfect." Heather patted Aden's shoulder. "When the wound in your leg completely closes, we can begin here in the dance studio with exercises and dance steps that will strengthen your back. In the meantime, I want you to be fitted with a back brace to support the lumbar muscles while you exercise and walk around midtown."

"Walk around my neighborhood in a clunky back brace? I don't think so," Aden huffed, rejecting any appearance of disability.

"Aden, Lindy's Restaurant is right downstairs on the corner of 7th Avenue. Take the elevator down, eat lunch, and take a walk. Wear the back brace for additional support."

Aden smiled slightly as a new, creative thought stitched a new seam in her mind. "We'll see," she said with her gravelly voice. But the image she saw was not the picture Heather had painted.

CHAPTER SIXTEEN

Tuesday, October 25

Dr. Hammerstein had arranged for a medically trained vocal coach to come to Aden's home after lunch on October 25. Caleb would be there following the matinee, perhaps by 5 p.m., to grab a cup of coffee and a quick bite before the evening performance at the theater. Aden would have time yet that morning to work through an idea.

Years ago, Aden's great-great-grandmother hitched her horse, Dolly, to the buggy and trotted along the dusty Ohio farm roads selling vanilla and other spices to her neighbors. For her sales, she earned an occasional prize. One cherished possession was a desk. That small, red antique desk now sat against the wall in Aden's living room. The desk had one drawer under a drop-down writing panel. Behind the slanted desktop were several cubbyholes. Her grandmother stored thank-you notes, birthday cards, paper, envelopes, and postage stamps in the tiny cubicles. Grandma Malloy gave it to Aden since it was just the right size for a New York City apartment and perfect for the current generation. Aden put computer paper and extra ink cartridges in the cubbies. She removed four or five sheets of printer paper and a number two pencil with a great eraser. The computer lap desk tucked behind the secretary would make a firm surface. Curling up on the chair that matched the sleek sofa, she propped her leg up, rested the little lap table on the chair arms, and sketched. She wasn't an artist, but she knew what she wanted to see.

Aden worked on her project for the rest of the morning until she had drawn the exact diagrams in her creative mind. Would she be able to talk loud enough if she made a phone call?

When she finally found the number in her phone's contact list, her voice was weak but had more volume than she would have imagined. "Bobbette? Hi, this is Aden Malloy." After not hearing the sound of her own voice very much for days, she was surprised. "Yes, I'm doing okay. Say, I have a project I want to run past you. Can you meet me at Lindy's for lunch in . . . 30 minutes? … My treat. … Great."

####

It didn't seem to Aden that she would ever leave her home again, certainly not leaning on a cane. She didn't think she could tolerate the humiliation of an ugly aluminum stick leading her around the neighborhood. But there she was, at ten 'til twelve, carefully stepping off the elevator onto the lobby floor. A long black skirt from the back of her closet concealed and protected the huge bandage surrounded by a walking brace on her leg. In her cane-free hand, she carried a portfolio. Ralph, the doorman, opened the door onto 53rd Street and waved her through.

Ralph, in a red jacket with brass buttons, smiled. He bowed in a great theatrical pose. "It is good to see you out and about, Miss Malloy. If there is anything you need, you let me know."

"Thanks, Ralph," she mouthed. As she struggled onto the sidewalk, she wondered if her invitation to meet Bobbette was too soon. Would her friend be able to hear her above the clatter of plates and other restaurant conversations?

It was a mid-October morning, fit for any aspiration, even those dreams that had dimmed on awakening. Aden pulled her fedora hat down farther, hoping no one would recognize her. *Who do you think you are, Aden Malloy? Your brief moment in the spotlight wasn't enough for anyone to recognize you. You only stood at center stage for a flash.*

As she walked along the avenue, the autumn sun glanced off the windows around her, sending flashes of sparkling light her way. She felt warm and invigorated, even though it took her three times longer to walk to the corner than it would have before life changed. As people passed, they seemed to fix their eyes on her. Their lingering glances made her nervous. Who were they? Was her attacker among them? Maybe she imagined it all.

When she stepped through the doors of the historic restaurant, she was glad Lindy's had reopened with the same nostalgic decor. It felt warm and familiar, like home. Inside, framed photos of famous stage stars and movie actors who ate at the longtime restaurant in the past lined the walls. *Maybe someday I'll be on this wall,* she thought as she looked for Bobbette, the costume designer for the *Honeysuckle* musical. Aden smiled when she spotted her friend seated at a black leather tufted booth under a photo of a smiling Grammy Award soloist.

"Aden," Bobbette said, beaming broadly. She stood and reached for her newest star. "How are you doing?" She quickly eyed the cane.

"Don't look at it," Aden growled as she removed her hat. "If you don't acknowledge it, it might go away." Opening her arms to hug her friend, Aden dropped the embarrassing stick on the hardwood. "Sorry," she apologized as the cane clattered onto the floor.

At the rude announcement of her presence, most lunch patrons, obvious out-of-towners, just turned and watched. Several patrons, no-doubt locals, smiled and clapped. A few tables away, a woman called out, "Hope you're feeling better, Aden."

"Thank you," Aden mouthed the words. "Sorry for the racket," she whispered.

A man at the next table jumped up and retrieved the loathsome walking device. "Miss Malloy, it's good to see you." He motioned to the woman who sat with him. "We heard about the incident in the alley. I hope you're getting along okay."

Aden took the cane, placed it in the booth beside her, and sat down. "I am, thank you." She eyed the man who recognized her and positioned herself, so he was not behind her. Even though he seemed nice, she had to know where he was and what he was doing. After all, he recognized her. Safety was everything.

"We are all glad to see you in the neighborhood, Miss Malloy." The waitress smiled as she approached the booth with a pad and pencil.

Aden blushed. "That's very sweet, Rachel." Aden maneuvered into a comfortable position. Her eyes scanned the restaurant. She knew she hadn't made a stealth entrance and wondered about every eye in the room.

Bobbette smiled in surprise. "You must come here often. You even know the waitress's name."

"I live nearby," was all Aden offered. The truth was, she was addicted to Lindy's New York-style cheesecake. "I'll have the fruit plate and cottage cheese. Oh, and coffee."

"No cheesecake?" Rachel questioned with a wink.

Aden sighed dramatically. "Probably. I'm not sure if I have my appetite back. I'll order the sweets later."

"And you, ma'am. Are you ready to order?" Rachel paused.

Bobbette handed her menu back to the waitress. "Yes, I'll have the same." When Rachel crisply walked away, Bobbette asked, "Aden, you said you have a project? The accident only happened a week and a half ago, and you are already planning new adventures?"

"It wasn't an accident, Bobbie." Aden stopped; her jaw set in anger as she looked around. "I was attacked."

"Aden," she gasped, "I didn't know. Who would do that?"

"I have no idea. So far, the police have no suspects." Aden shuddered. Just forming the word *attacked* brought some deeply buried, shadowy memories to the surface she didn't want to expose.

"I'm sorry I said it was an accident." Bobbette apologized quietly.

Aden's eyes scanned the room for anyone or anything that didn't look like Lindy's. She hadn't even noticed how full the dining room was when she came in. Nor was she aware of the scrumptious smells of food that floated in the air. "It's not your fault. The news reported all kinds of stories. I'm sorry I got cross with you."

"Never mind all that," Bobbette brushed off. "I hope your project is more pleasant." She stopped. "You know, Aden, that was your third 'I'm sorry' since I got here. Why do women think they must apologize for everything, even things beyond their control? I don't know. Maybe they still think it's a woman's job to make everyone happy."

"Maybe," Aden thought aloud. "For now, you don't need to make everyone happy. I just need you to construct some things for me."

"Sounds interesting." Bobbette sat back when Rachel returned with cups of steaming coffee. "Aden, what did you have in mind?"

Aden brought the portfolio onto the table, then rearranged the coffee cups to make room for everything. "There," she whispered and smiled.

The two friends sipped their fresh, hot coffee as Aden continued. "My physical therapist came this morning. She said my orthopedic specialist wants me to wear a back brace while I exercise and walk around town. Can you believe a big, black, in-your-face back brace?"

Bobbette looked at Aden over the top of her large, horned rim glasses. "I gather you don't want to wear one."

"You gathered more than others did." Aden opened the binder and pulled out the two pages she had worked on. "I'm willing, a little, to wear their sterile, weak-sister back brace while I'm working out at home. But I will not wear the thing while I'm out and about." She smoothed the papers with her fingers. "Could you make these two belts for me? I might design more, but these are the beginning. They will be made of copper-infused polyester with some spandex for tightening them. Can you get that kind of fabric?"

"Spandex?" Bobbette laughed. "The entire entertainment industry is clothed in spandex. The infusion of copper is different than what I have on hand, but I can run downtown and get some."

"Good," Aden said softly.

Bobbette patted her hand. "You're talking too much, Honey."

"I know. Give me a minute to finish going over these. Then, I'll yield the floor to the gentlewoman from Manhattan Costumers and some tales of her three-year-old niece." She turned the first sheet of paper over. "I want you to make wide belts for lumbar support out of the fabric we talked about. This first one will be in a peasant, waist cinch design, with low straps in the back that wrap around to the front to pull it tight."

"Oh, Aden, this is wonderful," Bobbette said excitedly as she inspected the design. "It will support your back without drawing attention to your injury."

"Thanks, Bobbie. This one," Aden drew out her description of the second design, "will be made of wide, braided leather strips in the front, with the same back support and cincher straps in the back. You can border the back in buttonhole stitched thin leather strips. The closure is a gold loop in the center front." She chuckled and pointed to the drawing. "I'm no artist. I couldn't get the leather braid to look right. I gave you the suggestion of braided leather strips. You can follow through on it much better than I can draw. What about it? Can you do it, and how long will it take?"

"Of course, I can do it, Aden. Do you doubt me?"

"Never, that's why I'm buying your lunch. It would be a poor investment if I didn't already know the payout." She picked up her coffee cup and ran her finger around the rim. "Bobbie, I really need those belts."

A man in black pants and a sweater entered the restaurant and looked around. It was when he fixed his eyes on Aden that she began to tremble.

"It's all right." Bobbette immediately saw Aden's reaction and turned to see who had frightened her. "Look, he's meeting some people at a table in the back." She pointed to a lovely blond woman who was waving the man over.

"Okay, okay." Aden gave in and tried to calm down. She sipped from her water glass and quickly glanced at the couple.

"You absolutely would benefit from these wonderful therapeutic belts." Bobbette reached over and patted Aden's hand. "If I have the fabric, Jill, my seamstress, can make them up, and I can bring them over this evening. I'll call the loft before I leave here and check our stacks of fabric and leather. If I have to get supplies, the Wholesale Fabric Outlet is on 37th Street, just the next street over from my design loft. I can pick up the things we might need on my way back to the loft. If I have to stop for materials, it might be tomorrow morning before I can drop the belts off. Jill has to leave early today." Bobbie pulled a small card from her pocket and handed it to Aden. "If you need to call, you have my number. The number on the back of the card is my business partner's cell. Jill can answer any question you may have, too."

"Either will be wonderful, Bobbie, this evening or tomorrow morning," Aden murmured softly. "I had no idea you could do it that quickly. I have your number already, but I'm glad to have Jill's. I'll try not to call and interrupt either of you."

"Two fruit plates," Rachel announced as she put the colorful meals on the table. "I'll bring more coffee." The colorful fruit was served on large white plates. Around the outer edge, tangy pineapple chunks lined up beside slices of apple, bananas, and large red strawberries. A mound of cottage cheese, with a hint of salt and cinnamon, was formed in the middle.

"Thanks," Aden said as she smiled at Rachel. "And Bobbie, thank you, my friend." Aden put her fork into a small banana piece and a dollop of cottage cheese.

The conversation turned to Bobbie's niece as a small helping of hope filled Aden. *Dwell on the positive,* Aden reminded herself as stories of Bobbie's Little Pumpkin, as she called her niece, dominated their table talk.

CHAPTER SEVENTEEN

After lunch, Aden walked back to her condo. Somehow, she felt safer, yet nothing had changed. Her attacker was still unknown. But there was a feeling beginning to reassert itself after creating the belts and putting their creation into action. She was beginning to feel in charge of her own life again.

Back in her home, she stood at the sliding doors leading out to the terrace and stared at the large, plump jars of flowers. She was determined to win the battle of wills. She repeated silently; *I am not afraid of a porch, even with a fancy name like terrace. I spent every summer sitting and playing on our front porch at home. The wide, concrete railing formed the fantasy horse and saddle I rode for hours on rainy days.*

Looking at the beautiful chaise lounge she found after a week of shopping when she first moved in, Aden came to a conclusion. Her anger didn't have anything to do with fresh air or sunshine and had everything to do with her attacker and … that garden.

Aden spent many summer weekends in the small garden her grandmother planted every year in Greenville. But in Mimi's yard, it was different than on Aden's own terrace in New York. Along the longest part of the Ohio garden, facing the street, Grandma Malloy always planted flowers of various colors. Behind the blooms were the vegetables, some that Aden had to learn to appreciate, like broccoli and onions.

If someone hadn't stabbed and beaten Aden, her grandmother wouldn't have come and planted a garden. The potted plants seemed to tell Aden that she was a homebody with nothing to do but putter around in her garden. When she looked at the raised beds and large pots, she didn't really see beautiful blossoms. She saw everything she had lost, her legs and back strength for dancing, and … her voice.

Even the glass door onto the terrace seemed especially heavy as she struggled to open it. She stepped out and walked past the loathsome furniture where she was supposed to practice breathing. Bellying up to the glass-protective railing, she gazed at the city she loved. Several years before, she came to conquer that city but only won the first battle. Through the autumn wind blowing along the canyon streets far below, she thought she heard the wild applause of opening night still clinging to the mild afternoon air. A faint smile was on her lips as she inhaled the autumn day.

Aden wasn't ready to sit down and practice Pilates breathing and core building. She walked over to the corner of the balcony and looked toward the Whiteway Theater. If she was ever going to return to that sweet stage, she would have to make peace with her body. And making peace meant giving in to the experts. She won her spot on the New York stage by taking charge of her life. Going out on her own, when the odds of success in show business were not in her favor, was how she succeeded.

"I do not have to be told what to do. This is my decision," Aden assured herself. "I determine what is best for me. And I prescribe therapy, exercise, meditation, and quiet out here in my flower-covered garden."

She sat down on the chaise, placed her fingertips on her lower abdomen, and pulled in her core … one, now push out, pull in, two, three, four …. She closed her eyes and soaked in the sounds of the city.

The lounge chair was low. When it came time to stand up, Aden was stuck. She tried to get her feet tucked under her, but the walking brace on her right leg made it hard to pull her foot back farther. The brace was there to protect the damaged nerves and muscles. Now, it was interfering with her ability to get up. What was she going to do?

I can take care of myself, she remembered trying to convince her mother. Now, here she was, in the city that amazed her, unable to get up off the porch furniture.

Inside, she could feel the trembling of approaching waves of tears. She wanted to give in to a salty stream. Instead, she became determined to solve the problem … but how? She thought for a moment, pulled her feet as far back as possible, kept her head down, rocked back and forth, tried to stand, and fell back on the chair. "Grrr," she growled.

She tried again. "No!" Aden screamed silently into the far canyons of the Big Apple. "I can do this," she muttered with determination. Leaning farther forward, looking down, Aden stood up and then straightened. With her cane above her head, she Victory-danced around the terrace, weaving in and around the garden path.

When Aden checked her watch, it was two forty-five. The voice coach would be there at three. She had time to pour herself another cup of coffee before Geraldine arrived. First, she slowly walked through her small garden and cupped a flower blossom in her hand. The sweet fragrance almost won her over. Peace filled her as she bent over one bloom after another. Her favorite hymn, *In the Garden*, sang like a lullaby in her memory.

> I come to the garden alone,
> While the dew is still on the roses;
> And the voice I hear, falling on my ear,
> The Son of God discloses.
> And he walks with me, and he talks with me,
> And he tells me I am his own,
> And the joy we share as we tarry there,
> None other has ever known. [1]

The doorbell suddenly rang out with, *The hills are alive* …. The thought of someone at the door to her safe haven made her hold her breath. *Am I having another panic attack? Oh no, not again.* Aden gasped inside as her chest tightened when the doorbell rang a second time.

Limping to the door, she frowned. Was this going to be her reaction every time a visitor came? Slowing as she neared the door, she knew she wanted to ignore whoever was there.

She began a short self-reprimand. *Wait, stop it, Aden. You are expecting someone who might be able to help you with your voice.* Surrendering to the doorbell, Aden peeped through the door viewer. "May I see your identification?" Aden's voice did not cooperate. Her panic only made talking harder.

"Sure," the woman held up her driver's license. "I'm Geraldine Garver—your voice coach."

Aden unlocked the deadbolts and opened the door, still struggling to breathe. "Come …"

"Aden," Geraldine said as she put her arm around Aden's shoulder. "Are you all right?"

"I … can't … breathe," she gasped.

"Sit over there," Geraldine directed toward the couch. She placed the square white box she carried on the coffee table. "Sit back so you're comfortable. With the neck brace, you can't bend or turn. Just close your eyes and see your throat like a shiny open pipe."

Aden tried to breathe more slowly with her hand on her chest as she walked over to the sofa. "I can't … lower my head."

"Oh yes, I know. Dr. Hammerstein told me about all of your injuries. No bending, just relaxing. Remember the pipes." Geraldine turned and looked around the condo. "Do you have any paper bags?"

"Maybe. Mostly plastic. Geraldine, try…kitchen," Aden gasped as she pointed over her shoulder. She smiled a little when she remembered an old public service announcement. *No plastic over your head.*

Geraldine picked up the box and hurried toward the kitchen as Aden sat back on the couch and closed her eyes. She knew from stage prep, if she slowed her breathing, she could slow the pounding of her heart that might come with stage fright. Aden tried to put it in reverse. She saw herself beating her own heart like a drummer on a snare drum. *I come to the garden alone,* she sang inside. *His voice to me is calling.* As the melody and words filled and warmed her, she slowed her beats to a new tempo. Finally, she was able to catch her breath. Then, the sweet aroma of cinnamon and sugar caught up to her.

"I'm sorry, Aden," Geraldine called, "I can't find any bags." She started back to join Aden. "And call me Gerry."

"That's okay," Aden whispered in soft, slow tones. "I'm doing better."

Gerry flopped down on the couch beside her. "You'll have to tell me sometime how you did that." She smiled as she patted Aden's arm.

Aden smiled at her new voice coach. She had taken voice lessons since she was fourteen years old. What would this new coach have to teach her to gain back even a few notes from her top register? Suddenly, the aroma of some kind of dessert hit her. "I have a detective nose for sweets, Gerry. Did you bring something in?"

Geraldine jumped up and started for the marble-top counter in the kitchen. "Pecan cinnamon rolls, my dear." She opened a few cabinets, took out two small plates, and dropped a scrumptious nutty pastry on each. Back in the living room, she placed Aden's roll in front of her with an air of accomplishment. "Here ya go."

"It looks wonderful." Aden hadn't regained her appetite, but there was something extra yummy about the roll's aroma. For the first time since the attack, Aden could taste her food, the nuts, the cinnamon, and the caramel. Taking a bite, the many flavors blended together into a familiar enjoyment.

"Tell me about your voice training, Aden. I know the beautiful results of all your hard work. I was at the

Whiteway Theater that first night." Gerry bit off a piece of roll and winked.

Aden stopped chewing and put the rest of her roll down. "You were there on opening night?"

"I sure was." Gerry closed her eyes. "The cast, the music, the book, the costumes, everything was wonderful." She leaned toward Aden reassuringly. "And you were magnificent."

"Thanks, Gerry." Inside, Aden tried to stay positive. She knew that was a major part of healing. "One night. After all of my hard work, I got to star in the musical for only one night. I had a three-octave range, Gerry. From the F below middle C to the F above high C. I cannot sing at all now."

"Aden, of course, you can't," Gerry took her hand in hers. "Your doctor told you that someone cut your throat. First, it has to heal."

"Then what?" Aden asked as her eyes filled with tears.

Gerry hesitated for a moment. "To be honest, I don't know. But I believe you are such a good performer you will sing again. Right now, I cannot tell you your range."

"Honeysuckle is written for a high soprano, Gerry."

"Let's worry about that when we have nothing else to worry about, Aden." Gerry paused, seeming to search for the right words. "Your musical career isn't over, you know. But you might have to be willing to adjust your life."

"Adjust?" Aden didn't say any more. Her shoulders fell as the weight of all that was taken from her threatened to crumble her resolve. But she refused to show any more weakness. She had already been adjusting. She couldn't walk without a cane, and she certainly couldn't dance. Her voice was barely a whisper, and her back hurt.

A smile crossed Aden's face as she remembered her new beginning had already begun. In full shape and color, a laced bodice and a braided leather belt waltzed through her thoughts, and she had a new plan. Maybe the belts could help other people, too. Perhaps she had already embraced a new way of facing life.

Gerry stood up and tapped Aden's foot. "I think you're ready. Let's begin."

CHAPTER EIGHTEEN

Gerry looked around the room. "Where do you normally vocalize each day?"

"There at the piano." Aden pointed to the Yamaha Clavinova against the end wall opposite the small bedroom. "There are mirrors on those doors." She pointed to a narrow, angular set of double doors that opened into a triangle-shaped closet. "If I need to practice with visual feedback, it's all right there."

Gerry studied the rosewood digital console. "Do you also play the keyboard?"

"Yes … well, some. With the ability of the Clavinova to fill in the more difficult background, my playing sounds okay." She smiled as she thought of the hours and hours of practice she had put in for the musical long before the full cast rehearsed. "I had digital support to practice my solos."

"That's wonderful, Aden," Gerry said encouragingly and paused. "Dr. Hammerstein went over your prognosis very carefully with me."

Aden said nothing and asked nothing more. For the most part, she focused her gaze out the window. While Gerry chattered, Aden watched a gaggle of wild geese fly by, detoured from their flight along the coast. She smiled inside when she thought of an old Disney movie about a girl leading her geese through the canyons of New York City. *What was Gerry saying?*

"The cut on your leg will heal. Your back, hopefully, will eventually be as good as new. But, your voice …"

Aden's attention snapped back to Gerry's words. "My voice? But…? Will I sing again?"

"Obviously, we'll know more when the incision in your throat heals. Dr. Hammerstein is sure you will be able to speak without hoarseness. The attacker only nicked your vocal cords, and that was repaired."

"And … singing?" Aden realized she was holding her breath but found it hard to exhale.

Gerry reached over and took her hand. "Yes … but Dr. Hammerstein doesn't know when your upper range will return."

Aden jerked her hand away. "I'm a dramatic soprano with a powerful voice. I can sing right over the orchestra," Aden whispered as hot salty tears, not of sorrow but of anger, rolled down her cheeks.

Gerry reached for her hand again in encouragement. "Yes, right, Aden. That's wonderful. Your type of voice also has a comfortable lower tessitura, or vocal range, with a darker timbre."

"Timbre?" Aden spouted out through clenched teeth. "My tone quality has always been great for the theater. Will that change? When will I get it all back? Now what?"

"No, Aden. The doctor believes the timbre will stay the same. It's the range she's uncertain about. We won't know for about a year."

"A year? Do you mean I won't have my upper tones for a year? What about returning to *Honeysuckle Rose*?"

"Let's not go there yet." Gerry put her arm on Aden's shoulder. "Dr. Hammerstein suggested that I prepare you for a lower register."

It all had to be part of the awful nightmare she had been living. "Lower?" she gasped in disbelief. "The solos for the female lead in a musical are written for a high soprano. I'll lose my role."

"Maybe not," Gerry encouraged her. "We can talk to the producers about rewriting your music."

"Like … second lead, second soprano range?" Aden felt the tears flow and flood her face.

Gerry pulled her new vocal student over and hugged her. "No, Sweetie, like low alto … or tenor range."

"Gerry, no," Aden sobbed with her hands over her face.

"It's been done before," Gerry soothed.

Aden looked up and out toward the terrace garden. "I am not Karen Carpenter, Geraldine. I am Aden Malloy."

CHAPTER NINETEEN

Tuesday Evening, October 25

It was only 5:15 p.m., but the city's tall buildings blocked the remaining sunlight. The sun was on the other side of the building, making Aden's condominium shady and beginning to darken. Aden hated darkness, even in her melancholy, where shadows were often welcome to feed the sadness.

When the doorbell rang, she tried to jump up, forgetting she wasn't jumping up for anything. Aden wasn't sure which was more painful, her leg or her back. She knew she couldn't stand up straight and hated her crumpled posture. That made two things she hated, darkness and her back. Aden couldn't remember hating anything or anyone in the past. She always took life as it came, with a positive attitude. When the bell rang again, it only scratched her anger like an annoying itch.

At the door, Caleb appeared at the peephole. Aden hadn't seen him since she left the hospital. Flinging the door open, she leaped into his arms, dropped her cane, and clung to him. The familiar spicy leather and pine scent of his aftershave lotion filled her with joy. "It is so good to see you," she squealed.

"Good to see you, too." Caleb kissed her cheek and then quickly helped her get her cane. "I don't want to hurt you. Are you sure you should be standing like that?"

"Standing?" Aden asked with disbelief. "Caleb, how do you think I got to the door?"

"I just don't like seeing you in pain."

"Is your emotional pain greater than my physical pain?" Aden asked under her breath.

Caleb sighed dramatically. "You know I didn't mean that." He watched her move. "Are you taking your pain meds?"

"I don't want to take that stuff," she began rubbing her hands together.

"You have to head off the pain before it comes," his insistence was firm.

"I am not going to take pain pills to ensure I don't get any pain." If she could have stomped her feet, she would have. "I took the narcotic in the hospital, but I'll deal with the pain now that I'm healing." Silence soon hung over the room.

Outside, the sun would set in an hour, when the streetlights would begin to glow, and the city would turn into a magical world of twinkle lights. In the condo, the shadows only brought evidence of the depression Aden didn't welcome.

"I'll turn on the light," Aden offered. "It's getting dreary in here."

Caleb smiled and spoke softly. "I thought it was romantic."

"Dreary is not romantic, Caleb," she snapped. "Dimmed light is romantic, not wondering who or what may be lurking in the darkness."

"Lurking, Aden?" He followed her to the lamp, then plopped down on the sofa.

She stopped and stared at him. "Caleb, I was attacked by someone just a few days ago. They still don't know who the attacker was. I have a right to be afraid."

"Come." He patted the cushion beside him. "Sit here beside me."

Aden eased down slowly and carefully leaned back on the couch. She felt stiff with Caleb, both physically and socially. *What's wrong? How did things change so fast?* She felt his arms around her as he tried to draw her closer. But Aden soon discovered she couldn't bend in his direction, literally.

"Honey … you're tense," he complained."

"Caleb …" Suddenly, a new understanding crossed her mind. "You really have no idea what happened to me, do you?"

"Aden, of course I do. Remember, I was with your parents when we found you. When I heard someone cut your leg and throat, I was worried sick. I could hardly perform the next day. All I could think about was you not being there. I had to get adjusted to the understudy."

Disgust mounted within Aden. "Basically, you were worried about yourself." She crossed her arms and clung to her body.

Caleb straightened his back. "Aden, explain yourself. How can you possibly think that? Give me some evidence."

Aden laughed. "I don't need to validate my beliefs. And I don't owe you an explanation for what I think and feel, Caleb Johansson. You owe me the respect of accepting my opinions." Even before the attack, Aden became angry when Caleb insisted that she defend her position on everything. Now, she heard herself finally speaking the words she had only thought in the past months. A new strength grew within her, if not in her physical body, at least in her psyche. Maybe that's where new energy needs to start.

"Well, that's a new you, Aden," Caleb smirked.

"Good, I needed a new *me*." She took a deep breath. "Someone tried to kill me, Caleb. Maybe a newer, stronger, more assertive *me* is just what I need."

Caleb reached over and took her hand. "Then you wouldn't be my Baby Girl anymore, Sweetie."

"So …" Aden drew out slowly as she pulled her hand away, "we aren't a couple unless I'm weak? Unless I fall into step within your shadow?"

He reached for her hand again. "No. When you put it that way, naturally, I don't want you to be weak or in anyone's shadow."

Aden straightened her back, at least in her resolve. "Then think about what you want, Caleb. Because when you see me, you'll see someone who can stand on her own two feet."

"Well, not quite yet," Caleb quipped as he pointed to the orthopedic brace around her leg.

Aden glared at him but said nothing.

"Sorry … that wasn't funny," he apologized.

Aden sat there for a moment until the silence became deafening. Pulling her feet under her, she leaned into the motion as she started to stand up.

"Wait, Aden." He patted her knee. "You've been through a lot and still have a way to go. I am sorry. You need as much strength as you can muster. If I can help you in any way, I want to be a part of your healing."

"Thanks." She placed her hand on top of his. "Most of me will heal," she began. "But—"

"But?" Caleb's eyes snapped to meet hers. "But? But what?"

"Well, the first *but* is, my attacker is still out there. He didn't even try to rob me. He left my cell phone and my walking around money and jewelry. I know he'll be back if he intends to kill me."

"Sweetheart, I am sorry." He put his fingers in his hair and stirred, embarrassed and frustrated. "I never thought about him coming back."

"And … there's another *but*." How was she going to tell him? The terrace twinkle lights snapped on and made Aden think of the lights on the stage in scene three.

"And …?" Caleb waited impatiently for the rest of the *buts*.

"Dr. Hammerstein doesn't know if I'll get my singing voice back," she blurted out and began wringing her hands.

"What does that mean?" Caleb asked, blinking nervously. "Will you be able to speak … no laryngitis?"

"Yes." She rubbed her hands together and massaged her arms nervously. "But the upper register of my singing voice may never come back."

"That won't matter," Caleb added with empathy. "Well, it will matter to you, of course. I meant they can rewrite your upper notes and pitch them a little lower."

"It isn't a little lower, Caleb," she spit out in disgust. She leaned on him and heavily on the arm of the couch as she struggled to stand up. She looked around frantically. The only place she could see to escape was the terrace. She grabbed the door latch and stepped slowly out onto the balcony. Caleb shuffled his feet and followed her.

"Aden, the balcony is beautiful," he marveled when he saw the autumn flowers and pots of herbs. "When did you do all of this?"

"I didn't do it." She paused and thought for a moment. "Maybe that's the problem. It's my garden, but I didn't plan it or plant it." She walked over to the New York asters and lightly touched their delicate blooms. "This is my new life, and my grandmother jumped in and took over."

"Took over?" Caleb shook his head. "Took over what? A few plants for your terrace?"

"But, it's my terrace, Caleb? My home is the only safe place in the whole city, and someone else shouldn't change it." She hissed through gritted teeth. "And it's the only place where I have control. My control. My home. Otherwise, I feel helpless."

"Did you think … maybe you're supposed to learn something from all of this?"

Aden was incredulous. Was he making a kindergarten lesson out of a vicious, near-death attack? She stomped her cane on the terrace deck and shook her head. "I can't think of life lessons right now, Caleb. I have other concerns."

He raised his hands in surrender. "Okay, okay. Maybe a few notes off the top won't be bad."

Suddenly, she felt trapped. She wanted to escape back inside, but Caleb stood between her and the door. "Caleb, I'll … only be able to sing in the second alto or … tenor range."

"What? But the lead is written for a soprano," he gasped.

"The female lead in a musical always is high, Caleb," she whispered as tears of disappointment and betrayal streamed down her face. *Betrayed? That's silly.* Why did she feel that someone had been disloyal?

"Geraldine Garver … Gerry, said, when my voice is ready, I should try singing an octave lower like Karen Carpenter." She slumped down on a terrace chair and looked at her beloved city.

"Don't dismiss that idea so fast," he said slowly. "It could work."

"How? How could that work? Melody is above the baritone, Caleb," she mocked with anger.

"Oh really? I didn't know that," the rich baritone voice sassed back.

"I'm sorry." Aden stopped talking and pulled inside her own protective shell.

"I just meant you could still sing the melody, under the harmony, not on top. That would make close, harmonic chording when the baritone is singing with you."

"Do you think?" She rubbed her eyes on a tissue. "It might work."

CHAPTER TWENTY

Caleb left, and Aden was alone. Bobbette called and said she had finished the belts and would drop them off on her way home from work. Aden couldn't wait for Bobbie to deliver the belts. Her excitement mounted. It was the first time in days that she had something to look forward to. Even though a mild cloud of depression was beginning to gather, Aden would have to wait. More alone time. More empty space to let fear and disappointment creep in and rob her of health, strength, and energy.

Her laptop lay on the coffee table where she had left it many days before the attack and the painful nights in the hospital. She hadn't even noticed her notebook computer when she gained more energy and started moving around the house. The very slim, ever-present, gray box of memories, research, and imagined plans, disappeared into the room and into the back of her mind. Her eyes hadn't even been able to focus, and her mind refused to concentrate since … well … since that Friday night. She wondered if reading a computer screen would be possible. She checked the clock again and sighed.

Slowly, resentfully, Aden dragged the small computer onto her lap. Why? She didn't really know why. At least, her conscious self didn't know the reasons. She seemed to be subconsciously streaming her old life into automatic movements without purpose. With her computer all booted up, she absent-mindedly logged onto video chat. Before she was aware, Grandma Mimi appeared on the screen.

"Hi, Sweetheart." Rosemary Malloy's dear face beamed.

"Hi, Mimi." Weak and gravely, Aden's voice cracked. "Hope you can hear me."

"No hearing aids needed here, at least not yet." Her grandmother's eyes narrowed as she studied Aden. "Your black eye and facial bruising have improved. There's been some fading. That's good."

"Do you really think so?" Aden's gaze darted across the room to the wall mirror. Even at a distance, it looked like her face belonged to someone else. Perhaps she had been a boxer in a previous life before the attack. "I haven't seen any improvement."

Mimi was slow to ask the next question. "Honey, have you thought about what you're supposed to learn from all of this?"

Aden stiffened. Caleb had just asked her the same question. Inside, she was angry that Mimi would agree with Caleb. But she didn't want to honor the connection by speaking of it aloud. "I can't see it." She squinted again in the mirror, but the ugly orange, deep reds, and browns of the bruises on her face and blackeyes were still there. She blurted out, "Do you really believe God sends evil into our lives to inflict pain and injury just so we can learn a lesson?"

"No," Mimi spoke calmly and softly. "Absolutely not. Life happens, Aden. And God is with us through it all. But we can learn valuable lessons about ourselves during the injury and agony."

"Right," Aden agreed. She'd heard those gems of wisdom her entire life and didn't feel strong enough to hear them repeated again and again. Maybe the words exhausted her because she clenched her fits, ready for a fight, every time the phrase tumbled out. The same words, like a spilled box of anagrams, scattered the same message in her path.

Mimi's voice was soft. "Rumor has it you aren't very pleased with your garden."

"It's confusing, Mimi. The garden is beautiful but represents so much junk: fear, pain, loss, and confinement. It was planted to pretend nothing happened. It's hard to enjoy it."

"I understand." Her grandmother paused a second. "Honcy, I didn't plant the garden to deny the reality of anything that happened in your life. It was planted for you to enjoy and see the outside as a safe and beautiful place. I have an idea. Why don't you come up with four or five positive words to describe the garden?"

Aden sighed deeply. "Homework on the aftermath of everything else?"

Mimi muffled a laugh until she found a straight face. "Well, I wouldn't call it that. I know. Why don't you re-label it? Homework on seizing control of your future, whatever that may be."

When the doorbell rang, Aden was expecting it. "Mimi, there's someone at the door. Gotta run."

"Okay, call again." With that, calm and patient Mimi was gone. But the person at the door seemed impatient as the doorbell rang again.

Aden wasn't expecting the face that peered back at her through the peephole. The same guy came to the door earlier, looking for someone.

Aden forced her voice through the door. "I told you. I don't know Carol and Chris Foy." The strain of being heard without opening the door hurt. Following surgery on her throat and vocal cords, even clearing her throat wasn't recommended. She coughed a little and shuddered.

"Maybe I could come in and use your telephone," he said smoothly.

"No." She yanked her cell phone from her pocket, brought the camera to the peephole, and snapped the camera. "Ask the doorman downstairs to use his phone," she offered as calmly as possible. She believed she was safer if she didn't show fear.

"What was that?" the man asked when he saw the quick flash of the camera.

"Oh, sorry. I was trying to find an earring," Aden's whisper trembled. "My flashlight got away from me."

She watched through the door as her neighbor, Carl Fritz, came out into the hall and stopped. "Can I help you?" Carl asked the man. "My neighbor isn't feeling well."

"Sure," the stranger said, smiling. "I'm looking for friends."

"Who are they?" Fritz asked.

"I thought they lived here," the man said boldly. He rubbed his chin awkwardly and asked, "What is the lady's name who lives here? She won't open the door."

"If she isn't the person you're looking for, it really doesn't matter what her name is, now does it?" Carl asked. "Who are you looking for?"

"Like I said, Carol and Chris Foy," the man glared.

"And, your name is?" Carl asked.

"If the Foys don't live here, it really doesn't matter what my name is, now does it, Carl?" he growled back.

"Well, now," Fritz smiled, "I guess you will be on your way then." He stood there, planted in front of Aden's door, as the man walked toward the elevator. Through the door, Fritz whispered, "Don't open up until he's gone."

"Believe me, I won't," Aden finally exhaled. "I should call the detective on my case, but I'm expecting company."

Through the tiny hole in the door, she could see Carl watching the man all the way down the hall. Carl scratched his head, "How did he know my name?"

Aden laughed softly, watching her neighbor through the security hole. "Carl, I wouldn't need a hole in the door to know it was you talking. I hear that distinctive voice on the radio every day."

"Right," Carl shrugged. "I suppose." When the elevator doors closed, taking the man out of the hall, Carl whispered, "He's gone, Aden. You're safe."

She opened the door a crack and looked into the hall. Except for Carl Fritz—*Your late-night radio news source,* on station WBKR, it was empty. She opened the door a little farther. "Thanks, Carl. Do you have time to come in a minute?"

He checked his watch, "Sure. It's seven-fifteen. I have just that minute you need."

Aden opened the door and looked down the hall for any reappearance of the man who continued stalking her. "Come on in." She snatched up the colorful blue blanket she had thrown down on the couch and led the way through the living room to the terrace door. "I know you and Lynn have a terrace garden. I want your advice."

The open door to the balcony let in the sweet evening air. As amazing as it could be, the city breeze that drifted far above the street had filtered out the taxi and bus exhaust. Funny, Aden hadn't noticed before; the terrace smelled like a garden.

"Aden, this is beautiful," Carl exclaimed as he went from the first planting bed to the next.

She walked past each flowering pot and bed of blooms. "I thought you could give me some ideas … like, I don't even know if I should water them or let the natural rain do the job."

"Who planted all of this?" Carl asked. He sniffed the blossoms and the long-bladed leaves as he walked through.

"My grandmother designed the entire terrace," Aden sighed. "I guess she thought I could use the added work."

"Work? No … Aden." Carl smiled gently at the green leaves that caught the rain. "The garden adds joy, peace, and the privilege of putting your fingers in God's good earth."

Aden smiled as she remembered something. "Grandma used to say, 'Plant your love and harvest God's.'"

"I like that. You're creative. Why don't you make a sign out of wood or some weather-resistant material and put it in your garden — The Garden of Aden? Make the outside yours." He checked his watch again. "As to watering the plants, the garden on our terrace is on the other side of the building. It gets different light, and rain comes in at another angle. Treat the terrace as if the garden were in your grandmother's backyard. Get out your watering can when the plants look like they need water. and the soil is dry." He started back inside the condo. "I'll have to hurry. Can I tell my listeners that you are up and around, working in your garden?"

"Sure, that would be very nice. It may keep my name before the public. My work here on the terrace will be more like physical therapy for a while. I'm to stretch across the planting beds and use my core properly as I reach to weed the pots. And, Carl, please don't tell your listeners I'm your neighbor. I don't want anyone to be able to find me."

"Absolutely," he said over his shoulder as he went to the door with Aden following. When he opened it, a woman was there carrying a long, lumpy sack.

"Bobbie," Aden squeaked. Any surprise sent her into panic mode. This time, the person behind the door was an expected friend. "I'm glad you're here." She pulled her friend into the foyer.

"Carl, wait a minute," she said as she quickly introduced him to her friend. "This is Bobbette Carpenter, the show's costume designer. She's a genius."

Carl touched his hat. "Good to meet you. My wife and I saw the show. I know how great those costumes are. You're busy now, Aden. I'll call the police for you from the taxi on the way into the studio. I saw what that guy looked like. I can give them a description." He smiled, waved over his shoulder, and hurried to the elevator.

"The police detective's name is Alverez," Aden called after him in a coarse voice. "Detective Angela Alverez. Thank you. You were a lifesaver. Perhaps literally."

CHAPTER TWENTY-ONE

"What happened?" Bobbette asked as she watched the elevator door close, carrying Carl away. "Why does he look and sound familiar?"

"You probably saw his face on the side of a city bus," Aden lightly chuckled, then coughed. "That was Carl Fritz of WBKR."

"Oh," Bobbie blurted out. "Carl Fritz, your late-night radio news source."

"Exactly," Aden chuckled softly. As she led Bobbette into the living room, she thought aloud, "I think that was the first time I've laughed since the attack."

"Then, I'm glad I came." She gave Aden a sideways hug. Bobbie looked at every corner of the room as she sat on the sofa. "Okay, I can't find the game station."

"And you won't find a game console in my home," Aden said with a smile as she tried to muffle another cough. "I don't have time for games. I used to play a little while growing up in Ohio. I was pretty good, too. Now, I don't even know the names of the most popular electronic systems." She shrugged a little. "Maybe someday this Broadway star-thing will lose its luster, and I'll need other forms of entertainment to keep me going."

"Well, you have another distraction now. A great one," Bobbette said with an excited twinkle. "Okay, my friend, I brought the belts for your approval or disapproval with suggestions—and that's fine, too. We have a moderate learning curve here. I've made many peasant belts. The shape of this one is just a little higher and made out of different fabric," Bobbie said with pride.

"Let me see them," Aden said softly.

Bobbie put the sack beside the laptop on the huge circular live-edge wooden coffee table. "I hope I was able to make what you had in mind. Your drawings were great." She removed the belts, placed one on top of the package, and handed the cinch belt to Aden.

"Bobbie … it's beautiful," Aden gasped as she picked up the wide, lace-up beauty like a fine piece of art. "Now, let me see …" she paused as she pushed herself off the couch and wrapped the wide belt around her. Closing her eyes, she sighed, "Yes … it works. I can feel the support without looking like I just stepped out of a convalescent facility." Aden filled with joy when she caught a glimpse of herself in the mirrored closet door. "It looks great. Sorry to say, looking like a little old lady is my greatest worry at this point in my young life." She moved a little in front of the mirror and smiled. "Let me try the other one."

Bobbette stood and helped Aden remove the cinch. "Can you feel a difference with the belt on or off?"

"Yes, I can," Aden gasped in surprise and satisfaction. "And it's not wishful thinking, Bobbie. I really can feel the support in the cinch."

Aden wrapped the braided leather belt around her and flashed a grin that lit up her face. "It is wonderful," she drew out slowly as she looked in the mirror.

"You look fantastic in both of them, Aden," Bobbette said as she admired her artistic handiwork. "I can make as many as you want in various colors and materials."

"That would be more than I had even hoped for," Aden agreed as her smile filled her face.

"What about this?" Bobbette thought out loud. "You design them; I'll make them, and we'll sell them on your website with your name on them. There have to be a lot of women with sore backs but want to look young and healthy."

For the first time in days, Aden's thoughts were other than her post-surgery pain and the loss of everything important to her. She actually had something else to fill her thoughts. "We'd need someone to monitor the orders that come in and then ship them out. What would that cost?"

"If they sell as fast as I think they will, price won't matter. I have space in the loft to set it up and get it going. My niece, Shamone, can fill and ship the orders to begin the business. She needs a part-time job for college, and her salary would be covered by the shipping and handling charges on each order. It would work. What do you say?"

"I have to have something to look forward to besides the physical therapist's visit. A small business would be great. Yes, I'm in," Aden squealed hoarsely and then covered her mouth.

"I'll bring a camera tomorrow evening after work, and we'll take pictures of you wearing these two. If you come up with other designs, I can make those in a few days, and we can have them on your website by next week."

"Amazing!" Aden whispered. "I think we can pull this off." She rotated her body in front of the mirror, careful not to twist, and loved what she saw. Her image revealed how much weight she had lost following that night in the alley. She thought of Scotty. He knew that dancers are usually thin with all their long and rigorous dance routines. *Skeeter, I want you to stay healthy. Don't get too thin.*

"Bobbie, I just can't believe it." Aden posed some more, patting and caressing the belt around her middle. "If you haven't eaten yet, let's celebrate. Angelo's Pizza, down the street on Broadway, will deliver the best pizza you've ever eaten … unless you have to get home to family."

Bobbette whooped and threw both hands in the air. "Brice took Ian to his game and won't be home for hours. Pizza sounds wonderful. I am starving."

"Then, life-changing decisions have been made in a matter of minutes." Aden giggled. With her hand to her mouth, she looked at her reflection in the mirror again. "All in all, this has been a good day."

CHAPTER TWENTY-TWO

Saturday, October 29

"Hi, Cindy," Aden bubbled in a fizzy voice into her cell phone when Cindy Streeter called three days later. "It's good to hear your voice."

And it was true. It was wonderful to hear Cindy's familiar voice. Until last week, Aden and Cindy would have run their errands together. Their business would have been shared fun. But the musical, *Honeysuckle Rose,* seemed like something from the distant past, a far-off memory, yesterday's joy. Aden smoothed her hand across the middle of her white silk blouse and raked her fingers through her hair.

"Everyone wanted me to call," Cindy said encouragingly. "We all miss you so much." There were a few seconds of silence. "We heard that you might not be able to come back to the show, Aden."

"Only Caleb knew about my condition, Cindy." Aden's heart fell. Had the cast gossiped about her, unable to walk or talk while in the hospital? They might have started a pool about how long it would take before she was dropped from the show. Aden didn't like the thought.

"I'm your friend, Aden. I don't want to get in the middle of anything," Cindy apologized. "Everybody is hoping you are all right. We just want what's best for you and the show."

Aden relaxed and gave in. "I know you do, Cindy. I'll be out for at least a few weeks. The issue will be how soon I get my voice back. Since I'm alone most of the time, I've been able to rest my vocal cords more than the doctor expected. But when I first return to the role, I might have to sing a full octave, or more, lower than how the score is now written."

"That's your singing voice. Sustaining a note for a long time might be hard in a low key." Then Cindy asked a question that had not occurred to Aden. "What about your speaking voice? Will those in the theater balcony be able to hear your lines?"

Aden held her cell phone even tighter. All she had been thinking about was singing. But that wasn't all she would need. "Obviously, I won't be able to take to the stage if no one can hear me."

"Oh, Sweetie, I am so sorry," Cindy apologized, full of energy and zip. "Listen, I have to run. I'll come over real soon if that's okay."

"You know it is, Cindy. Before, you were over here all the time," Aden reminded her.

Cindy lowered her tone. "But you said being alone and not talking is how your voice can improve fast."

"You're right. But my needing to be alone doesn't count you. Let me know when you're coming." Aden reminded her. "Call first. I have some projects in the works with appointments around town. I'll tell the doorman you're coming." As she pushed the red disconnect button, she felt weak and deflated.

The condo was growing dreary as over-cast clouds began to darken the room. Aden wouldn't stay positive without more light flooding her space. She turned on a table lamp and tried to smile. Caleb hadn't stopped by since Tuesday, the day Bobbie brought the great belts. Yes, he had texted Aden several times a day, saying how busy the show had kept him. Caleb bragged with an air of humility about spending extra time on late-night talk shows after the evening performances. The special commitments, plugging the show and himself, kept him busier than ever.

In her quiet time, when the phone didn't ring and her physical therapist or voice coach didn't come, Aden sketched four additional support belts. One was in black elastic that tapered down in front to two large rhinestone-studded circles connected by a sparkling crossbar buckle. The second was the same design in gold tones. But the third was of stretchy, copper-infused denim fabric in indigo blue, alternating dark brown woven leather every six inches, with an oval buckle in silver set with turquoise nuggets. The last was a simple black design with three parallel leather straps, each with its own front buckle and wider, lumbar supporting back.

Aden was pleased with the creations for several reasons. The belt project gave purpose to her days. And it fed her need for creativity like sweet-smelling homemade bread is a familiar life-sustaining staple.

She called Detective Alverez the day before, but Angela had nothing new to report. No one had seen anything or knew anything about the attack. Aden wondered if anyone cared.

CHAPTER TWENTY-THREE

That day, Aden started dance-barre work in the studio, where she practiced hand and arm movements. The doctor gave her the go-ahead to twist but not to bend. Touching the familiar wooden barre felt comfortable, like running her hand up the smooth handrail that led upstairs to her childhood bedroom. The first position of her routine was executed with her arms relaxed and oval-shaped, her elbows slightly bent, and her fingers curved below her navel. Then she progressed through the second, third, and fourth positions to the fifth, where both of her arms were softy rounded above her head, with her fingertips a hand width apart. She liked this final position since it was the one a ballerina used to display her beauty and strength. It made Aden feel whole and free again as she looked at herself in the mirror. The gash in her leg had closed, and the muscle was healing. In another week, she would begin a simple plié with her heels together and a slight bend in the knees. And then a grand plié in which she would gradually let her heels lift as she went down. The two discs in her back were healing fast. Simple laser spine surgery corrected that injury at the time of the attack. But the muscles in the lumbar area were badly sprained and strained. Wearing the cinch belt protected her lower back and gave stability to her walking and dancing until strength returned.

Aden watched her every movement in the reflective glasses around the rehearsal room and tried to perform the positions correctly. She knew if she practiced incorrectly, her muscle memory would store those false moves. It was a truism she'd learned in the theater. Never rehearse a scene or a song when you don't have the words memorized. Unlearning those mistakes is harder than learning them correctly in the first place.

Even the muscles not affected by the fall during the attack screamed in pain as she turned carefully and posed her hands. Some areas in her back felt like she was repeatedly snapped with a rubber band, snap, smack, crack. Other bands of muscle burned like acid flowed through her veins. She thought again of Scotty on the high school stage. With Scotty holding her close, they waltzed around the stage, bending, swaying, and gliding smoothly to the melody of the songs.

But in her condo, the pain, stiffness, and limitation in some dance moves made her both sad and angry. Some days, her grief nearly overwhelmed her. Aden knew she could not dwell one second on despair. Depression and despair would only yield weakness, exhaustion, poor health, and slow healing.

After lunch of a turkey sandwich on whole wheat bread and an apple, Aden went out onto the terrace. On the chaise lounge, she did many repetitions of core-building exercises and stretching movements over the plant beds. She was thankful the flowers were still in bloom because of her addiction to color. Aden used to tell her mother that she was "color deprived" in Ohio's winter white and gray. She solved the lack of color by whipping out watercolor sketches on cotton art paper and filling them with the garden's blues, browns, and greens.

In the lonely condo, Aden carried her cell phone with her everywhere. When it rang, she thought it was Cindy calling again. Maybe her plans had changed. That would be a disappointment. She was glad somebody, anybody, was stopping by.

"Hello? Daddy?" she asked, surprised but happy to hear his voice.

"How are ya doing, Honey?"

"I'm glad you called," Aden's voice was a little stronger and less hoarse. She certainly hadn't overused it, alone in her condo.

"You sound better than you did the other day," her dad said with an upbeat tone. "Your mother was concerned when she talked with you yesterday." He was silent a second and then asked, "Are you able to stay busy? Have you gone to church?"

"I've stayed in the condo, except for walks to Lindy's for lunch," Aden admitted softly, not because of a strain in her voice but because she didn't like the meaning of her words. She had never been a hermit. Aden had always been out and about. As a teen, she was either at after-school activities, Saturday voice lessons across town, or church services and activities on Sunday. She also took long walks along the creek near her home, where milkweed pods reached out of earthy-smelling, damp ground. It embarrassed her to think of all she was not doing now.

"Sweetheart, you need to get out, to church, down to the theater, go backstage to greet your friends. Take long walks by the waterfalls in Central Park. Go, go, go."

"I'd still have to use that awful cane, Daddy. I hate that thing. Around the house, I don't need it."

"How much longer does the doctor want you to use it?" Miles asked.

"He won't say," she drew out disgustingly.

"He won't say? Or, you don't like the answer?" her dad asked.

"You know me too well, Daddy," she said as she laughed quietly. "What the doctor said was: I will know when I don't need it anymore. I don't need it if I have balance and don't use the stupid thing to lean on."

"Then, that sounds great. It's a good reason to double up on your therapy." He slowed and added, "I know you're aware that walking will be the best exercise you can do."

"I know, Daddy. The doctor told me, and the therapist said the same thing, but … I don't want anyone seeing me broken and weak and … old."

"Old?" her father asked and laughed.

"Yes, Daddy," Aden admitted as her eyes rimmed with tears. "When I pick up that cane, I feel like I'm ninety-five years old."

"Then get a fancy one, Honey. One with color and design." He laughed out loud. "You could design one yourself that reflects more of you."

"Speaking of design," she began just as the doorbell rang. "Oh, I'll tell you more another time. I'm expecting someone. Gotta run."

"Okay, Honey. Bye."

As Aden went to the door, she was excited. She missed the activity and bustle of the city. Cindy had told her she was bringing a surprise, something someone had left at the box office. Cindy said it would give her a chance to see how Aden was doing and not just hear her voice. Perhaps she'd brighten the dimmed star at the same time.

Aden put her phone back in her pocket and went back inside. This time, she paid closer attention to how she was walking. Her balance was good, but the strength in her legs was not quite there. When she got to the door, she was formulating a plan. She would get outside, somehow.

Peering through the peephole, she smiled. "Hi, Cindy," Aden greeted as she opened the door. "Come in."

As they gave each other a friendship embrace, Aden noticed a familiar smell. Perhaps it was French perfume. Aden herself used to wear the same fragrance. Now, perfume was the last thing she thought about. But she did wonder about the package her friend had in her hand.

Cindy smiled broadly. "I have something for you."

"Bring it in here," Aden suggested as she led the way into the living room and sat down.

"Aden, your place looks beautiful," Cindy marveled. "If I had been through everything you have dealt with recently, my apartment would have been stirred and turned upside down."

"Thanks, Cindy." She patted the couch cushion beside her. "Come … sit. Tell me about the production. How are things going?" Aden held her breath. She wanted the show to continue to be successful, so there was a production to return to. But she felt empty. The success of the show was no longer of her making. It belonged to those who remained with the cast.

Cindy shook her shoes off vigorously and sat on her legs. "It is wonderful, Aden. The audiences continue to roar. They are so supportive."

"There is nothing like a New York audience," Aden marveled. And she was right. But what she really needed to know, she was afraid to ask. With a lump in her aching throat, she said, "I haven't asked anyone how my understudy is doing." Aden wanted to hear about Hailey's performance. And yet, not knowing felt safe, too. "Is Hailey's performance … super?" Then she quickly added, "Of course it is. What am I asking? Don't answer that."

"Yes, I will answer that," Cindy jumped in and edged up on her knees. "Hailey Daniels is a fine actress and singer. She's doing a good job. But … I don't know. The chemistry with the whole cast isn't the same without you."

"Oh," Aden sighed. She needed to hear that but didn't like herself for feeling good about what she heard. "What about the chemistry between Caleb and Hailey?"

Cindy rolled her eyes. "You know Caleb Johansson."

"I thought I did." Aden was suddenly filled with doubt. "Sounds like the Caleb/Hailey duet can be very harmonious."

Cindy's eyes softened in empathy. "The rumor is, Caleb Johansson falls in love with all of his leading ladies."

"I don't think that's possible." Aden's jaw was set. "People can't fall in love with anyone when they love themselves more." She rubbed her hands across her eyes, then smiled. "Thanks, Cindy. I'm glad you told me before I had invested too much time and love into that jerk."

Cindy took a deep breath. "Aden, if Hailey leaves, I get to try her part until you come back."

"Cindy, that is wonderful!" Aden heard herself say. Strangely, she realized she had made an honest statement. She was sure it was because Cindy said, "Until you get back." She would definitely be going back. She just didn't know when or if her part would have to change.

"Oh, thank you, Aden. I was afraid you would be upset if I filled in for you." Cindy put her hand to her chest and exhaled loudly.

"Upset? No, no. Everybody has to keep the show going. I don't want it to close before I can get back to it." Aden laughed a little and settled back in relief. A wave of guilt flooded her. She was only thinking about herself. What she told Cindy sounded like the play had to continue for Aden to meet her own needs. That wasn't right.

"I brought this for you." Cindy pointed to the long white box with a red ribbon around it toward one end. "Chandler, out in the box office, said the box just appeared on the edge of the ticket booth last night when he was really busy. He didn't see who left it."

"Wow," Aden said with a smile, "a mystery. As dull as my days are, a mystery would be nice." She didn't pick up the box for fear of appearing too eager.

Cindy patted Aden's arm. "I hadn't seen you since the accident, and—"

Aden felt her skin crawl. Anger rose up inside her until she slowly erupted. "Why does everyone call it an accident? What happened was not an accident. I was attacked, Cindy, by a deranged sicko," she whispered insistently.

"I'm sorry, Aden. I guess … I don't like thinking about it like that. Who would attack anyone I know? Even, like you said, a deranged sicko." Cindy paused for a minute and added, "They're probably just upset about something."

"Upset?" Aden gasped in disbelief. "Would you stab someone and slit their throat if you were just upset with them?"

"Oh, Aden, that sounds awful." Cindy turned away and buried her head in her hand.

"It feels awful, too," Aden whispered through gritted teeth.

"I'd better stop. I just can't talk about your being attacked. I put my foot in my mouth every time I try." Cindy patted Aden's arm and smiled. "Just know, I'm glad you are healing."

"Thank you," Aden said softly.

"Now to the box commanding too much attention in this room." Cindy pointed to the box and chuckled. "I'm done talking about blood, guts, and gore." She reached over and handed Aden the box. "Now, open this thing."

"I will," Aden squealed as best she could.

The box was heavier than Aden thought a box of flowers should be. "There must be six dozen in here," she added. "But that many long-stemmed roses wouldn't fit."

She pulled the ribbon off the end and threw the satin strip on the coffee table. Removing the lid, she pulled back the inner white paper and stared at the contents. It wasn't roses, after all. Aden pulled out a rhinestone-studded collapsible cane or walking stick with a handle. "Who knew I was going to look for a fancy cane?" she marveled.

"No one knows who left it," Cindy stated again. "But it sure is fancy."

Aden waved the cane back and forth in the air. "A little more acceptable than a clunky aluminum stick," she stated. "In fact, you're right. It is beautiful." She stopped when she saw a piece of paper at the bottom of the box. "What is this?" Carefully, she unfolded the half sheet and read aloud.

"Aden Malloy, the beautiful new song and dance Broadway star. I silenced your voice once and crippled your tapping. Here's a cane to help you get around since you can't walk without something to lean on. And, if you ever show yourself in a theater again, you will no longer walk at all." It was signed, *Not an admirer*.

Aden dropped the note on the floor as she grabbed her throat. She couldn't breathe. Reaching in her pocket for her cell phone, she dialed 9-1-1.

A female voice crisply answered, "9-1-1, what's your emergency?"

"Aden …" she gasped for air, "Aden Malloy."

"Yes, Ma'am. Are you hurt?"

"Yes," she sputtered. "Police, Detective Alverez, please."

"We have your location. We'll have someone there immediately. Are you still in danger? Are they still there?"

"No … a friend is here."

"Stay as calm as possible," the operator assured her. "An officer will be right with you."

"Aden," Cindy picked up the note from the floor and wadded it up. "Who could be that cruel?"

"No," Aden struggled to speak while pointing to the paper wad. "Police will want that."

Cindy also retrieved the cane from where it had fallen on the floor. Holding it out at arm's length, she said, "At least this is a real beauty."

"They'll dust that for fingerprints, Cindy," Aden reminded her.

"Sorry, you're right." Cindy fumbled as the cane dropped with a clatter on the hardwood floor.

CHAPTER TWENTY-FOUR

When the doorbell sent out its melodic announcement, Aden was still picking the cane off the floor to replace it in the box. Cindy offered, "I'll get it." She unwound her legs, jumped up, and darted to Aden's front door. She didn't look through the peephole but popped the door open without a thought.

"Cindy, no!" Aden shouted as her voice reverted to a squeak. But it was too late. With her protection breached, Aden shrunk behind the door and waited.

"What?" Cindy asked, confused. "Why?"

"You called 9-1-1?" A police officer stood at the open door. "I'm Officer Eric Grant. This is Officer Al Warnock."

"I called," Aden admitted as she moved out from behind the door. "Thank you for coming so fast. Please, come in."

The officers, dressed in regulation blues, stepped inside, and looked down the short hall. "What seems to be the problem?"

"I'm sorry," Aden apologized as she maneuvered past Cindy. "Please, come in here." She led the way into the living room to the coffee table and the box. "I'm Aden Malloy. Someone attacked me a few weeks ago in the alley beside the Whiteway Theater. The police haven't found him yet, but I got this package today." She gestured toward her friend, "This is Cindy. She brought the box by, thinking it was flowers."

"Cindy?" Grant asked as he took out a pen and a small pad of paper. "And, your last name."

"Streeter," Cindy watched over Officer Grant's shoulder as he wrote down her name.

"And where did you get the package?" he questioned Cindy.

"Someone dropped it off at the theater box office," Cindy offered. "The man in charge of the ticket booth gave it to Hailey Daniels, and she found out I was coming over here, so she gave it to me."

The officer removed some latex gloves from his pocket, put them on, and picked up the box. "That's some chain of evidence." Turning to Aden, he asked, "What theater is that, Ma'am?"

"Actually," Aden was shaken by the note and what the officer said. "I'm not a Ma'am."

"Yes, Ma'am," the officer responded without blinking or pausing. "The theater?"

"Like we said," Aden offered, "the Whiteway Theater."

"Whiteway?" Al Warnock asked. Then his eyebrows raised in recognition. "You're the new Broadway star who was attacked after opening night," he stated.

"Yes," Aden agreed as she reached into the box for the fancy cane. "But I prefer to make a name for myself in more positive ways."

"Yes, Ma'am. Glad you're doing better," he commented.

"Thanks," she said as she handed the cane to Officer Grant. "This cane was in the package, not flowers."

Grant took the fancy cane carefully. "We'll have to take this along and test it for fingerprints."

"Our fingerprints will be on it," Cindy offered. "And the box, ribbon, and note."

"What note?" Grant asked.

Aden reached for the small piece of paper at the bottom of the white cardboard box and smoothed it against her thigh. "Cindy wadded it up."

"Yes, Ma'am," Grant repeated again. Reading the note, the muscles in his jaw flexed. His anger was evident. "I'll take this, too. And, you be careful, Miss Malloy. The attacker has made it clear. He intends to attack again if he sees you. Maybe we'd better post an officer outside your door."

"No, please … no," Aden spit out gruffly.

"Okay … for now," the officer agreed. "I'll report this incident to the detective who's over your case, Miss Malloy. I'm sure he or she will follow up with you."

"Thank you. It's Angela Alverez, Officer. I feel safe here in my home. I have good neighbors." Then she stopped and remembered the man from before. "Oh, yes, I don't want to forget. A man has stopped here twice, demanding to see Carol and Chris Foy. I don't know them. I have lived in the building for about a year."

"Foy?" Grant asked as he took out his paper and pen again.

"Yes, Carol and Chris."

"I'll also put that in my report as an additional incident. Is that all?"

"That's all I can think of." Aden thought back through the last week.

"Officer," Cindy quickly began to ask before he could leave, "don't you think it would be better if Aden stayed in … where the man who stabbed her can't see her?"

"Yes, Ma'am," he agreed. He looked around the living room and out toward the terrace. "You have a nice place here—plenty of space. Staying in would be good."

"Thank you, Officer Grant." Aden smiled as she led him to the door.

"I have to go, too." Cindy started to walk out and then turned. "Aden, I'm sorry you were exposed to trauma again. I was the one who brought that box to you. You have been through enough. Now, you're confined to your home just when you could get out."

"No, Cindy," Aden spoke softly but with steely determination. Many ideas flashed through her mind. "I will not be confined anywhere. I'll come and go as I want to."

"Please be safe." Cindy kissed Aden's cheek and followed the officers out the door.

Watching the flashy cane leave her condo, a new plan began to form. "Hide in my condo?" she growled at her empty rooms. "We'll see about that," she hissed. With the cell phone still in her hand, she punched another set of numbers. "Hi, Bobbie? Aden here. Please bring another item when you stop with my second set of belts. See you Monday."

CHAPTER TWENTY-FIVE

Monday Morning

"Bobbette, I'm glad you're here," Aden giggled as she checked through the security peephole, opened the door, and pulled her friend inside. "I see you brought everything." She felt like an ungrounded fifteen-year-old. It felt good to have something to look forward to, to get excited about.

Bobbie hurried in with a carry-on suitcase, a camera around her neck, and a fancy cane under her arm. "I have it all."

"I want to see the cane first." Aden took the cane case and rolled the carry-on toward the sitting area.

Reaching for the cane, she clutched it like a Tony Award. The fancy walking stick was similar to the one Mags Ferrell used in her Get up and Dance tour. The handle was different. For the grip, the one Aden held had a soft, molded crystalline rose in soft pink and silver. Fine green rose leaves formed an extended handle, making it easier to hold. The collar, between the shaft and the handle, was a silvery, glittering band. The shaft was of clear carbon fiber polymer encrusted with white, silver, and pale pink glitter. The cane's tip was a faceted rubber that shone like a diamond.

Aden's eyes filled with tears, and her heart, joy. "A blubbering fool is not the look I was going for," she stammered as she mopped her face with a tissue. She caressed the cane like a newborn baby and brought it close. "It's even more beautiful than the one Cindy brought. I had to turn that one over to the police." She tapped the tip of the cane on the floor and smiled. It was strong yet delicate, both beautiful and utilitarian. "Bobbie … it is magnificent. Did you make this?"

"I had bits and pieces around the studio and put them together on a cane base, so yes, I made it," she beamed with pride. "Are you ready to see the other four belts?"

"Yes, I guess," Aden agreed as she stood in front of the closet mirror, admiring how the cane looked in her hand. It made her look and feel elegant, stylish, and whole again.

From the carry-on, Bobbie removed the belt made of gold elastic fabric. It had double gold buckles and closures. "Here, try this on to get the entire superstar effect."

"Rebecca Portman?" Aden asked, while her smile only grew broader.

"Sure," Bobbie agreed. "*A Day in the Park*. Not the same cane as the one in that movie … but the same elegance."

Aden wrapped the belt around her waist, tapped the cane on the floor, and tipped it at an angle. She was stunned and at a loss for words. "You are so special," Aden sobbed on Bobbie's shoulder. "You knew what was in my mind and created a perfect copy."

Bobbie handed Aden a folder of the drawings. Her smile was warm and broad. "You drew amazing sketches with every detail. I just transposed them onto the belts. You designed them. I only followed your sketches." Bobbie snapped multiple pictures of Aden in the magnificent supportive belts.

"We have to talk." Aden pulled the camera from Bobbie's hand and led her back to the couch.

"What's going on?" Bobbie asked. "You seem … determined … assertive, the old Aden."

"Thanks, Bobbie." Aden raised her right hand, pledging a continued resolve. "I needed to hear that. Actually, something bad is going on, and something good."

"Okay, tell me more." Bobbie made hand gestures, drawing Aden out.

"Number one, a man keeps coming to the door asking for a man and woman who have never lived here. My neighbor across the hall stopped him the second time he showed up. Then, Cindy Streeter …"

"I know Cindy," Bobbie agreed. "She wears that green lamé body suit when she dances."

"That's right. Wow," Aden marveled, "with so many people in the cast, I'm amazed you remember one costume."

"I worked very hard on those costumes. Trust me, I remember each of them," Bobbie said with pride.

"Anyway," Aden continued, "Cindy brought me a package that someone dropped off at the box office. No one saw who had left it. Chandler said the box appeared when he turned around the other day. He gave it to Hailey, who gave it to Cindy since she was coming over here. It looked like a box of flowers, but it held a beautiful cane. There was a threatening note inside the box that said I'd better not show up at the theater or go out in public. The police took the cane to dust for fingerprints."

"Aden, no. You've been threatened?" Bobbie asked.

"Yes, and the note terrified me. But I will not be intimidated. Thank goodness you brought this cane today. I won't go out in public leaning on a granny stick. Enter … your beautiful new one."

Bobbie snapped to attention and sat up straighter. "You are going out? Where, Aden? It won't be safe for you."

"The theater is one destination. I want to wish everyone in the cast continued success and … make sure they don't forget me. I'm coming back to the show, eventually." She paused as she pulled the other belts out of the carry-on. "I'm going to call my agent tomorrow and see if she can get me on a morning show to introduce our belts. I'll give contact information for orders."

Bobbette shook her head. "Are you sure you're not a producer rather than an actress?"

Aden laughed. "Business is certainly not my talent. I have to deliberately do what I do not naturally do. I've thought it through. These broad, lumbar supporting belts will help many people. We'll register a copyright for my original designs and trademark our label."

Bobbie agreed. "I can't wait."

"Right," Aden said with a dry chuckle. "We should start this project while it's obvious I need to use the belt myself. They'll sell better if I model them. A lawyer can get the company all set up. I don't plan to be incapacitated forever."

"I'm willing to gamble if you are," Bobbie agreed as she slapped her hands together.

"Now, what do we call our brand?" Aden asked as she went over and looked in the mirror. "I'm thinking of … Waist Knots."

"Aden, that is perfect." Bobbie bubbled with enthusiasm.

"We'll put a Celtic button knot on the front of each belt as a logo." Aden's smile spread. She'd conquer her fear by taking advantage of it. If she had a limp, she'd walk all over town, regardless of how much she disliked her stride. Like someone joking about their handicap before others tease them, she would use her own need for a back brace to her advantage. Aden was determined. She would be in control.

CHAPTER TWENTY-SIX

Bobbie left after a tea-time snack of chicken salad on club crackers and carrot strips. It sounded mid-western to Aden, but that made it taste better. *Comfort food*, she concluded as she scooped the rest of the salad onto a few more crackers. She especially liked the little bit of onion she had added. Mixed with the buttery taste of the crackers, it was perfect.

Running the hot water in the kitchen sink, she rinsed the dishes and put them in the dishwasher. Sure, she knew it was a wasted step, but that's how her mom always did the dishes. Following a system was how she captivated New York and got her picture on billboards all over town.

Aden wandered onto the terrace, thinking she would do another round of core building. But those flowers she at first resented drew her to the planting beds. The aroma wafted up and filled her senses with joy, nostalgia, and anger. She was just six blocks from the south end of Central Park, just past Rosie O'Grady's Restaurant. The amazing perfume of Black Angus filet mignon, her favorite whenever she stopped in with her parents or other visitors, was intoxicating. Since the attack, she had been stuck in her condo for weeks with frozen meals and whatever she could have delivered or picked up at Lindy's. The perfume of all the varieties of food New York restaurants offered didn't reach the high-rise condo.

She had called Grace, her agent, and now wondered how she could stand being isolated until Grace called about a possible TV appearance. She knew being alone was best for her. Her vocal cords were healing fast, with no one to talk to most days. That didn't mean she liked the loneliness. It usually came over her like a great fog of despair. She hated it. Reading was an escape, and the belt designs kept her busy. The new designs were completed, and sample belts were constructed, waiting for her appearance on some television shows.

She found some peace on the terrace. Before, the garden had invaded her life. It was now a tranquil oasis between the inside and the greater outside world.

The music from her CD player seemed to get lost in the peace of the evening. A late autumn breeze blew through the garden's pedals and stems, sending specks of orange and yellow blossoms into the air. They fluttered over the world, fifteen stories below, and danced their way to the sidewalk. Again, the words of a familiar hymn filled her with solace.

He speaks, and the sound of his voice
Is so sweet, the birds hush their singing;
And the melody that he gave to me
Within my heart is ringing.

She smiled as the often-sung words filled her soul. She wondered what others draw on for comfort if they have no songs buried in their heart. She walked around the garden from flower to flower. Like a butterfly gathering nectar from the sweetness of the garden, Aden harvested her inner strength from the air around the plants.

God, will I ever heal all the way? Will I be me again? Like the presence of a friend, Aden knew He was there.

The air stirred, sending dry crimson leaves from the terrace above her condo into a swirl around her feet. The wind in the overhang hummed through the garden, singing a melody that planted its roots inside her.

Aden's moment was suddenly shattered by the ring of her cell phone. She pulled the phone from a sweater pocket and answered with a sigh. "Hello?" A second of silence on the other end sent chills down her back.

"Hi, Aden, it's me," Scotty said in a soft, embarrassed voice. "I told you I'd call soon. I'm sorry it's been so many days."

Aden took a deep breath and decided it was not the time to scold him. "I'm just glad you called, Scotty."

"I like how those words sound. When you say my name, it's like music." Scotty's voice was soft and mellow.

"That's sweet," Aden said as she felt her face grow warm. With the phone to her ear, she walked back into the house.

"Aden," he began, but he sounded hesitant, cautious. "Thursday, I'll be out of here. I won't have much money, but if I can stay with you, I'd like to come for the weekend. My weekend this time will be three days."

"Stay here?" she blurted out. "Scotty, I'm still having trouble getting around and have to preserve my voice."

"I know, Skeeter," he said with a smile in his voice. "I called your mom."

"You did?" Aden asked, surprised.

"Skeeter, I've known your mother as long as I've known you," he said with a chuckle. "When you guys moved into the parsonage, I inherited a second family."

"Right," Aden responded as she thought through the long weekend, especially the Friday before.

Scotty sounded amused. "Besides, I promised your mom, if you let me stay, I'd take care of you while I'm there, not the other way around. I live in an apartment with three other guys. I've had to learn to cook. Do they have grocery stores in Manhattan?"

Aden curled up on the couch with the phone tucked under her ear, comfortable and homey. "Of course, silly. You can ride my bike. Thornburg's Supermarket is one street north and several blocks west. Of course, my bike is a girl's model."

"Is it pink?" he asked, sounding like he was holding his breath.

Aden shook her head. *There goes Scotty being Scotty again.* "No, in fact, it's blue."

"I'm just kidding," he said, teasing. "I have my car. I'll drive. Is there a garage near you that won't cost me the price of a semester's tuition?"

"As a matter of fact, my condo building has a garage, and I have a parking space. I use buses, the subway, and taxis to get around town. I'll call Ralph, the doorman, and tell him to have any car moved that might be in my space." She spoke softly, but her tone had a lilt of joy. "Since I don't have a car, I allow him to loan it out for a resident's guest."

Scotty paused for a minute. "I wouldn't want to inconvenience anyone."

"No, no, Scotty. It's great you can come, and I'm glad I have enough space for you." Then she remembered. "Speaking of space, I have two bedrooms, but the second is a dance/therapy studio. You'll have to sleep on the couch, or there's a Murphy bed in the studio. But no sleeping in late since I exercise, do therapy, and dance there."

He was quiet, then whispered, "I'll sleep on the floor if you say I can stay."

Aden's heart flipped a little. "Scotty, yes, yes. Please … come."

Scotty's exhale was heard all the way to New York City. "It's an Interstate all the way. It should take me about eight hours. I can leave at about eleven in the morning after I wrap up some things around here. One quick meeting with a professor, and I'm in the car. Depending on the traffic, I'll get to your place around eight p.m."

"Great, I'll thaw something great for you," she said and laughed. "Scotty … no, since it's you, I'll order something from Lindy's."

"Will that include cheesecake?" he asked mischievously.

"Absolutely," Aden drooled. "Yummy, sweet, and syrupy, blueberry?"

"Perfect." Scotty's voice sounded as sweet as the dessert.

Aden said *goodbye* and smiled. She felt warm and safe as she put her cell phone in her pocket. Aden got up from the couch and picked up the sparkling staff. Like Fred Astaire wearing a top hat and tails, she raised the cane to her shoulder. Admiring herself in the mirror, Aden moved around the room. Hesitantly, carefully, she tried a soft-shoe dance step she hadn't used since before she went into the hospital. Since the soft shoe wasn't done with taps, she loved hearing the light, smooth scraping, and leisurely cadence on the hardwood of her dance studio.

Stepping forward with her left foot, then shuffling forward and diagonally with her right, she began the familiar steps. She accomplished the ball change with her weight on her left foot and then on her right. She smiled broadly through tears. Now she was sure she was home.

CHAPTER TWENTY-SEVEN

Thursday, November 3

Aden had just completed her exercises at the dance barre the morning of the new day and made a decision. She opened the closet door and removed her nude-colored, two-and-a-half-inch healed Capezio tap shoes. The wooden stool in the corner of the room served many purposes, including a fancy dance step while seated and moving in a circle. This time, she put her foot on it while securing the single buckle on her shoe. She hadn't even put tap shoes on since the attack. They felt good.

Her leg was healing nicely, but she still felt very stiff. Aden was thankful her weak back felt supported while wearing one of her belts. That was good for her posture and pain relief and great for the new business. She knew she wasn't strong enough to break into a full dance routine. But Aden could stand with both hands on the barre and tap out a rhythm on the floor, dancing to some parts of her show performance. *Easy, easy, tappity tap, tappity tap, tappity tap, tap, tap.*

It was Thursday. She knew what was on television that evening. Confined to the house since opening night, she had watched way too much TV. Aden told herself she was just catching up from not having watched many programs in the last three busy years. Scotty said he was coming. She hoped he would get there in time to save her from an evening in front of the plasma screen hanging on the wall.

She ate lightly for lunch, planning to have a large supper with Scotty. Would he come? Since high school graduation, Aden hadn't been able to depend on him. He had promised to come to New York several times during the last five years.

Carl Fritz's wife, Olivia, brought over some salmon she had prepared for Carl the evening before. It smelled wonderful. The salmon was smothered in a honey sauce with the zest of a lemon. It was easier to fix two small casseroles at once than to try to think up another dish to share. Aden fixed some asparagus spears to round out the meal. Olivia stayed and ate lunch with her.

"Olivia, your casserole was wonderful. Thank you so much." Aden said as her neighbor prepared to leave.

Olivia had spooned the leftovers into one of Aden's dishes, so she could take her dish home. "Carl wasn't going to be home. I really appreciated eating my lunch with you."

Aden stepped into the hall and checked for anyone who might be there. "And, thank you for watching out for me. It makes me feel safe knowing you two are close."

"Aden." Olivia stopped and touched her friend's arm. "I am glad we are neighbors. Carl and I hate what happened to you. If there is anything you need, just let us know."

After Olivia left, Aden watched a Hallmark movie. The pictures and characters floated in front of her eyes, but her mind was on Scotty. When her cell phone rang, she jumped and pulled it out of her pocket, fumbling with it.

"Hello?" she answered, dreading it might be Scotty explaining that he couldn't come after all.

"Hi, Aden, this is Grace. I have news." The voice was female and really upbeat.

"Oh, Grace." Aden felt relieved when she heard her agent's voice. "I'm already shaking. Is the news good or bad?"

Grace's voice was playful. "Why are you shaking … like … you're nervous … scared … sick?"

"Excited, I guess, Grace," Aden admitted. "An old friend is coming for the weekend. I've been in solitary confinement for weeks, except for a few hours of release time for permitted visitation."

"I hear ya," Grace said with a smile in her voice.

"Okay," Aden calmed herself as she swallowed hard and closed her eyes tightly. "I'm calm now. What's the news?"

"Tomorrow morning, at eight-thirty, we have booked a spot for you on America Today. A scheduled guest had to cancel, so they were thrilled you were able to come. There will be a *Morning Brunch* segment on Sunday at eight-fifteen. Be at the studios, in makeup and ready in the green room, at least a half hour before your spot," Grace said, practically all in one breath.

"Oh fantastic, Grace," Aden gasped. Then she stopped. "Tomorrow?"

"Yes, is there a problem, Aden?" Grace asked. "Please tell me, 'No.'"

Scotty's smiling face popped into her mind. "My guest will be here … but I will make it work."

"Bring him along. He can wait for you." Grace gave her the directions and time of arrival. "This will be wonderful for you."

They talked for a few more minutes and then hung up. Aden could not believe what was happening. What had started on opening night as a disaster had turned into an opportunity she had never dreamed of.

It was only about six in the late afternoon. The setting sun hid behind tall buildings until time for it to disappear. Her excitement and extra tap dancing had tightened the muscles in her legs and gnawed at her back. With her fancy cane in her hand, she stood in front of the mirror, looking tired and bent. Leaning on the cane for balance, she stretched and strained to pull herself up to her full height. Every bit of strength and energy she could muster only held her completely upright for seconds before she could see herself wilt again.

Feeling giddy inside, Aden hurried back to her bedroom and chose a powder blue tunic-length, long-sleeve top with roll-up sleeves. She paired it with the denim belt and turquoise buckle. In the back of her mind, Aden anticipated a little dancing that morning when she got dressed and put on one of the new belts. She was excited about wearing the belt during her therapy routine. Her black leggings would work for therapy and when Scotty was there. Truthfully, she wanted to look her best for Scotty. She smiled when she checked her reflection in the long wall mirror.

With her Waist Knot's comfortable support, she walked back through the living room. The twinkle bulbs on the terrace drew her outside as darkness settled over the city. Magnificent lights turned on in the streets below and in the windows around her. They all glistened in the lamplight. The night air brought a chill. Aden wrapped her arms around her middle to hold in her own body heat. The face of Marilyn Hall, the choir directed at Aden's home church for as long as Aden could remember, came to mind with a rousing downbeat. The choir led the congregation in singing the old familiar hymns. *I'd better go in,* she thought as a smile crossed her lips.

> I'd stay in the garden with him
> Tho the night around me be falling;
> But he bids me go; thro' the voice of woe,
> His voice to me is calling.
> And he walks with me, and he talks with me,
> And he tells me I am His own
> And he walks with me, and he talks with me,
> And the joy we share as we tarry there,
> None other has ever known. [1]

Reluctantly, she stepped back into the condo and slid the door closed. The coolness of the evening surprised her. But then, it was November. Thanksgiving would come soon with turkey, pumpkin pie, and the Macy's Thanksgiving Day Parade. She jumped when the doorbell rang.

"Caleb," she was surprised when she peeped through the door and saw him standing there, leaning on the doorjamb. "I didn't know you were coming. Come in."

She saw him walk back and forth in the hall but stepped no closer. Aden looked at her watch and was glad it would still be a while before Scotty arrived. "Well, come on in. Don't just stand there."

"Well, just for a minute. I don't have much time."

"I know," she answered with a strain in her voice. "You're … busy," she mocked. With all the strength in her body, she straightened her back as tall as possible. She was not going to wither, not in front of Caleb. It felt like she was holding her breath to keep from inhaling contaminated air. "Sit down," she nearly ordered, and Caleb obeyed.

"Well, all right … for a minute."

"Why did you come if you didn't have time to spare?" she asked with a hoarse gruffness.

"I know … I haven't stopped by. But …"

"You've been busy. You said that already," Aden jumped in. They both laughed, relaxed, and settled down on the couch.

"Aden … I hate to do this, but I have to ask … in two and a half weeks, it will be Thanksgiving … the parade and all. The cast will perform on the stage in front of Macy's Department Store. Since you have been out, Hailey Daniels has been filling the lead. She's doing great."

"Yes, Cindy Streeter told me Hailey was holding her own." She leaned back and covered her eyes with her hands. "Good grief, Caleb. Is there anything else I can lose?"

Caleb's question was awkward. "Then … you haven't considered quitting the show?"

"Quitting?" Aden jumped up faster than she knew she could. "Why would I quit after hanging on by my fingernails all these weeks? Are you saying you think I should drop out?"

Caleb looked away. "Well, it is hard getting adjusted to a new co-star. I have to—"

"You have to adjust? This is all about your comfort?" She couldn't believe his selfishness. Or maybe she was the one being selfish. Then she remembered, "Were you and Hailey dating before I came along?"

"Dating? I wouldn't call it dating. Dinner a few times, a weekend in Vermont to attend her mother's birthday party."

"To meet her parents? Caleb …" When her voice cracked, she put her hand to her throat.

"I'm sorry, Baby Girl. Rest your voice. You're not ready to talk, let alone sing. We … hey, Aden …" he gasped as he jumped up. "Let's think about this. We'll have to do everything electronically when we perform, lip-syncing it anyway. There's no way to get balance in the sounds out there in the open. It's always done that way." He started to pace again. "Remember, I brought that CD to the hospital that the theater engineer prepared for you. That's you on that disc. You can lip-sync your own song." Caleb reached over and gathered her in his arms.

Aden wrapped her arms around him. "Yes! It could work." She leaned back, looked into his eyes, and smiled mischievously. "I tried tapping this morning. I'm rusty, but I can work on it. With any severe twists, you can just dance around me."

"That's it then," Caleb announced. "I'll let Floyd Blackstone know he may need to modify a few dance steps. We'll do it." He smacked his hand on his knee. "What about costumes? You look like you have lost some weight."

"I have some new belts. I'll wear one of those. They can hold up, or hold in, the costume." She smiled to herself without saying any more about the Waist Knots. "I assume we're going to rehearse to block out the scene in the smaller space."

"We have a practice … tomorrow afternoon, at the theater. We can see how the CD works, what moves need modification, and if your costume needs altering," Caleb offered.

Aden thought for a second about the threat she had received if she were to go back to the Whiteway. She also thought of Scotty. He would be here in a few hours and, of course, through the weekend. But she didn't think very long. Answering immediately, she said with enthusiasm, "Sounds great." Suddenly, the America Today appearance popped into her mind. "What time?"

"We'll meet about 4:30," he said, checking his watch. "Can't stay much longer." He ran his hand over the back of his neck. "The cast will come to the theater after lunch and before the evening performance."

"Okay," Aden said, carefully choosing her words. "A friend is coming for the weekend. We can pop in early, go backstage, and tour the theater."

Caleb started toward the door as he said, "Can't be late. I'll see you tomorrow and … bring her along. She might like to visit your dressing rooms."

"Sure," Aden said, smiled, and didn't offer another word. Tomorrow would be soon enough for Caleb to find out the "she" was Scott Russell. Goodness knows, Aden had talked enough about Scotty when the production was in the first rehearsals. Caleb should feel like he knew Scott already. *That's okay, Caleb Johansson,* she thought to herself. *Scotty has called me more than you have since the attack. A surprise might be good for you.*

CHAPTER TWENTY-EIGHT

Thursday Evening

Aden started watching the large wall clock long before eight p.m. When the condo began to turn a dreary gray, table lamps were switched on. Aden not only hated the dark, but she also had a fear of tripping over something in a dimly lit room. There was no way she wanted to strain or sprain something just as she was healing.

When the minute hand ticked past the hour and started slipping down the clock face, Aden became anxious. Was this going to be an encore of Scotty's previous songs? In the past, he had said many times he would come to New York and then never showed up.

At twenty-two minutes after eight, the doorbell rang. Aden grabbed the doorknob and twisted it without a thought to the peephole. She smiled as she flung the door open, hoping … assuming. Thank goodness it was Scotty. She threw her hands up joyfully and jumped into his arms as he waited there, standing in her hallway. Since he drove all day, his beard had grown scratchy, yet it felt as soft as the boyish stubble he tried to grow in high school. He smelled new. His men's cologne was still woodsy. It reminded Aden of the many times they spent around the fire pit in her family's backyard.

"Aden Malloy," he whispered. "You feel wonderful." Standing back, he looked at her up and down. "How do you feel?"

"You just said I feel wonderful," she said as she threw her head back and laughed.

"Oh, Skeeter," he sighed as he pulled her to him again, "I missed you so much."

"Me, too, Scotty," she admitted. With his hand in hers, she led him over to the couch and gently pushed him onto one of the cushions.

"Come," Scotty coaxed as he patted the seat beside him. "Sit by me." His eyes glistened as they locked onto hers. "I'm going to sit here and pretend there isn't a new baritone in your life," he whispered, warm and tender.

Aden didn't respond to that comment. After Caleb's visit earlier, she no longer knew if he was part of her life. Not a *special* part, anyway. She and Caleb were both excited about the Parade Day show, but there was something different between them. Seeing Scotty took her back to a time of security and love with no qualifiers.

Aden leaned her head on Scotty's shoulder. The aroma of his leather jacket filled her with memories. It felt like late evenings in her parents' living room until she remembered, "How early can you get up tomorrow?"

"I get up at 5:00 a.m. every morning," he boasted. "I run for an hour, shower, and study … study … study."

"Wow," she leaned back and looked at him. "Where did my old Scotty go?"

"Your Scotty?" he asked through a wry smile.

Aden lowered her gaze and felt her cheeks heat up. "I'm sorry. That's just a saying. I'm sure you're dating someone special."

"No … Aden … someone special isn't in Ohio anymore. I completed three and a half years of college in much less time. I earned two degrees … business and music. I immediately started Law School and just finished my JD Like I said, I've been studying." He paused and reached for her hand. "Now that I'm finished with my studies, I'm going home. Skeeter, I hate to see you in such pain. Why don't you come home, too?"

"Home? I thought you would understand. I came to New York to act, to sing. Not to run home when things get tough."

"I'm sorry, Aden. I do understand." He took her hand. "I'm just talking about coming home for a rest. I know almost nothing can pull you away from this city. You want to sing."

Aden was hurt. She thought Scotty, more than anyone, would know she couldn't leave the city, not now. She needed to sing. Right now, even an Ohio visit would seem like a retreat or a surrender. They had talked about her plans as children while riding the bus into town to see a favorite movie. On Sunday afternoons, they would borrow the *New York Times* from the man next door to Aden's house. Together, they'd spread the large sheets of newspaper on the floor to pour over the classified ads. Apartments with bathroom doors that banged into two-seat sofas in tiny living rooms were researched for possible places to call home before her *big break* came in. If anyone could understand her loss, it should be Scotty. She quickly changed the subject. "You took another major in music? Why?" Aden couldn't believe what he was saying.

"I have been writing some music, Skeeter. I wanted to have legitimate credentials." He traced an infinity sign on the top of her hand.

His touch was exciting. "What? What have you written?"

"Some songs … for you."

"Scotty … that's beautiful." Salty tears gathered in her eyes. "What key are they in?"

"They are for you, Skeeter. I can pitch them in any key you want, from coloratura soprano to bass."

"You're getting close," she said as she breathed slowly. "I may never get my upper register back … ever. Right now, I sing in the … tenor range, if I dared to sing at all." She put her hand on her throat unconsciously to protect the asset that put her on Broadway in the first place.

"Really?" Scotty burst out with a broad smile. "Aden, one of my songs would be perfect for you in the lower range. I can lower them all if you want me to or if that would be more comfortable."

Aden exhaled deeply. "Do I *want* you to lower them? No. *Must* they be lowered?" Her gaze fell to her hand entwined in Scotty's. It looked natural, familiar. "Right now, I'm not even supposed to talk very much. If I'm going to be able to sing your songs …" her voice dropped lower and lower, "they have to be keyed as low as possible." Finally, she laughed. For the first time in weeks, there was something about her voice she found amusing.

"Skeeter, it's good to hear you laugh. If I came for only that reason, your laugh would be good enough for me." He wrapped his arms around her and snuggled her close. "Okay, now, why the question about how early I can get up."

"You're going with me someplace in the morning." She paused for dramatic effect.

"Okay, I give up … where?"

"I'm going to appear on America Today in the morning." She giggled with glee.

"About your return to the show?" Scotty asked with equal enthusiasm.

"No … about my side company, Waist Knots." Aden anticipated Scotty's reaction.

"Waste not?" His face formed into a question. "Is it a cause you're supporting—about not wasting valuable resources?"

"No … w.a.i.s.t, and k.n.o.t. We'll put a Celtic knot on the front of each belt as a logo. Bobbette and I have gone through an attorney to protect our designs. We're set."

"Bobbette? Belts?" he asked, his face drawn up in confusion.

"Exactly. Bobbette is a costume designer. The entire cast of *Honeysuckle Rose* was dressed by Bobbie and her staff of seamstresses. I designed the belts, drew the sketches, and she made them. They are not orthopedic. We make that clear," she stated emphatically with a wave of her arms. "But they do help support sore back muscles in the lumbar area. Obviously, that's where I need the additional help."

"Aden, I don't know what to say. I'm speechless. I always knew you were, and are, creative. But a business … that is fantastic. With my business degree, if there is anything I can do to help, just let me know. We can correspond by phone, Instant Message, email, Snapchat, or anything you need. I would be honored to help you." Scotty was so excited he moved to the edge of the couch.

"That would be great. But Scotty, I would have no money to pay you for your expertise."

Scotty's face became animated as he raised his eyebrows. "Pay? I didn't say pay. Did I say pay? I said *help*. It could be a blast! I could use my new marketing skills to get those belts into therapeutic outlets and clothing markets. Do you have any stores willing to handle them yet?"

"Bobbette contacted a huge department store chain just the other day. They're accepting one-thousand units to put on their website." Aden smiled at the ease with which she rose from the couch. With a little curtsy, she patted the belt around her waist. "This is one of them. Olivet Department Stores will carry them in this and five other styles in several sizes."

Scotty jumped up and smoothed his hands over the belt. "Aden, Oli's is carrying it? That is fantastic!" He swooped her off her feet instantly and twirled her around. "Oh, Skeeter." His joyous expression turned to fear and guilt. "I am sorry." He said as he quickly and very carefully put her back on the floor. "Did I hurt you?"

"No," she said with a surprised giggle. "I don't feel hurt at all."

Scotty bent down to Aden, the beautiful girl of his teen years, and kissed her powerfully yet tenderly.

The eagerness she put into kissing Scotty back shocked Aden. He felt good. She had only remembered the muscular contour of his shoulders and chest in her dreams. She was confused.

Pulling away, Scotty apologized. "Sorry, Skeeter. It felt natural."

Aden smiled coyly. "It did, didn't it." She reached for her phone and said, "I'd better call for dinner to be delivered … unless you want to go out."

Scotty put his warm hand gently on her shoulder. "You know I'd love to eat in a New York restaurant, but by the time I shower and get ready, we'd both starve."

"Okay, good. We'll eat out tomorrow." She tapped in an auto-dial number. "Rachel? You're still there." Aden looked up at Scotty and blushed. "This is Aden Malloy. I had ordered a delivery. Will you tell them we're ready for it? Thanks."

She put the phone on the coffee table. "The restaurant is just downstairs and around the corner. They'll be here in about fifteen minutes." She just stood there, close enough to feel his breath on her hair. At first, they didn't move. Then she touched his chest and said, "You can put your stuff in the closet in my dance studio."

"Great," he said, looking around. "Your own dance studio?"

"Don't get too excited. It's small." With a shrug and a smile, she led the way to the small bedroom. "See?" She pointed inside the door. "The closet is there on the right." Stepping out of the way, she let Scotty pass.

"You didn't dance a lot in high school," he said softly as he studied the long dance barre.

"I did a little. I took dance lessons on Thursday evenings in elementary school and junior high."

"Thursday evenings, I took guitar lessons," Scotty said with a knowing smile.

She added, "I didn't have time to continue dance classes in high school" There was a wishful sound to her voice. "I'm finding I really love it."

"That's great," Scotty answered. When the doorbell rang, Aden moved past him again. It felt so good to be close; she no longer thought about food but guessed Scotty was hungry.

"I'd better get the door," she sighed.

A young delivery boy wearing a baseball cap and athletic jacket stood at the door with two large sacks. "Hi, Kyle." Aden was glad the boy came in time to break up the embarrassing moment between her and Scott. "Thanks for the delivery." Kyle handed Aden the bill. She signed it and handed it back while Scotty took the containers. As she closed the door, she pointed to the left, "The kitchen is right around the corner." Following him, she laughed, "I know. Neither your mother nor mine would say this little room qualifies as a kitchen. But my micro-kitchen has a refrigerator, stove, dishwasher, microwave, sink, and cabinets … well ... some cabinets."

"Plates? Silverware?" Scotty put the containers from Lindy's on the counter and started toward the cabinets.

"Right here," Aden offered as she opened the cabinet door to the right of the sink. She removed two white plates, another coffee cup, and forks and knives from the drawer.

"What do you think?" Scotty looked out toward the garden. "Will it be too cold to eat out on the terrace?"

"I can put on a sweatshirt. Will you be warm enough?"

"I have my jacket." He went back into the living room and retrieved his brown leather jacket. "It's the food that might get cold."

Aden walked into her bedroom to get the gold, autumn leaf-decorated sweatshirt she had picked up weeks before when her life was normal. She called over her shoulder. "In the front closet, behind the mirrors, there's a small room heater. Get it out, fire it up, and then take the food to the terrace. I'll be right back."

Scotty slipped his jacket on, removed the room heater from the closet, took it out to the garden, and looked for an outlet. There was one in the corner. He turned it on and positioned it where the terrace railing curved and supported a small round table and chairs. Scotty rubbed his hands together as the heater quickly started getting hot.

"This is perfect," Aden said as she came out onto the terrace with two small boxes in her hands. "You can bring the rest of it out. I have the important course, dessert. Our cheesecake is blueberry and cherry."

From the kitchen, Scotty returned with the place settings balanced on top of two additional white boxes. "Don't know what you ordered, but it smells great," he swooned.

"It had better," she chuckled. "I cooked all day."

"Right," Scotty agreed with a fun, sarcastic tone.

With the table quickly set, Aden opened the boxes. "New York strip steak, French fries, grilled vegetables, and garlic bread. I sure hope you're hungry."

"I am famished." Scotty cut into his steak and closed his eyes, savoring the bite. It was seared and browned to a scrumptious caramelized perfection. They settled into the full meal. "This is beautiful out here," Scotty sighed after eating several mouthfuls.

"I love the terrace. At first, I resented the garden," Aden admitted.

He stopped with his fork in one hand and his knife in the other. "How can you resent a garden?"

"You can't," she agreed as she placed her fork on her plate. "I was angry with God. I guess I blamed him for the attack. I figured I had worked hard and deserved to avoid bad things. An entitlement claim, I suppose."

"God doesn't help us to avoid life, Skeeter. He helps us march through the toughest parts of life, promising to be at our side."

"I know. But … I had gotten pretty uppity, as Mimi would say. I thought I should be above the hard things people go through. I was angry that God didn't see life as I did. He measures fairness differently."

"And … I was angry with me," Scotty whispered.

"You - why?" Aden was amazed.

"In round-about thinking, I figured if I had come to New York with you as we had planned that night after the prom, I could have protected you from all of this, from whoever attacked you." Scotty reached over and took her hand. "Skeeter, I did come to opening night. I just had to see you fulfill your dream. When I saw that special something between you and Johansson, I couldn't interfere with your special night. So, I left. I haven't stopped kicking myself yet."

Aden finally had to know what she had suspected all along. "Did you come to the hospital?"

Scotty grinned. His eyes grew wide with surprise. "Did you know I was there? Why didn't you say something?"

Aden looked down, avoiding his eyes. "I thought you were a dream."

"I didn't think you were conscious enough to know I was in the room." His voice faded to a whisper. "After singing the little song I wrote for you, I left." He looked into the night, where the city lights hid the stars. "If I had stayed around at the theater on opening night, I could have walked out that side door with you. Even if we weren't together, we could have been together in that alley. I would have protected you. I have felt awful."

"Scotty, it was not your fault. In fact, Detective Alverez has no idea who did it." Aden's voice drifted off as she looked out at the lights. "I'm not going to worry about the *who* of it anymore. It happened, and I'm adjusting."

"You sure are," Scotty agreed. "The belt business, for one."

"Waist Knots," she corrected. "And … I'm going to perform with the cast at Macy's Thanksgiving Day Parade."

"Aden," he hooted. "Fantastic!"

"Tomorrow, we'll go to ATN for America Today. Then, after lunch, we'll go to the theater. We'll block out the opening musical number for the smaller space we'll have on the stage in the street in front of Macy's. After that, you and I can do something you would like to do." She popped a bite of meat into her mouth.

"Okay, the city will be mine for the evening. Think of the possibilities." Scotty tapped his finger on the table. "After watching a live TV show and walking up onto a

Broadway theater stage, I'll have the city in the palm of my hand."

"I am looking forward to whatever you choose. There are many wonderful places you might want to go. And I've probably never been to any of them," Aden admitted. "I've done nothing but work since I got here," she said wistfully. "It will be a weekend vacation for both of us."

They were quiet while they finished their food. But it wasn't that awkward kind of silence. It was the familiar peace of being with an old friend, someone you didn't have to prove anything to, the kind of person who already thought you were the lead singer in their life.

"Tomorrow will be a big day for me," Aden sighed and gathered up her plate and silverware. "I'm going to have to go to bed."

"Great. I'm tired too," Scotty said as he took the plate from Aden and stacked it with his.

"There is a blanket in the hall closet and a pillow," she reminded him as she closed the sliding door. "You can use them on the couch or the Murphy bed in the other room."

"Tonight," Scotty began as he studied the sofa with sleepy eyes, "I'll take the couch."

The doorbell rang just as Aden started to turn off the side lamp. Her heart stopped as she started for the door. Who would be at her door at that hour of the night?

"Wait, Aden. Don't bother. I know who it is," Scotty said with a flourish and fanfare. He stepped in front of her, checked the peephole, and opened the door. The doorman stood there with a giant grin, holding a fuzzy blanket in his arms.

"Ralph, it's late," Aden said cautiously. "Is something wrong?" Then she saw what he was really carrying.

"I believe this is yours," Ralph said with a smile as he handed her a long-haired, black-and-white, fluffy dog.

"I'll take him for you," Scotty said apprehensively. "Hope it's okay that I brought her. I asked Ralph to wait until ten to bring her up."

"She's your dog?" Aden asked as she reached out and nuzzled the dog under her chin. "What a cutie."

"Well," Scotty drew out slowly. "I'm hoping … she's not my dog. She's yours. I thought the little one might help as you heal. She's trained as a service dog."

"She adorable," Aden whispered. "I can't bend over to pick her up, though."

"Thanks, Ralph," Scotty said. "Would you please bring up the other stuff?"

Aden looked from Scotty to Ralph. "What other stuff?"

Scotty nodded to Ralph, who turned and left. "He'll bring up the sleeping crate, feeding bowl, and dog food I brought to get her started."

"She's a cockapoo, right?" Aden asked. She sank onto a chair, reached down, and nuzzled the dog behind its ears.

"I can keep the dog with me in the living room," he offered. "That will give you some time to think about dog adoption."

Aden didn't say anything for a minute as the sweet dog put her head on Aden's knee. The little animal seemed to know that Aden was in pain, and the dog was there to love her and bring her peace.

"She is beautiful, Scotty." Aden smiled at the dog and said quietly, "Sit."

The dog immediately sat down in front of Aden while keeping her chin on Aden's leg. The continuously wagging tail was evidence that she had found a new friend.

"You are full of wiggles. That's a good name for you," Aden said with a smile. She looked up at Scotty. "I think you can put Wiggles' bed in my room, against the wall. The room isn't big, but I'll make room for her."

When the doorbell rang again, Scott hurried to answer. Ralph came back with full arms. The dog crate had two bowls and a sack of dog food. "I'll put the food in the kitchen, Miss Malloy."

"Thanks, Ralph," Scotty offered. "Aden. I'm going to put the dog bed and sleeping crate in your room."

As Scotty walked toward Aden's bedroom, she watched the doorman. "Thanks, Ralph." She wanted to walk Ralph to the door but wondered if the dog would dart out. She turned to Wiggles. "Stay," she commanded and smiled. After Ralph left, Aden locked the door and threw the two deadbolts. "Good, dog," she rewarded Wiggles with praise.

"She's all set up, but I can move her in here," Scotty said again. "I didn't ask you if you had a dog or wanted one. But I thought she might make you feel safer." He studied Aden's face. "Is a surprise dog present okay with you?"

Aden had never even considered having a pet. Miss Fluff, her cat in Ohio, was special, and Aden loved her dearly. But a dog didn't use a litter box. Aden had no time to walk a dog, take her to the vet, or the groomer. She couldn't get down on the floor to toss a rubber ball or play tug-of-war with a knotted rope. Everything now would have to change. Looking back at the cocker spaniel/poodle mix, her heart reached out for something other than herself for the first time in days. Maybe the little dog would bring something else to her condo, a sense of family. She smiled and whispered, "Yes. A dog present is perfect."

CHAPTER TWENTY-NINE

Friday, November 4

"Okay, do we have everything?" Aden asked Scotty as she checked her pockets for an extra tissue and looked for her purse.

"I hope so." Scotty reached down and picked up Aden's new dog. "Wiggles and I went for a nice walk this morning. And," he teased, "we wrestled on the living room floor." He started for the bedroom, "I'll put her in her crate."

When Scotty came back into the room, Aden felt like she couldn't breathe. "I am so excited. I don't know if I can make any sense on camera," Aden gasped as she put her hand to her chest and tried to inhale.

"Skeeter, you can go out on a New York stage, dance yourself around in circles, and deliver an entire libretto without a single mistake." Scotty took her wool cape and helped put it around her shoulders. "Besides, I'm with you. It's Skeeter and Scotty again."

The brown leather of his jacket felt soft under her fingers. "Skeeter and Scotty," she echoed. "Those few words speak volumes."

Scotty gathered her in his arms and pulled her close. "Aden, I can't let you go just because you're a big star now."

"Scotty, you let me go years ago. And I can't talk about that right now," she said with another sigh. "We have to leave." She shook her head to clear her thoughts. "ATN Studios is down at Time Square, on W 44th Street. We'll take a taxi, so we don't have to wait at a bus stop."

Scotty didn't ask other questions and only changed the subject. "I'm hungry," he complained as they went out into the hall and walked to the elevator. "We didn't eat breakfast."

"Same old Scotty." She pushed the elevator button to take them to the lobby. "Jewel Razor's Steakhouse is right across the street from ATN-News …" They stepped on the elevator and rode down to the lobby. "But Jewel Razor's doesn't open until 11:00 a.m. You'll love it. We'll try to go there sometime this weekend."

Scotty smiled but offered a more immediate solution. "Maybe they'll have doughnuts in the green room at the studio."

Aden elbowed Scotty with a teasing nudge. "Maybe. If you pass out from hunger, I'll get someone to pull you off the floor," she said with a chuckle.

Downstairs, Ralph led them through the revolving door and into the glorious autumn morning. Birds flew low along the sidewalk, pecking at bits of food dropped by those who enjoyed the pretzel and nut vendors along the sidewalks. The beat of a bongo drummer echoed from the next corner to the south. "It is great to see you out, Miss Malloy," Ralph said enthusiastically as he flagged down a taxi for her. "You look really good. I like that fancy cane. You look like a true Broadway star on an outing."

"Thanks, Ralph," Aden said and smiled, feeling she had accomplished the effect she wanted. Ralph's compliment had nothing to do with her limitations. It had everything to do with her glamorous image.

The fall air was crisp, a perfect November morning. Women in expensive business suits and sneakers on their feet hurried by on their way to the office, carrying their fancy stiletto shoes in a tote.

"We'll find something for you to eat, so you don't starve," Aden promised. She smiled as the doorman opened the taxi door. "Thanks, Ralph." She got in, smoothing her skirt. "There might be a snack at ATN, or we'll find something when we leave."

"Hopefully," Scotty weakly put the back of his hand to his forehead, "or I might perish."

"Don't snap, gingersnap," Aden said as she slid across the seat. "We'll find food before you dissolve in your milk."

CHAPTER THIRTY

"No doughnuts, no pastries," Scotty moaned as they walked into the green room at *America Today.*

"True," Aden agreed. "But there is a large pot of coffee. That should fill you up and hold you over. Just remember where the bathrooms are. Caffeine is a diuretic, you know." She did one dance step, waved her cane, and whispered, "Ba, bum, bum."

"Bathroom … right," he repeated as he checked over his shoulder for restrooms. "Remember that Saturday we went to the mall right after lunch?"

"You mean the incident right after you got a refill on your super drink?" She elbowed him lightly in the ribs. "You couldn't find the restroom fast enough."

"The key word is *couldn't.* The first thing I bought was a new pair of Levi's." His mouth curled tightly at the corners in an embarrassed, playful smile.

"Well … maybe. But—"

"Welcome," *America Today's* news producer greeted with an outstretched hand and a smile.

"Thank you," Aden offered her hand while her fancy cane sparkled in her left. "I'm glad to be here. I'm Aden …"

"Aden, the whole world knows who you are. We've had tons of emails since we announced yesterday that you'd be here this morning. I'm Thalia, the producer."

"Thank you," Aden felt her cheeks grow warm. She was surprised, thinking everyone would have forgotten her. Or, worse yet, they never remembered that she was the one who stared in *Honeysuckle Rose.*

"And you are …?" the producer asked as she reached out her hand to Scott. Spotting Aden's bag, she said, "If these are the belts, I'll give them to my assistant to arrange."

Aden nodded as she handed over the Waist Knots. Apologizing, she added, "I'm sorry. I'm a little scattered. This is Scott Russell … a friend from Ohio."

"It's nice to meet you." Thalia put her hand behind Aden, directing her toward the studio. "Are you going to be on camera with Aden?"

"No, she's the star and designer, not me," he explained as he poured a large mug of coffee.

Aden was both surprised and pleased Scotty didn't try to up-stage her or take over her story. The Waist Knot belts were hers. She was the one who found a way to begin to live again.

"Well, come on in the studio, Aden. We're at commercial. There will be time for you to meet Jocelyn ahead of the segment." Thalia patted Aden's back.

"Aden Malloy," Jocelyn called out as Aden approached a small area in the studio where two chairs sat in a grouping. At the center of the conversation area, a low coffee table held an artful display of the Waist Knots. "We are all glad you are doing better," Jocelyn said as she hugged Aden.

"Thank you, Jocelyn," Aden sputtered. "I'm still getting used to the idea that people know who I am."

Jocelyn took Aden's arms and held them out gently, studying her. Laughing, she added, "Oh, trust me. People know who you are."

"So they tell me," Aden said as the sound tech attached a lapel mic.

"Aden," Jocelyn began, "we have it all worked out the way your agent and our producer discussed." She checked the clock on the back wall and added, "We're on in twenty seconds."

"Great," Aden agreed and smiled. She sparkled when she saw Scotty come into the studio and position himself behind the cameras.

Jocelyn raised her eyebrows. "Someone you know?"

"Yes," Aden said as she sat on one of the set chairs. "I definitely know him. He's been my friend since we were about eight years old, Scott Russell."

Jocelyn smiled a knowing smile. "Our cue." She pointed to the director and spoke into the camera. "I'm here with Aden Malloy, the fantastic new Broadway star of *Honeysuckle Rose* who was attacked on opening night. How are you doing, Aden?"

"I keep improving," Aden offered and heard the hesitancy in her own voice. *No, I'll not be weak.* With a firm voice, she continued. "My voice is much stronger, and I put on my tap shoes the other day." She chose her words carefully. "I'll rejoin the cast for our production in the Macy's Thanksgiving Day Parade."

"Wonderful!" Jocelyn's eyes lit with enthusiasm.

"I am excited." Aden's eyes flashed.

Jocelyn reached over and touched Aden's arm. "I know it might be hard for you. We won't take too much time looking back. This segment is about going forward. But I have to ask; have the authorities been able to narrow down a suspect? To recap what happened to you for our viewers, you were alone coming out of the stage door into the alley, right?"

"Right." Aden didn't expect a question about her attacker. Would she be able to hold herself together? "I had just stepped out of the theater when someone tackled me. And, what is strange about the night, I don't remember any of it."

"You don't remember it, but you are overcoming what that monster did," Jocelyn said. "I see you are still using a cane," Jocelyn mentioned as she pointed. "That is the snazziest cane I've ever seen. Where can I get one of those?"

"We hadn't planned to offer razzle-dazzle canes … but we might," Aden held her cane out in front of her and swayed it back and forth. "I'm here to talk about our Waist Knots." She looked back and saw Scotty beaming at her.

"You designed these?" Jocelyn asked as she picked up several styles and inspected them carefully. "They're amazing. What prompted you to design them?"

"When I was assaulted, the attacker ruptured two discs in the lumbar area of my back. A surgeon used laser surgery to repair them. Also, some muscles in my back were strained and sprained. The discs are actually healing nicely, but the sprains are taking longer. Depending on the day, I use a cane when my back feels weak and painful. At first, I refused to go out in public with a cane until I contacted Bobbette Carpenter, the talented designer of all the costumes for *Honeysuckle Rose*. I told her what I wanted and needed. She also brought this beauty over." The camera panned down to the glittering walking stick Aden had in her hand.

"It is beautiful. Now the belts, Aden," Jocelyn began with animated hands. "These are gorgeous!"

"Thank you." Aden could not have smiled more broadly. "My orthopedic doctor thought I'd be more comfortable with a back brace. You have got to be kidding me," she sputtered and laughed. "There is no way I'm going to walk around New York strapped into a big black brace. Let me assure you, the damage done to my back did not require a regulation, orthopedic back support. My back is sore and weak. That's why my doctor thought I'd benefit from a brace. I drew some designs, and Bobbie made these wonderful wide belts with support in the lumbar area. They have a Celtic knot on the front as a logo—hence—Waist Knots."

"Waist Knots? Wonderful," Jocelyn said as she put her hands together. "We brought in some young ladies to model them."

"While the girls model the other five, I have on the sixth design." Aden stood up and turned, letting the camera see it from all sides. As the models walked in front of the camera, Aden continued. "Please remember, these belts are not for therapeutic use. They are not equivalent to a back brace from your surgeon or one you'd get through your physical therapist. But they do provide comfort for those with a weak and painful back."

Jocelyn and Aden walked over to the women modeling the Waist Knots. Aden had chosen to wear the one with woven leather in the front, high support in the back, and cincher straps. Her design included a border in a buttonhole stitch, with a thin leather strip woven through. The closure had a gold loop in the center.

"Amazing, Aden." Jocelyn turned quickly to the models. "How do they feel, ladies?"

Each chattered out, "It is so comfortable." And, "They're beautiful."

"Okay, thanks to all of you," Jocelyn offered. "We don't have much time. Aden, tell us why you started this company and where to get one of these Waist Knots."

"Sure. The *where* is at Olivet Stores online and on our website at Waist Knots. The *why* is more complicated."

"Oh, Oli's online store handles them in addition to your website. Wonderful." Jocelyn stopped for a minute. "Now for the *why*. It's important to our audience that you tell them the *why* of your business. You are still recovering. You're the star of a big production. You are busier than anyone could imagine. Why Aden?"

Aden thought for a minute. She knew why but wasn't sure she could explain it. Since the attack, Aden hadn't talked to anyone about how it had affected her life. "Jocelyn," she began looking confidently into the camera, "I will not be a victim. I will decide how I will deal with what life hands me. We are created to be problem-solvers, not whiners."

"That's wonderful, Aden," Jocelyn concluded and shook Aden's hand. "Many in our audience needed to hear your story. We'll watch for you in the Thanksgiving Day Parade."

Aden hugged each of the models and thanked them for their professional display of the belts. Scotty followed close behind as Aden waved to everyone and hurried off the set. Once out in the hall, she jumped into his arms, trembling. "I did it, Scotty. I went out in public wearing one of my belts and carrying my cane. No one laughed at me."

"Of course, no one laughed," he whispered enthusiastically, brushing her hair with his cheek. "They were inspired by what you said about being strong. They loved the belts. And frankly, we might see others with sparkling canes around town."

"Oh Scotty, I lo—" She stopped herself, but neither was lost on the words left unsaid.

CHAPTER THIRTY-ONE

In the ATN-News Studio lobby, Aden searched the sidewalk beyond the windows as they started toward the door. "Dunkin' Doughnuts isn't far from here." She touched her stomach and added, "I'm finally hungry, too."

At the entrance, Aden balanced the door and her cane. But the walking stick got stuck in the opening.

Scotty reached out and took her right hand. "Does this help?" he asked. "You can take my arm like Grandma used to do if that's better for you."

"Grandma, is it?" Aden sassed as she bopped him with the rose handle of her cane. "I remind you of a seventy-year-old? Thanks, friend."

"No … not even a little bit." He squeezed her hand warmly. "You remind me of my Skeeter." They walked a few steps slowly in comfortable silence. "But—if you need extra strength for walking, I can hold your hand, or you can take my arm."

"Taking your arm might help me walk faster, but I like holding your hand." Had she really said that out loud? Caleb held her close just yesterday. Hadn't she enjoyed that, too? She felt both confused and alive at the same time.

They reached Dunkin' Doughnuts, where Scotty opened the door. Aden liked the gallantry. Many of her friends didn't want help with doors, chairs, or carrying packages. But she was glad to have assistance, given her situation. Ordinarily, she was perfectly capable of pulling a door handle herself. But there was something intimate about the old-fashioned attentiveness from someone who knows and appreciates that you are there.

Inside, Scotty rested his hand on Aden's shoulder as he studied the menu above the counter. His touch made the contact that connected them as a couple. It felt to Aden that they belonged together.

"Every doughnut looks great." Scotty drooled over the bounty of sweetness.

"They do, don't they?" Aden scanned the entire list of wonderful treats, starting at the end and working forward, the same way she read a magazine or a catalog. She guessed she didn't like surprises. As she studied the menu, her cell phone vibrated.

"Oh, hi," she said into her phone. Aden could see Scotty watching her cell interaction in what looked to her like his well-practiced indifference. He always gave her space. She would be careful. Caleb was on the other end of the line, and she had no intention of creating a jealousy incident. Turning to talk with a modicum of privacy, she faced the front of the store.

The morning sun streamed through the windows sending strips of shadow and light between and around the paper ads that hung on the glass. Pictures of the magical pastries included peaches and cream, snickerdoodle pecan, and ooey gooey caramel. The sun's glare was so bright it was hard to see through the display case.

"Hi, Baby Girl," Caleb spoke softly into her ear. "Just wanted to remind you about the rehearsal after lunch today. Be at the theater about 4:30 p.m."

"Okay," Aden drew out slowly when she spotted someone standing outside. A man, with his hands on his hips, stared into the store right at her. The sunlight was so brilliant the person was mostly a glare. She could see he was about average in height with a heavy coat, work shoes, and a team cap pulled down low with the *CUBS* logo on it. She felt her stomach churn and her heart race faster and faster. It seemed to Aden that there were suspicious people everywhere.

"Aden? Are you still there?" Caleb asked, sounding concerned.

"Yes," she mumbled as the man outside turned and ran down the sidewalk. "Yes. I'm okay," she whispered hoarsely.

"Good," he offered quickly. "Gotta run."

"Wait," Aden called after him. "Did you watch TV this morning?"

"TV? No," he said as he yawned. "Slept in. Just woke up."

She was determined not to brag. If Caleb was interested in what she was doing besides singing the melody to his harmony, then he would already know about the Waist Knots. He would have known about her appearance on *America Today*. Maybe the presence of the possible stalker outside made her go limp. Shame on him. But she was not going to inflict weakness on herself. That would mean shame on her. As her career developed, she knew she would have to get used to people watching her. She put the cell phone in her pocket and sat down on the first chair she came to.

"Skeeter?" Scotty asked as he flexed his knees and dropped down beside her. "What's wrong?"

"You didn't ask if there *was* anything wrong. You knew." Aden took a deep breath as she steadied her hand on Scotty's shoulder. "There was a man …"

"A man? Where?"

"Outside … watching me." She took a tissue from her pocket and blotted her eyes. "Since you're with me, you need to know what's happening."

Scotty reached out and took her hand. He said nothing but seemed to wait for her to take the lead.

"Since the attack, I've gotten a package and a note. The box contained a cane. The note said I'd better stay inside and away from the theater, or I would never walk again," she blew out a short, anxious puff of air. "And someone has come to the condo twice looking for a couple I've never heard of. And now this guy who may be stalking me."

"Then why are we going for a walk in Times Square? Why did you appear on TV this morning? And why are we going to the theater if you're supposed to stay away from it?" Scotty smiled a knowing smile.

"Because … no one tells me what to do," she said with a firm set to her jaw.

"I remember that." He caressed the top of her hand. "Skeeter, I'm worried."

"Worried for you ... or worried for me?" she asked as she searched his face. Scotty always told her the truth, mostly because he knew she would know if he wasn't being honest.

"For you!" he insisted. Shrugging, he added. "No one cares what I do."

"But you could get caught in the crossfire," she insisted. Scotty had to understand what danger he could be in.

"Good." His smile penetrated her fear. "If I'm in the crossfire, then you aren't."

"Scotty," she said as she stood and embraced him, "you are amazing."

"I know," he said and laughed. "Now, let's order our food and sit in the corner, out of sight from the street."

They moved back farther into the store and sat at a small table. Scotty motioned for Aden to stay seated. "Tell me what you want, and I'll order it."

"Um, I'd like a powdered sugar doughnut and a small orange juice."

"Is that all … no coffee … another doughnut?" He listed many possibilities.

"Yes … yes, coffee and … what I already said, and two powdered sugar munchkins." She got up and moved to the other side of the table, where she could see the front windows and door.

"Let me sit on that side, Skeeter," he offered. "You don't need to worry about who is coming and going."

"No, I'm fine. I know I would recognize only a handful of people in a city this size, but at least, I would recognize that dozen or so." She patted the table firmly. "No, I'm staying right here."

Aden said no more but planted her feet firmly on the floor. An ardent people-watcher, she didn't let the bright sun interfere with her favorite pastime. Once the stalker or nosey gawker left, she dismissed him from her mind and enjoyed the dazzling blue sky. Scotty brought over their order with a tray in each hand.

"Do you have enough to eat?" Aden joked when she saw Scotty's order of coffee, a large orange juice, and three huge doughnuts. She thought the pastries looked like the largest in the case.

"Maybe," he said as he placed her food in front of her. "I can always stop at a sidewalk vendor for a pretzel or hotdog if I get too hungry."

They shuffled the food items back and forth, trying to make space for everything on the small table. Aden laughed. "It's like the guy with the shell game down on the corner."

They said little as the two hungry old friends bit into their delicacies. Aden savored the taste and amazing aroma of cinnamon, sugar, and Scotty's Boston cream filling. "Oh, ah," they exhaled in unison. Laughing, Aden remembered the times they had enjoyed their favorite foods together.

"Ah, Scotty … I remember it all." Aden bit off a large piece of doughnut.

"Mm-hmm," Scotty agreed quietly. "I think about you every day of my life, Skeeter," he admitted.

"That's sweet," she sighed and looked away, embarrassed. She didn't want to go further down Reminiscence Lane. "Have you thought about what New York site you want to see before we go to the theater?"

"What's close?" he asked as he bit into his cinnamon doughnut. "I don't want you to have to walk very far."

"Thanks, and you're right. Rehearsals will take more energy than I've used in a long time. But, getting back to a rigorous dance routine will be important, so I can participate in Macy's show. It will get my name back out to the fifty-million people who watch the parade on television."

"Okay … I get that." He thought for a minute. "What could we see where I could push you around in a wheelchair?"

"A wheelchair? You have *got* to be kidding," Aden said as she nearly choked on a bite of food. She washed it down with juice. "That isn't going to happen."

"All right then," Scotty began again slowly. "I know. The Museum of Modern Art is on this end of Manhattan. We can sit down a lot and admire the displays."

"Great idea," she agreed. "We can take a taxi, and I won't have to waste energy and strength just getting there."

They had a plan. The two would spend the rest of the morning enjoying Cubism, Matisse, Monet, and other masters like Paul Gauguin and Vincent van Gogh. But, best of all, Aden would spend the morning with Scotty Russell, something she thought she would never do again.

CHAPTER THIRTY-TWO

The collections at the Museum of Modern Art became food for Aden's soul as she and Scotty walked through the galleries and witnessed the various works of gifted artists. She inhaled every ounce of creative elixir she could squeeze out of each exhibit. When they came to a masterpiece that fueled her healing engine, they would sit on a nearby bench and savor the energy the piece emitted.

On their way out, the museum gift shop had an array of prints from the masters. "Look at all the colors," Aden marveled. She and Scotty weren't in the shop to buy anything. Aden called it window shopping, even though there were no windows. It was an opportunity to have a massive injection of creativity, filling the right hemisphere of Aden's brain with the fire of healing through inventiveness.

"Let's take a cab," Scotty suggested later as they prepared to leave the gift shop and head toward the door. "We've spent hours in here. I don't want you to use up all your energy."

"I appreciate that, kind sir," she countered. "If I'm going to dance a little during rehearsal, I think a taxi would be the perfect pre-exercise solution."

Outside, they laughed and jostled each other back and forth. They were like two pop bumpers in a pinball machine as they neared the curb and waited for a cab.

Scotty opened the door, and Aden stumbled a little as she started to get in and banged into him again.

"Oh, Skeeter, I am sorry," he apologized as he grabbed her arm. "You almost fell … and it would've been my fault."

"Don't worry about it. I wasn't being careful." She straightened her cape and carefully got into the cab. "I'm just having fun. I'm not focused on me and my injuries."

Scotty took her hand there in the cab. "I'm glad you're not dwelling on the things that hold you back. Isn't that the whole point of getting outside, outside your condo, outside your hyper-focus on yourself? Keep fun in mind as we go to lunch. Be careful but don't dwell. Now, where to?"

"Jewel Razor's Steakhouse, driver, on Broadway in Times Square," Aden told the driver. She heard what Scotty said about focusing on fun, sat back, and relaxed.

A light rain misted the windows as they neared the same part of the city they had left a few hours past. When Aden got out of the cab, the sidewalk smelled like fresh cement. Tiny rain puddles gathered at the curb and waited for more drops to fall. They hurried into the restaurant and dashed up the interior steps to the dining room above the entry and gift shop. Once they were ushered to their table by the window, they sat down and watched the doors at ATN-News across the street for any famous celebrities they might recognize.

"Hi, Aden," the waiter said when he stopped at the table.

"Alex?" she asked, her eyes wide. "I didn't know you worked here."

"Just started last week," he said and smiled. "My show closed. Every little bit of work helps until another part comes along."

"Great," she agreed. "I know how that goes. I did my share of waitressing while waiting for my big part."

"Well, it sure fell into your lap, Honey," he nodded, pulling his order pad from his belt. "Do you guys know what you want yet?"

"In a minute," she said. Then turning to Scotty, she added, "This is my friend, Scott Russell, from Ohio. When I first came to New York, Scott, Alex and I met in drama class."

"Scotty?" Alex rolled his eyes. "I heard about you every day for months," he said and laughed.

"Oh, really?" Scotty asked with a twinkle in his eyes.

"Never mind all of that." Aden blushed. "I'll have iced tea first. Now," she gestured with her hand, "take your opinions and run."

"Make that two," Scotty dittoed.

Aden turned, trying to hide a little grin, and looked out the window. "It looks like the rain has stopped."

"I don't want to talk about the rain," Scotty jabbed. "I want to talk about how much you missed me when you left home."

"Well, I don't want to talk about that," she insisted and pushed a menu in his direction. "I know what I want to order," she barked with a tilt of her head. Grabbing a crystalized, three-inch tall resin diamond at the end of the table, she flipped on the little switch at the bottom, lighting the jewel at the top.

"What's that for?" Scotty asked with a wary eye.

"Any waiter will stop and see what we need … and I need lunch," she answered with a self-satisfied wiggle.

"What a clever idea," he said with a smile, ignoring Aden's in-control attitude.

Suddenly, Aden's body went rigid as terror filled her eyes. "Scotty," she choked out, shifting her stare from the entry to the dining room to the windows.

"What do you see?" Scotty asked as he spun around to see what was causing her stress.

Aden relaxed. "Sorry. It isn't who I thought it was, that stalker from before." Anxiously wringing her hands, she wondered how long she would dissolve into fear when someone she didn't know or dressed like someone else came near.

Alex stopped again at the table and poised his pen over the order pad. "Yes, ma'am?"

"Well, at least someone is giving me respect." Aden didn't even stop to check Scott's expression. She caught her breath and went on. "I'll have the bourbon-kissed filet mignon with mashed potatoes." She folded the menu and handed it back. "I'll get enough exercise to work off all those calories."

"You've practically wasted away to nothing, Skeeter," Scotty said as he looked at Aden up and down. "Some food will be good for you."

"I haven't been able to eat very well for weeks," she admitted as she rubbed her stomach. "My appetite is coming back."

"And you, Scotty Dear?" Alex teased.

"I'll have the same."

As he turned, Alex grinned knowingly and said, "Somehow, I knew that."

CHAPTER THIRTY-THREE

Forty-Fifth Street brought up waves of nostalgia Aden hadn't expected. Whiteway Theater had been her home for a long time, long before opening night. During those early months of show-prep, she spent hours each day attending to the details of getting a new musical ready for production. There was stage blocking, line rehearsals with a complete read-through as new parts were cast, and costume fittings, among the many details.

Aden and Scotty didn't use the alley entrance. The cabbie let them off at the main entrance, where theatergoers, the non-performers, entered the Renaissance-style theater. Aden knew she wanted to avoid the stage door. The memories there were more like post-traumatic stress disorder than the excitement of a dream fulfilled.

Aden stood back and inhaled the sweet and spicy fragrance of the musical theater. When she saw the marquee above the front of the theater, where thousands of people passed, her shock was overwhelming. Hailey Daniels' name had replaced Aden's spot, reserved for the female lead. The reality of her place in the cast emotionally crippled her.

She missed Caleb, her many dancing friends, the glorious music, and the majestic theater itself. But she had managed to push the sorrow and dark clouds of homesickness back into the unknown reaches of her mind.

That afternoon, at the Whiteway Theater, it gushed in so fast she couldn't stop the flood.

"Skeeter, what's wrong?" Scotty grabbed Aden as her knees buckled under her.

"I don't know." Her mouth went dry, and weakness overtook her whole body.

"I assume you still want to go in." Scotty put his arm around Aden's waist and raised her off her feet.

"Scotty, yes, yes," she breathed hard and fast.

He looked around at the billboards and marquee. "I didn't know there was a matinee on Fridays."

"Normally, there isn't. But when Cindy came over, she said they added a Friday 1 p.m. performance to thank the theatergoers for their loyalty to *Honeysuckle*." Her voice drifted off. "They'll probably cut the Friday matinee when I return."

"I cannot imagine embarking on a terrible marketing move like that," Scotty said with his arm around her shoulder. "They should continue with the extra performance, at least for the first few weeks. It would be an opportunity to welcome you back."

Inside the lobby, the matinee goers had cleared out, and the area was empty. The thick red floral carpet silenced their entry, making Aden feel even more frightened. If she could walk right in without detection, so could anyone.

"Aden?" Chandler called out from the box office. When the side door opened, he burst through and lifted her off her feet. "Oh, my goodness." He put her down as quickly as he had picked her up. "I didn't hurt you, did I?"

"No, Chandler. I'm fine. I'm not in pain, just as stiff as Grandma's ironing board."

"Glad to hear that," the ticket manager said with an embarrassed smile. "Not glad to hear how stiff you are, but that you are fine. Your attacker must have wanted to slow you down, not knock you down."

Aden's eyebrows raised, not understanding Chandler's meaning. "Slow me down?"

"Can't catch someone running as fast as you." Chandler gave her another hug. "You'd better go in. They're waiting for you."

Scotty opened the huge, heavy doors from the lobby into the auditorium, helped Aden into the standing-room area at the back of the house, and squeezed her shoulder. "What an odd thing for that guy to say. The attack sounded more like a game to him than an assault that nearly killed you."

"I can handle my healing if I stay positive." Aden steadied her hand on the back of a theater chair. "But, Scotty, the least little negative thing, any weakness, sadness, and all the junk of life come flowing in. I could drown in all that muck."

Scotty held her close. To Aden, it felt like he rowed over and gathered her into his lifeboat.

"Here, let's just rest a minute." He helped Aden into the end seat of the last row. Some dancers were warming up on stage, even though they had just closed the curtain at the end of the earlier performance.

Her cell phone rang just as she sat down. Looking at the screen, to her surprise, her agent was calling. "Hi, Grace. I'm at the theater for a rehearsal."

At the other end of the phone, Grace babbled, "Great. I'll be quick. An editor at *People Magazine* called and wants to interview you—they saw your spot on the morning show. They like your spirit and love your belts."

"Fantastic."

Grace rambled on. "They were able to arrange a photo shoot tomorrow around noon with their photographer. They're putting you on the cover. Get there as soon as you can. They will do the interview on Monday. That way, they'll be able to get you in the next issue."

"Oh, Grace, yes, yes. Text me the time and place." Aden's smile let Scotty know something special was happening.

She turned back and stared up at the ceiling for a few minutes. The high-capacity air filters were artfully surrounded by art deco moldings that added to the décor of the huge auditorium. But she couldn't study the ceiling all day. She was there to rehearse regardless of how she felt. "Scotty, I can't just sit here. They'll think I can't perform."

"Scoot over." Scotty motioned for her to move. "I'll sit, too. It'll look like we're watching the others and waiting for the rehearsal."

"Thanks. And, Scotty … thank you for not even suggesting that I should go back to my condo. You know what I want to do."

"Sure, Skeeter." Scotty squeezed her hand.

"You're here, Baby Girl." Caleb ran easily up the aisle. "Are you sure you're ready for this?"

Aden looked at Scotty and smiled. She would be assertive and strong. "You know me, Caleb." The words came out, but the meaning was lost. "Is the cast ready?"

Caleb turned his eyes on Scotty, even while talking to Aden. "Floyd Blackstone is working with the backup dancers." He faced the stage, then whipped back to Scotty.

"Caleb," Aden stood and touched Scotty's shoulder, "I'd like you to meet my friend from Ohio, Scott Russell. Scott, Caleb Johansson."

Scotty jumped to his feet and put out his hand. "Caleb. Good to meet you. Thanks for taking this much younger actor under your wing and mentoring her."

Caleb's jaw tightened in apparent anger. "You must be the kid our Aden went to school with."

"That's me," Scotty spoke with a firm, confident tone. "Now, I'm the man who just graduated from the Law School at Ohio State University."

Caleb seemed to have no words to up-stage Scott on that pronouncement. "I imagine that was hard for you."

Scotty's eyes met Aden's. "I graduated summa cum laude with my bachelor's degree." Scotty smiled confidently. "I imagine it would be hard for some."

Aden gently poked Scotty in the back as she moved out of the row. She knew he was jabbing at Caleb's sarcastic remarks. Then she turned. "Scott, before you got here yesterday, I hadn't seen you or heard from you for all these years—nearly seven. I had no idea you went to law school."

Scotty looped his arm through Aden's. "Didn't your mother tell you? She and I have talked about it. I finished undergrad school in three years and went straight to law school. Your mom has been very supportive."

"Mom was careful not to mention you to me," Aden said softly.

Caleb blew over Aden's comment, seeming not to hear. He did jump on what Scotty was saying. "You know Pat and Miles, Aden's parents?" Caleb's eye twitched a little as his body grew visibly taunt.

"Caleb," Scotty's tone was dismissive, "Miles has been my pastor for many years. Pat taught my seventh-grade Sunday school class. Aden and I have been friends since we were eight years old. We've been in each other's childhood homes hundreds of times. Well, more than that. Every day." Scotty put his arm around Aden's shoulder. "Are you about ready to rehearse, Skeeter?"

"Skeeter?" Caleb gloated with a snide smile. "That's a nice name for an eight-year-old."

"And, what age does 'Baby Girl' fit?" Scotty squeezed Aden's shoulder.

Celeb didn't answer but took Aden by the other arm. "Let's go down to the stage." Turning to Scott, he added, "Why don't you find something to do and come back. Aden can call you or meet you someplace."

"I'll stay," Scotty stated with a warm smile. "I'll sit quietly in the front and promise not to direct the scene from the seats."

"Yes, Scott, please stay." Aden knew she would limp and fumble all the way down the aisle. But she was determined to show no weakness. She hurried in Caleb's direction and tried to keep up. "Caleb, where's the race?"

"Sorry," Caleb snapped. "I thought you were ready for this performance."

"Caleb," Aden stopped and pulled away from his grasp. "What was that about?"

"What? Do you mean with your college man? Nothing." He looked at Scotty following close behind. "Sorry, Ba—" He pointed to the end seat in the Orchestra section for Scotty but said no more.

Aden froze at the foot of the stage steps. She pretended to stop and watch the cast as she caught her breath.

"Well, come on," Caleb snapped. "They're waiting for you."

"Caleb," she scolded, "there's no hurry. They're not even all on stage yet."

"Aden," Floyd Blackstone greeted with open arms. "Get your gorgeous self up here on your stage."

Hailey Daniels was close enough that Aden knew she heard what Floyd said. She worried about how an understudy, who had carried the show in recent weeks, would feel. But Aden could only know her own feelings. She knew how she felt when unspeakably evil had robbed her of the show after only one night. She didn't know what to say to Hailey. *Thanks for holding onto a goldmine for me. Now give it back.*

"Aden," Hailey squealed as the original star stepped onto the familiar stage, leaving Hailey as the *after-market* choice. The stand-in's expression revealed she felt the slight.

"Hailey." Aden wrapped her arms around her very talented understudy. "It's good to see you." Overwhelmed by a homesickness Aden didn't even know had possessed her, she embraced as many of the cast as she could. Suddenly, she was aware of her body. It wasn't magical. It was real. She had forgotten about her injuries, the stiffness, and sore muscles once she stepped on the stage's apron.

She was relaxed and transformed. Her focus was on everything else, the music, the sets, everything … not herself.

"You look at home," Scotty spoke from the front seats. His voice was as warm as the key light above.

Aden knew where she belonged, and it was right there. Scotty was right. She was at home.

CHAPTER THIRTY-FOUR

Aden was excited. Her new life had been given a do-over. She turned and waved at Scotty just as Floyd began.

"People, gather around. Aden, come and stand by me. I missed having you as my sidekick." To the entire cast, he waved his arms and pointed to various spots on the stage. "We will restage the opening number but not by much." Pointing to the gypsies, he turned and took in the entire stage. "We'll see how it looks if the chorus, the gypsies, dances and sings exactly as you currently perform it. Aden, you take center stage where you usually begin the number."

Floyd, the masterful choreographer who had created the gracefully complicated routines in the first place, began the process of re-blocking the dance steps for the show's theme song the cast would perform at Macy's. "We're going to change everything, yet nothing. Aden, your twists will morph into soft dance steps. Caleb will dance around you rather than you doing the fast, double-timing steps and circular twirls as I had originally created."

Floyd smiled and pointed to Aden's understudy promoted to star. "Hailey, move over here where you were on opening night." Floyd pointed to the first position with the backup dancers. "You've learned Aden's routine, my prima butterfly. Now, I want you to pick up some of Aden's steps from that original routine and incorporate those moves into your solo maneuvers. Aden will do the broader steps, and you fill in the more difficult fluff into what you learned for opening night."

"Hailey, would you?" Aden was thrilled.

"Sure." Hailey sounded surprised. "I had no idea—"

"Well, great," Floyd interrupted briskly. Chuckling, he added, "I'm glad we all agree." Blocking out the additional moves, he used every one of the dancers in the same yet different way.

"Singing the song … that's not my department." Floyd brushed his hands together as he called out to everyone. "Aden, you practice at home, lip-syncing the words from the opening night master tape. I'll send a copy home with you. If you have any questions, just give me a call. I'll come over and help. I know where you live."

"I have a CD of the theme song, Floyd," Aden reminded him. "The day I was fully conscious, Caleb brought a copy to the hospital that the crew here at the theater had made. I've listened to it … a lot."

"Great, Aden. You may be the most rehearsed of everyone. Thanks, Caleb."

After a fast hour-long run-through of lifts, twirls, double-timing tap, and Aden's graceful soft-shoe shuffle, Floyd called out his usual, "That's a rehearsal, kids. Let's all meet back here on Monday afternoon. The timer for the sanitizing fog will go off soon. Let's move out."

The steps down from the stage didn't frighten Aden as much as the steps up. She hurried down without a thought and met Scotty. "What did you think?"

Caleb darted in around her, wedging himself between Aden and Scotty. "I thought it was great."

Scotty sat in the third row from the stage and watched Aden rehearse. He beamed with every step and turn she took.

Aden knew Scotty had memorized the new blocking and would make a great rehearsal partner. Especially if he remained in New York, as he seemed to say earlier. Dare she ask about Scotty's plans?

Scotty threw his arms open for Aden but stopped when he saw Caleb. Reaching out, he took Aden's hand. "It was wonderful."

"Thank you." Aden felt the warmth of Scotty's hand in her heart. They didn't let go of each other. When her eyes locked on Scotty's, she saw the old boyfriend she had once planned to marry. Many cast members began gathering around, and Aden tried her best to focus on the show. "The music for the Thanksgiving program will be the recording. I don't know what they'll do when I'm actually back. Floyd said it would be soon."

"I can write the reverse harmonies for you if you want me to." Scotty's approval and encouragement made her feel more secure about returning. He watched as Caleb crowded closer, establishing his co-star role in his relationship with Aden.

"The composer will do that," Caleb's words were flat, like off-key clunkers on a piano.

Scotty smiled confidently. "That's all right, Caleb. I brought my computer along. It might give something for Aden to practice during the week."

Like a dancing feather, Cindy came fluttering up the aisle. "Aden, a note came for you today before the performance. Hailey handed it to me before the rehearsal."

"Before today's matinee performance?" Aden spluttered. "I thought the whole world knew I was out of the show for a while. Why would they think I would be here?" She panicked a little. The "fan" letter that came in the box with the cane turned out to be a threat. What would be in this one?

"Beats me, Aden," Cindy said with a shrug. "You are right. Every television station in New York and Poughkeepsie carried the story of your attack. Cable TV sent it around the world. Do you want me to read the note, Honey?"

"No … I'd better read it," Aden sighed again. "If he's threatening something, I want to know what it is."

Cindy gave a flourish of her arms and handed the folded piece of paper over to Aden. "Maybe it's from a fan who knew someone would know how to get it to you."

Aden reached for the paper excitedly. Perhaps someone had missed her and wanted her to know it. Staring at the paper, she froze. As she unfolded the small piece, Scotty took it from her hand.

"Are you sure you want to read this?" Scotty asked.

"How will I know if it's good or bad unless I see what it says?"

"I know, Skeeter." Scotty folded his hand around hers as if no one else was there. "Do you want me to read it to you? I'll stop if it gets too graphic."

Aden put her hand to her mouth, muffling a scream, and nodded. "Will this ever end?"

Scotty began to read. "Aden, I see you're healing." He paused and looked at Aden before going on. He scanned the page and read slowly. "You were cut up pretty bad." Scott stopped and jerked the note away. "Aden—"

"No, Scotty, read the rest of it," Aden insisted. "I have to know what that guy is thinking."

"Just remember," Scotty assured her, "I'm here this time."

The cast was silent and listened intently. "We love you, Aden." Hailey put her hand on Aden's shoulder in support. "The note was left at the box office. Let's all hear what it says. Go on."

Turning it over in his hand, Scotty looked at the paper. "Where's the envelope?" he asked as he looked at Hailey.

Hailey sputtered. She had handed the note to Cindy as a single piece of paper. "I don't have it. Ah," she threw her hand to her forehead, "ah, it wasn't sealed." She smoothed the hair back from her forehead. Snapping her head like she remembered something, she added, "Chandler said the envelope was torn up."

Scotty unfolded the paper again as he asked, "What was the return address?"

Hailey narrowed her eyes in concentration. "Aden," she gasped, turning toward them, "the envelope was on the box office counter. It was pretty ripped to pieces. There was no stamp, no return address, and only your name was on it."

Aden snapped her fingers. "Like the note in the cane box. Go on, Scott," she said as she turned back to the awful piece of paper in Scotty's hand, "finish reading that thing."

Scotty put his arm around Aden's shoulder in support and a measure of protection. Taking a breath, he read, "I saw you on *America Today*. I told you to stay out of the spotlight. You wouldn't listen. I'm forced to stop you myself."

"Aden," Floyd Blackstone stepped down from the stage. "Maybe you shouldn't be in the Macy's production. It might not be safe for you."

"I will not be threatened or terrorized, Floyd," Aden insisted as she stomped the end of her cane on the floor.

Scotty spoke up, "Mr. Blackstone, Aden will not be out of my sight."

"I thought you were just going to be here for this weekend," Aden whispered and squeezed his hand. "Thanksgiving is almost three weeks from now."

Scotty kissed the top of her head and spoke softly. "We'll talk about that later."

Caleb watched their every move. "If you have to leave, Scott, I'll be here."

"You *were* here, Johansson," Scotty said but added no more.

Floyd Blackstone studied Aden's face. Her jaw was set, and her eyes determined. "Okay, then, Aden. You have the role back again beginning on Thanksgiving Day. I know you are determined." He turned to the others on stage. "What do you say, cast. I don't know what will happen. Goodness knows; none of us knows what happened there in the alley. But there could be a chance, if Aden returns, we could all be in danger."

"Someone is blackmailing all of us?" the dancer at the end of the chorus line belted out in surprise and disgust.

"It looks that way," Floyd answered. "It's your call," he pointed in a sweeping gesture. "All of you."

The entire cast buzzed with anger and determination. "I support Aden," the plump raven-haired actress who played Nettie Clinker burst out. Other players raised their fists and demanded Aden's return just as soon as she was ready.

"That guy will not threaten all of us. We will watch your every move, Aden. Come on back. We can dance circles around you. You just have to sing, act, and be the star that you are."

"Oh, thank you," Aden said as tears of joy flooded her cheeks. "All of you." She stole a glance at Caleb. He was smiling, but his usual enthusiasm was gone. Or maybe it was just the glare in his eyes he had for Scotty.

Floyd gave Aden a hug. He smelled like his usual cologne, a blend of sophisticate Mets glamour and the high country of the Black Hills of South Dakota, where he was born. "I've seen you work hard enough to know you will be more than ready for the performance on Thanksgiving. All your fans watching the Macy's Parade will see your perfect performance of the theme song from *Honeysuckle Rose*."

Aden would certainly know her part. She had watched and memorized every step and position. Thankfully, Floyd's assistant had filmed the rehearsal that afternoon. The dance studio in Aden's condo would be the right size to practice the new moves. The performance had to look natural and full of energy. Audiences who returned many times to enjoy the production had to assume any changes in choreography were due to the smaller stage in front of the store at Herald Square.

"Okay then. I said it before, and I'll say it again, that's a wrap," Blackstone announced. "Everybody, practice your new moves. Take smaller steps but do them with panache."

Hugs, tears, laughter, and love were shared as the cast reluctantly gathered up their things. Hailey lingered back.

"Aden." Hailey was slow to approach, but Aden could see how much she wanted to speak to her. "I want you to know I am so happy for you and your improvement. We all love you, Aden."

"Thanks, Hailey." Aden put her hands on her friend's shoulders. "I do want to pass on some gossip," Aden said with a sheepish laugh. "Rumor has it, you have been doing a great job. Thank you for holding the show together."

Hailey could not hold back her tears. "Oh, Aden, I am sorry about what happened to you."

"I know." Aden joined in the tears. "Are you okay about dancing my extra steps on Thanksgiving?"

"Absolutely," Hailey's voice was firm. "In fact, I just may get some attention for my versatility. They might create a new Tony Award category for shadow dancing."

"I like that," Aden said.

Outside, a breeze blew softly on Aden's cheeks. Golden leaves from trees planted in fenced-off wells on the sidewalk blew the fragrance of autumn in her direction. It could not have been a better day. Well, it would have been a glorious day if her back and legs weren't aching from the rehearsal. Her body screamed at her with shouts louder than she could talk.

Scotty didn't take his eyes off her. "We don't have to go sightseeing just for me, Skeeter. You are adding strenuous rehearsals on top of healing. We can go back to your condo, and you can rest."

"I am tired," Aden admitted. "But I can compromise. We won't walk. We'll take a taxi again to the place you want to go. That will save energy and wear-and-tear … on me. Where to, my friend?"

"The iconic spot where movies are made." Scotty paused and laughed. "The Empire State Building. I've always wanted to see the city from up there. And it's good enough for Cary Grant and Tom Hanks, so why not. I know … everyone goes there. But I've never been."

Aden grabbed Scotty's arm. "I've lived in New York City all these years. And I have only been there once. I was too busy. Okay, then, 20 West 34th Street it is."

CHAPTER THIRTY-FIVE

The Empire State Building, an Art Deco, 102-story skyscraper, was eleven blocks from the theater in Midtown Manhattan. Between 5th and 6th Avenues, it was near Herald Square and Macy's Department Store. Aden was glad they hadn't walked. At the same time, she felt guilty for not using the city hike as one more opportunity to work out. She decided to waste no time or energy on feelings of guilt.

The Yellow cab pulled up to the entrance. Others who entered and left one of the nation's most famous buildings seemed to recognize Aden. Many eyes turned in her direction. Aden felt a chill run up her spine when her feet hit the sidewalk. What was it? Was she being watched? She knew she would have to get used to people recognizing her. She was famous now, or she was for a few hours many weeks ago.

"Hurry up." Aden nearly pulled Scotty into the building.

"Sure." he looked at Aden closely. "Are you okay?"

"Yep." She didn't want to waste time adding one more word.

Scotty stepped inside as soon as they cleared the door. "What is wrong?"

"I don't know," she whispered as observers passed, sheepishly watched them, and smiled at her. "It felt like someone was watching us."

"I won't pretend to know how you feel. But I believe you." Scotty hugged her, making sure he didn't draw attention to Aden. "I saw them, too. But they acted more like stargazers. I promise I'll help by keeping my eyes open."

Aden was silent as they rode up to the 86th-floor observation deck. She found security in Scotty's solid hand in hers and smiled. His years of playing the guitar, keyboard, and football quarterbacking, made him agile and strong.

On the observation deck, New York City lay before them in all directions. The setting sun made a rim of crimson on the horizon. The city's sparkling lights were coming on. Aden could see the Brooklyn Bridge. This suspension bridge spanned the East River between the boroughs of Manhattan and Brooklyn. To the north was Central Park, and to the south, the Statue of Liberty were all visible from their perch high about the city.

"Wow." Scotty's eyes danced with the magic of New York. "I've been missing all of this, the beauty, the power of the place." He whispered, "Most of all, I missed you."

People coming to the building would be mesmerized by the city at dusk. "Oh, Scotty." She put her forehead on his chest and whispered, "Why—"

"Aden," a young woman interrupted, "may I have your autograph?"

"How nice," Aden feigned surprise and joy. "Of course." Reaching into her purse, she pulled out a fine-tipped pen.

"I have a 3 by 5 card." The woman giggled. "My friend and I were trying to get recipes from some of the Manhattan restaurants. This is an extra one." She handed the card to Aden. "I'll frame it sometime next week when I get home."

"Where is home?" Aden thought she detected a slightly southern accent.

"Lexington, Kentucky, horse country." She pointed to the index card. "My name is Tracy if you want to personalize it."

"Perfect." Aden turned Scotty around and used the back of his shoulder as a firm writing surface.

"To Tracie. The girl who remembered me when I almost forgot who I was.

Many Blessings, Aden Malloy."

Tracie took the autograph and read it. "Aden," she said as she choked up, "your one performance will be remembered along Broadway for a very long time. May I give you a hug?"

"You sure can," Aden responded, realizing a connection had been made in those few seconds.

"You'll be back in the spotlight real soon," Tracie added. "Thanks."

"Thank you," Aden called after her as Tracie hurried to catch up with her friends. Aden felt honored yet confused. How could she have gained all she ever dreamed of and nearly lost it all in the same night? She smiled at the fan, who seemed to see no limp, nor did she acknowledge

Aden's raspy voice. She couldn't believe the woman's admiration and said, "That's sweet."

Scotty pulled out his cell phone and took pictures of the streets below and the panoramic scene beyond the building. "Beautiful. Now," he put his arm around Aden's shoulder, "let's go home. We can pick up some food, or I'll fix you something at your house."

"Are you sure?" She was ready to go home but didn't want to rush Scotty.

"Yes," he laughed. "Yes."

The ride down on the elevator was unsettling for Aden. The small square elevator car was crowded. The observation floor didn't close for hours. But many people appeared to maintain a mid-west schedule, heading for food at mealtime. Everyone seemed happy except the man in front of the elevator, against the wall. He was scowling. Aden had no idea who he was, but she had to get off that elevator and away from his negative spirit. When the elevator stopped on the lobby floor, she darted out and pulled Scotty behind her. Since she wouldn't have been able to run once outside the stuffed box, she flipped around and pressed herself against the wall.

"Aden? What is it?" Scotty folded himself around her, using his body to shield her from whatever she saw.

"I don't know." She grabbed her face and buried herself in Scotty's chest. "The man with the dark sunglasses, the crowd pushing us … it felt dark, suffocating. I couldn't breathe."

Her new-again protector gathered her in his arms and held her close. "I'm sorry I insisted we come here, Skeeter."

Aden smiled weakly. "You didn't insist. I did."

"Let's go." Scotty put his arm around her shoulders and eased her out of the building.

Though the air was cold, everything was beautiful and full of energy. The city was even more alive with evening people than when they went in. Some offices were beginning to close for the day. Junior assistants flooded out of the buildings and hurried to bus stops on various corners. But something made Aden's hair stand on end.

Suddenly, from someplace off to her left, Aden saw a man in black slacks and a tan zip-up jacket. She cringed when he moved in closer and bumped into someone beside her. The short man in an Iowa State athletic jacket on the other side of her grabbed his chest and staggered to his knees. A few people fled from the scene when they saw the man struggle and fall. Aden froze. Scotty grabbed her arm and pulled her behind one of the trees. The small wrought iron fence around the trunk felt cold and hard. She wouldn't be able to crouch down to hide. Her back and leg were too damaged. The guard at the door ran toward the man who slipped erratically through the crowd, pushing and shoving.

Aden's head was swimming, but she couldn't just leave. She dialed 9-1-1 on her cell and hurried to the downed man.

"Aden," Scotty pulled on her arm. "I have to get you out of here. The guy might come back."

"Are you okay?" she asked the man sitting cross-legged on the broad sidewalk just outside the door.

"Yeah," he leaned his head back on the wall. "It's my heart. When that man bumped into me, my heart flipped, and my pacemaker went off, throwing me to the ground."

A middle-aged woman dropped to her knees beside the fallen man. "Gary, are you all right?" She looked intently at Aden. "You called for help, right?"

"Yes," Aden whispered as her eyes darted around the small crowd.

"You're that musical star, aren't you? Malloy?" The woman soothed the man's forehead. "Look, Honey, It's Aden Malloy." She smiled at Aden. "The guy who shoved Gary might have been after you. You'd better leave."

Aden trembled. "What do we do, Scotty? Do we stay or go? I want to go home."

Scotty searched down the sidewalk. "The guard is coming back. We'll give him our names and contact information. The police can call us if they need our statement. It may have all been an accident from a clumsy walker, in a hurry, not watching where he was going."

"Okay," Aden nodded. She pulled a business card from her purse and pushed it in the guard's direction. "Here's my card. My number is on it. Can we go?"

The man looked at Aden carefully. "Aden Malloy," he said with a smile and pointed to the billboard high on the building across the street. "*Honeysuckle Rose.*"

Aden smiled. "Right. I really didn't see anything, but I'd be willing to talk to you or someone from the police if you have questions. I'll contact Detective Alverez."

Aden thought back over the last few minutes, beginning with her reaction to the crowded elevator. "There was a man. He made me nervous. He seemed to be alone.

Coming down on the elevator, he didn't seem happy. I only know that things felt … awful … scary. It sounds stupid … but it felt like a premonition of danger. I'm sorry, but I see scary men and danger everywhere these days. I didn't see anything else or anyone, just elevator-man. Outside, I only saw the man fall to the sidewalk. His wife called him Gary."

The guard also knew who Aden was. "You've been through a lot, Miss Malloy. Do you think the guy was looking for you?"

"I have no idea. I'll have to admit, when I'm out, I'm cautious of everyone."

Scotty stuck out his hand. "I'm Scott Russell, an attorney from Ohio and a longtime friend of Aden's. We just came out the door. I didn't see anyone either."

"Miss Malloy, you said, *him … I didn't see him.* The person who was pushing people around was a man?"

"I don't know," Aden shook her head slowly. "I only assumed."

"Mr. Russell, you can take her home. How do I reach you, sir?"

"I'm staying at Aden's for a while. My plan was to go back to Ohio on Sunday night. Now, I'm not sure the exact day I'll leave." He squeezed Aden's arm and whispered, "I don't know how long I'd be welcome."

"Put your name and number on the back of Miss Malloy's card." The guard pulled the small business card out of his shirt pocket. "That'll do it. It would be best if you could stay in New York a little longer and give Detective Alverez a full report on Monday."

Scotty looked at Aden and raised his eyebrows a little.

"Sure, you can stay." Aden felt some of the fear and stress drain from her. She patted the downed man on his shoulder. "I am so sorry. I hope whoever attacked me weeks ago didn't miss me today and hit you."

Scotty put his hand under her arm. "Come on, Skeeter."

Aden smiled and waved a few fingers at the two. "Okay. Let's go home."

CHAPTER THIRTY-SIX

When Aden got home, she hung her coat in the closet. "I'd better call Detective Alverez." Sitting at the red desk, she selected the detective's number from the last dialed list. "Detective Alverez? This is Aden Malloy."

"Good evening," Alverez replied. "I'm glad you called."

"Detective, I have you on speakerphone, and a friend is here with me."

"Thank you for telling me, Aden. That's the honest thing to do."

Aden looked at Scotty, who listened in carefully. "I want to be sure the officer told you what happened outside the Empire State Building a little while ago. We just got home."

"No, what happened?" Angela's voice sounded shocked. Obviously, the officer hadn't returned to the station to make the report.

"A friend was visiting the city, and I took him to the Empire State Building." Aden described the details of what happened as quickly as she could. "Gary, the man who fell, was taken to the ER I called 9-1-1. The lobby guard said he'll also make a report. If he's found any new information, you could call him. The man doing all the pushing and knocking down may have had nothing to do with me. But, with everything that has happened, I didn't know what to think."

Detective Alverez assured her, "I'll find out what I can. Also, I want you to know that I found out who that guy is who has come to your door several times. I ran the picture you took through your security peephole and got a hit. I also traced down Carol and Chris Foy."

"Wow, that was fast."

"First, the picture is of Harry Metzger, a loan shark. Interestingly, Mr. and Mrs. Foy borrowed money from Metzger, and the Foys did live in your building. Only, their condo was on the floor above yours. Metzger loaned cash to several people in the complex, including that radio guy, Carl Fritz."

"Carl?" Aden's head began to swim. "But Carl had helped me many times by getting someone away from my door. Why wouldn't Harry have recognized Carl when he talked to him outside my door? Carl is my neighbor. I never heard them argue like they knew one another."

"Metzger has quite a thing going. He has several young, clean-cut men and women in an expensive office with secretaries. They have all the legitimate trappings of a banking institution that takes applications for high-interest loans. The borrower only meets the boss, Harry Metzger, if they fall behind on their payments. Evidently, the Foy couple couldn't keep up their obligations, so Metzger came looking for them."

"He may not be the one who attacked me? I never had contact with Metzger. I never borrowed money." Aden began to choke up. "Angela, I hoped this would be over."

"I know, Aden. I had that same hope." The detective's voice softened. "I wish I could tell you more. Metzger isn't off our list yet. I'll inform you when we find out who was running through the crowd, perhaps pushing people."

"Thanks, Detective. Good night."

Aden looked up at Scotty, took his hand, and put it to her cheek. "Thanks for being here, Scotty." She shook her head and threw her shoulders back. Leaving her phone on the desk, she started toward her room. "I'm done with all of that for now, Scotty. I'll change. I'd better do my therapy before I begin to relax, or I'll never get up and do it."

"Therapy? Aden, you've been dancing and walking … and now, you need to do more?"

"Scotty, I have a routine. I'll have to stick with it. That's how I do what I don't want to do at that moment." She stopped at her bedroom door before putting on some workout clothes. "You know me. I have two levels of habits—total commitment and none."

Scotty threw his head back and laughed. "I remember. You didn't dare skip your voice lesson to shop in town or take in a movie. You'd want to ditch every lesson for many Saturdays after that. And your mom … wow, she knew if you weren't where you were supposed to be."

"That's because everyone in town knew my dad and mom. Those in Dad's congregation obviously knew me, too. It seemed they all needed to keep their eye on me."

Scotty nodded. "They knew how busy your parents were and wanted to help them."

"If you say so," she somewhat agreed, with mischief in her eyes. "I'll be out in a minute."

Aden changed from the leggings and short skirt she wore for the rehearsal into tights and a long-sleeved black leotard. When she came out of the room, Scotty was asleep on the couch, with his guitar across his lap. Aden smiled. When she went into her small dance studio, Aden made sure the radio music was low.

Lift, lift, lift, she whispered softly as she raised her right leg up to the dance barre and stretched her body out across it. Then she switched to the left leg. Her first set of exercises was stretching and limbering movements. The last positions were to strengthen the muscles in her back and a series of exercises for core building. It was a good workout.

Aden heard music from the living room when she turned off the radio. She didn't recognize the melody. What was Scotty playing?

In the living room, Aden saw that Scotty had gone out on the balcony. With her grandmother's Afghan from the back of the couch wrapped tightly around her shoulders, she went out on the terrace. The night air blowing across the garden was cold when she opened the glass door. Flowery perfume lifted from the remaining fall blossoms. Mimi had planted every late-blooming flower that could survive on a high-rise terrace in New England. Knowing the petals would eventually fade and fall, her grandmother had a creative idea. Mimi strung beautiful, colorful ceramic blossoms, connected by electrical wire, around the base of the planting beds. The ceramic flowers waited for the cooler weather, adding artistic warmth to God's beautiful garden.

When her grandmother planted the garden, she had lined the burst of colorful roses, poppies, and calla lily ceramic flowers with LED strip lights in orange, red, yellow, and blue. By day, the painted blossoms added invigorating hues to the garden. At night, the twinkling colors made the garden magical. Although Central Park had fallen asleep to color, Aden's Garden provided food for the color-deprived soul.

Aden paused after she closed the sliding door behind her and inhaled the beauty of her unique terrace garden. Scotty's melody added a musical accompaniment to the joy she experienced. "Scotty, what is that song?"

"I wrote it for you last week. Your mom told me about the garden your grandmother planted and the ceramic blooms she created to replace the live ones in the winter. And, by the way, it is beautiful. I'm surprised there are still a few real blossoms out here. Maybe the heat from the condo helps."

"Probably." But Aden was stuck on what Scotty had said about a song he had written. "You wrote a song for me?"

Scotty looked up and smiled. "Your mother said you would have to sing in a much lower key, at least for a while."

"My mother?" Aden lowered her gaze and teased. "You said you often talk with Mom."

"I do. I finished law school and wanted to take the Bar exam right away. The waiting period for each candidate's score is weeks long. I needed support and encouragement while I waited for the results. Your mother was on my side as usual."

"Wait a minute, weeks. That means you could have received your results already."

"Yes, indeed, I did."

"And …?" Aden gently popped Scotty on the shoulder with her fist. "So …?"

Scotty reached over and took her hand. "I passed it, Skeeter."

Aden clapped her hands together. "Oh, that is wonderful."

"I wanted to be able to practice law in several states, Ohio … New York."

"New York? Scotty, what are you saying?"

"It's just a thought right now." Scotty looked down at his guitar.

Aden didn't want to push him. He just said he was only thinking about it. Could he be teasing her or expecting her to choose for him? That would be another thing she would think about later. For now, she wanted to know about the music. "You said you wrote a song."

"I wrote it, then pitched it even a little lower after talking to your mom. I can even put the harmony on top rather than under the melody. That's what I had in mind for rewriting the music in *Honeysuckle Rose*. But like Caleb said, the composer will rewrite his own music."

"How did you know I need my songs pitched in a lower singing register?"

"Remember, I called you sometime after you got home from the hospital. You sounded really hoarse. It sounded like more than laryngitis you might get if you yelled too loudly at a football game. And … like I said, I talked to your mother."

"What did she tell you?"

Scotty didn't look up but watched the strings vibrate slightly as he gently strummed his guitar. First, there were chords. Then a melody emerged. "Your mom told me the guy who attacked you damaged your vocal cords. But no matter what happens to you, you always wake up every morning, opening up as one of God's own flowers."

Aden didn't know what to say. From all her years of performing, she knew one safe response. "Thank you, Scotty. That's beautiful." She felt uncomfortable, not knowing the meaning behind his words. She had to find something else to talk about. "You could do me a little favor and rework one of the shorter songs from the show. It would give Randolph, the composer, an idea of what you had in mind."

"Sure," Scotty's eyes danced. "It will be fun to write, and … it'll help you in the process." He started to speak, then paused and began chording again. "Seedlings are the talents with which God blesses us all. We plant them in God's Garden, where the stems begin to grow. When the blossoms open, we can claim them, with arrogance, as our own, or name them after Him who gave them." Scotty held the guitar closer and began to strum and then sing the song he had written for Aden.

Like the Rose

There were no words Aden could add to the beauty of the ones Scotty had chosen for her song. Tears ran down her cheeks. She got up and put the guitar Scotty held on to the table. Curling up on his lap, she sobbed. Aden knew, she surely knew, God always finds a way. And each time she would open the terrace door, she would find a way for Aden to be Aden again.

CHAPTER THIRTY-SEVEN

Aden woke up on Sunday morning, stretched, and smiled. Scotty was still there.

When the phone rang, she checked the screen. Caleb was calling. She rubbed her eyes to clear her mind. "Hi, it was good to see you and everyone last Friday."

"It was." His deep baritone voice flowed like maple syrup. "I forgot how much I missed you." Caleb paused, but Aden said nothing. "I got up early this morning because I was wondering if you would like to meet me for breakfast."

Aden didn't understand how Caleb could say that. He knew Scotty was there. Then she remembered what Caleb had said before the ill-placed invitation. "You're saying you forgot about me, Caleb?"

"Well, no." He sounded flustered. "I just got busy."

"I know you did." Aden truly did understand. She wondered if, in the future, Caleb would drift in and out of her life when he had time. Maybe. That's what casual friends do.

"Okay, then … breakfast?"

"No, Caleb, sorry." She wanted to sound sorry. After all, when she's back in the show, she will have to get along with everyone, including her co-star. "I'm going to be on *Morning Brunch* a little after 8 a.m. this morning. Then, Scott and I will go to church before lunch."

"*Morning Brunch*? I didn't know you would promote the show this morning." Caleb didn't hear *Scott, church,* or *lunch.*

"I'm not going to promote the show." She mentally repeated a phrase her mother gave her. *There he goes being Caleb again.* "It's not about the show or you. It's about me and what I've been doing since the attack."

Caleb's voice mellowed. "Oh. I know physical therapy and voice training have been hard. I imagine you've needed a lot of rest, too. Sleep heals."

"It certainly does." Aden tried not to laugh so Caleb could hear. Caleb seemed to have no idea how she had filled her lonely days. Maybe he was right. She hadn't seen the cast except for Cindy and Bobbie. "I've been busy designing fancy belts for those who need back support."

Caleb sounded positive as his volume raised with excitement. "That's great, Aden. We can promote those by just wearing them."

"There is no *we* in the belt project, Caleb. I designed them, and I wear them. They're for women." She stopped during the long moment of silence. "I still have to get ready. Caleb, Scott may be gone next week. Why don't you call again then?"

"Scott … is staying there?"

"Of course. Caleb, you know a night in a New York hotel can cost hundreds of dollars."

"Right … right." Caleb was silent again. "Okay, then … I'll call you next week. Bye, Baby Girl."

"Bye, Caleb." Suddenly, Aden didn't like Caleb calling her *Baby Girl.* She felt weak and helpless. Those were not feelings that would promote healing and health.

"Aden," Scotty tapped on the door. "It's 6:30. The coffee is ready."

"Fantastic. Thanks. I'll hurry and take a quick shower. Then you can use the bathroom. Coffee after."

The super warm water in the shower felt good on Aden's tired muscles. She had danced for the first time in weeks just the day before. Well, her form of dancing. Her back was stiff, and her leg was sore. The hot water soothed everything. She dried off, gathered up her makeup, darted into the bedroom, and slipped on her clothes. "Scotty," she called out into the living room, "the bathroom is yours."

Scotty came in wearing the dress slacks he would put on. His chest was bare. "Sorry," he threw the shirt he planned to wear over his shoulder. "Thought this would work."

"Scotty," she laughed and lowered her eyes, "I've seen you in swim trunks every summer since we were ten." Her smile changed to embarrassment as she looked away quickly. "Wow, Scotty, you're not ten anymore."

He bowed gallantly. "Thank you, ma'am." He took a step in Aden's direction.

"You …" she looked away and pointed at the bathroom, "better hurry with your shower. I can't be late."

"Umm, okay, Skeeter, get out of here then." He closed his eyes and stumbled into the bathroom.

At the mirror in the living room, Aden applied some makeup. She was careful about her application since she would be on television. But then, Aden was always minimal with foundation and eyeshadow. She never put it on with a frosting spatula.

When Scotty came out of the bedroom, he stood and watched her for a while. "You are … beautiful." Scotty brushed a stray hair from Aden's forehead, then kissed it gently.

"We'd better hurry and drink our coffee or leave." Aden knew how she was feeling. Scotty's actions and glances told her he felt the same way. The songs they sang to each other and the plans they made in high school streamed through her head.

When the doorbell rang, Aden was startled. Pulled away from her sweet memories and back into the past month's nightmare, Aden peered through the peephole and froze.

Scotty stopped and grabbed her waist. "Skeeter? Who is it?"

"Sorry to bother you," a man's voice called from the hall. "I was here before. I know Carol and Chris Foy live here. I want to talk to them. Just open the door."

Aden started to speak, but Scotty stopped her with his finger to his lips. He lowered his head and spoke as deeply as his voice would go. "We asked the police to check for us. No Foy family has ever lived here."

There was silence on the other side. The man put his hand in his jacket pocket. "I recognized your neighbor's voice. Carl Fritz, WBKR, confirmed Foy's presence in the building."

Aden trembled and shook her head *no*.

"No." Scotty punched 9-1-1 into his cell. "I'm checking with the authorities even as we speak," Scotty insisted. "Unless you want to explain it to the police." At that moment, a distant siren was heard on the road below, heading someplace.

Aden heard the shuffle of feet and the ding of the elevator. Then the hall was silent. She scanned through the peephole as far as she could see in both directions. All was clear. She grabbed her bag containing the belts and a small purse. "Let's get out of here."

CHAPTER THIRTY-EIGHT

It was still very early when they arrived outside Beacon News Studios on Avenue of the Americas. The lights from the stores, billboards, and trees still glowed gold, blue, and red in the next block. Aden stopped and studied the building, all forty-five floors. "First, *America Today*, and now *Morning Brunch* on the Weekends. Scotty, it feels like a dream."

"You're not dreaming, Skeeter. I know your life has been a whirlwind. You have worked harder than anyone I know. You have rehearsed for hours every day for several weeks and attended physical therapy and voice training. Now, it's time to shine. Come on, let's go in. I don't want you out in the open." He stopped abruptly. "I'm sorry. I'm not your daddy or your boss. It is your belt business, not mine."

"Thanks, Scotty. I don't need you to verify that it's been rough, and I've worked hard. I know who I am. But it is nice to hear that you are looking out for my safety. Thanks for recognizing me."

Inside Beacon Studios, some people spotted Aden as she walked into the lobby. "Miss Malloy," a couple in matching Indianapolis Colts caps called out. "You're looking good."

"Thank you." To be kind and yet convey her rush, she asked, "Where is the elevator?"

"Right there," they pointed.

"Thanks," Aden said and hurried on.

It was a short ride up to the mezzanine, but she knew she would get there faster than climbing the stairs.

A woman in gorgeous black braids approached them when they took their first step off the elevator. "I'm Yolanda. They'll be ready for you soon. Follow me to the green room." She looked back at Scotty. "Your friend can come, too."

Yolanda handed each of them a paper plate. "There are doughnuts and a complete tray of fruit. Help yourself. Aden, we'll be ready for you in about three minutes."

When Yolanda left the room, Aden handed Scotty the paper plate. "I can't eat if I'm going on in a few minutes. But you help yourself."

"Absolutely," Scotty beamed as he took his time with his selection.

Yolanda breezed back into the room. "We're ready for you, Aden. We're in a commercial break right now."

They entered the studio where Maria, the show's host, sat on one of two chairs behind a low table. "Aden," she stood and greeted her. "I am so happy you came."

"Good morning, Maria. I'm thrilled to be here."

"It looks like you are getting around faster than I would have expected after that terrible attack," Maria encouraged her.

"I keep improving. Yesterday, I rehearsed for the production of *Honeysuckle Rose* at Macy's Thanksgiving Parade. I even danced a little." Aden beamed. She enjoyed meeting Maria and was happy to report her progress in getting her legs back.

"You danced?" Maria asked excitedly.

"Ready in five," Yolanda announced.

"Okay, Aden. Let's see these belts." Maria rubbed her eager hands together.

"Well, I'm wearing this one." Aden took off her jacket and handed it to Yolanda. Turning, she modeled the combination braided leather, topped with a rhinestone buckle in the middle. In the back, it had a high sculpted contour that provided extra support.

"Aden," Maria's eyes lit up with excitement. "I would love one like that."

"Five, four," Yolanda called off, then silently signaled, *three, two, one.*

Maria looked into the camera and began. "I'm here with Broadway's newest star, Aden Malloy."

"Good morning." Aden smiled, happy to be on the show. But she wondered if she was the newest star or if the sparkle belonged to Hailey Daniels. Quickly, Aden redirected her focus. She was there to promote her belts. "I'm happy to be here. I certainly want to lift up the show, *Honeysuckle Rose.* But I'm here to introduce everyone to the belts I've designed." She pulled the belts out of her bag and arranged them on the table.

Maria picked up one of the peasant corsets. "Everyone was shocked to hear someone attacked you on opening night. Did your time recuperating prompt the idea for the belts?"

"The period I spent healing gave me time … time to think … time to create." Aden paused and wondered how much she wanted to reveal about the dark nightmare she had been through. She wasn't ready but willing to admit something about her character. "Maria, I'm young."

"Yes, you are."

"I mean … during the attack, I was flipped over a railing and bruised my spine. The doctor told me to help support my back when I'm out walking around, I should wear an orthopedic brace. I'll have to admit; I'm too vain to walk in some of the most stylish boutiques in the country in a clunky, bulky black back brace."

"So, you designed these wonderful belts. Will they replace the support of an orthopedic brace?" Maria held up the denim one and turned it around in the bright studio light.

"No. These are not for those who have had surgery. These are for those with sore backs and aching muscles. The Waist Knot gives a little help in holding them up." Aden stood up to demonstrate the one she was wearing.

"The one you have on is beautiful," Maria admired. "Aden, the report we passed on to our audience said you had a ruptured disc, maybe two."

"It turned out to be just one," Aden sat down again. "The ortho surgeon repaired it with surgical glue."

"Glue?"

Aden handed Maria one of the leather belts. "Glue. It's better than spit and bubblegum, but yes, glue. I wear one of these when I go out and often wear the plain one, without the bling, when I exercise or rehearse. Major back surgery with an incision and rods would need more support than these belts would provide. But if it's just back pain or muscle strain, these will provide the help you need. Always check with your doctor."

Maria took the Waist Knot and turned it over and over in her hand. "They are wonderful, Aden, beautifully designed. I like the Irish knot on each of them."

"That's our trademark, Maria."

"We're short on time. Where can we get one of these wonderful Waist Knots?"

"Olivet.com, or my website, waistknots.com. Either will work. They are adjustable but come in small, medium, and large."

"Well, thank you for coming, Aden. You have certainly decided you won't be a victim."

"I cannot be a victim, Maria. Victimhood would weaken me. It promotes poor health and lack of healing." Aden looked squarely into the camera. "I don't know who attacked me, but I will not let them win. I choose to be a winner, not a whiner."

"That's a lesson for all of us," Maria said in conclusion. "Take what life hands you and repurpose it into something to benefit yourself and others." The camera lights faded as Aden and Maria stood. "Thanks again, Aden. We all look forward to your return to the stage."

"I appreciate that, Maria," Aden said as she gathered up the belts and her cane. Maria hurried off to her next studio spot, and Aden handed Scotty her duffle bag full of Waist Knots.

####

Out on the street, the November day was crisp, almost biting. But the sky was blue, and that was enough. Still, there was something in the air that Aden could not identify. People enjoyed the day, laughing, talking, and hurrying from place to place. Others took the day at a stroll, stopping for a soft pretzel from a street cart or purchasing honey-roasted peanuts or almonds from a vendor. The salty aroma hung in the air like an expensive perfume.

Someone else was on the street, someplace. Aden could feel him behind her, around her—somewhere. Who was the man in the black slacks and tan zip-up jacket near the curb? Wait. Where did he go? She knew he was still there, someplace. She felt a chill run up her spine.

CHAPTER THIRTY-NINE

The morning was glorious as Aden and Scotty came out of the church around 11:30 a.m. The sun shone brilliantly on that fourth day before Thanksgiving. She smiled as she put on her sunglasses in November. Not knowing what to say, she was quiet. Scotty had booked his flight and would be gone soon. She'd have to adjust to losing him again.

"You're quiet, Skeeter." Scotty reached over and took her hand. "What was the most important point of the service today?"

"The music." She held his hand more tightly as people hurried along the sidewalk, crowding her toward the street.

"I'm sorry, Aden." A lady in a tan wool coat reached out and patted Aden's arm when she bumped it.

"I'm right here." Scotty's voice was soothing and strong.

"That's all right. I'm fine," Aden assured the woman as she hurried out of the church with the stream of others from the congregation. "It's funny," she whispered to Scotty, "when someone gets too close, I cringe. I actually begin to tremble on the inside. But it's getting better. When they call me by name, it still feels good, like they accept me."

The church wasn't far from Rosie O'Grady's Restaurant in the theater district on 7th Avenue. The familiar eatery waited for them with the flavor of roasted chicken floating in the air. At least, that's how it felt every time Aden went to Rosie's. Sometimes the cast would gather there late in the evening after rehearsals. Laughter filled the place and warmed her heart. Obviously, sidewalk dining was not available since it was November. But that was all right. Scotty opened the glass-framed door.

"I like the hardwood floors and white beamed ceilings." Scotty's eyes shone as he took it all in.

Aden slipped her hand more tightly into the crook of Scotty's arm. "I'm glad you like it."

Once seated at their white cloth-covered table, they quickly looked at the menu and ordered their meal. Aden knew exactly what she wanted. She had it before and had waited all morning for the familiar taste of grilled salmon Caesar salad. Scotty chose a steak and fries. After taking their order, Aden watched as the server walked away.

Aden was feeling restless. She admitted to herself she was anxious about Scotty's leaving soon. Aden could not hold back her feelings. Tears filled her eyes. To hide her emotions, she put the cloth napkin up to her face like she was opening it with some fanfare when the server brought their coffee.

Scotty didn't take his eyes from Aden's soft blue ones. He reached out his hand and placed it over Aden's smaller, softer fingers. "Skeeter, talk to me."

Aden tried to smile, knowing some in the restaurant knew her. The coffee would calm her, but the way she was shaking, she might spill it all over herself. Turning her face to the wall, she breathed in slowly and blew out through her mouth. "Wait a minute."

"Better," he whispered?

"I'm spoiling one of your last days in New York." The coffee was hot and brisk. She felt her inner self stiffening again, giving some physical support to her spirit.

"Don't worry about me. I'm having a great time. I'm just concerned about you."

"I don't want you to worry." Aden blotted her eyes again and emptied her cup as the server offered to fill it. "I just …" How was she going to tell him? Aden choked up. "It will be hard to see you go, Scotty. You're the only one I want to be here when I perform at Macy's." Her throat was so thick and tight that it choked off the words.

His eyes twinkled over the top of his cup. "I did promise to transpose your music into a lower key."

"Uh-hum," she nodded. "Create tight chords when Caleb and I sing and put the harmony on top in other songs. That would take some time."

Scotty added, "And you haven't had a chance to learn the new song I wrote for you—*Like the Rose*."

"No, not yet." She drank more coffee as she tried to pull herself together.

"Well, Aden," Scotty began slowly, "would I be in your way if I stayed here … worked on the music and had Thanksgiving with you?"

Aden was stunned. "Could you?"

"My law degree is finished, and I passed the bar. I hadn't started looking for a job. I … didn't know which state I'll practice in."

"Which state? You mean—" Aden paused when the server returned to the table with a plate in each hand. Aden looked up, "Thank you."

"You're welcome." The server pulled a piece of paper from her pocket. "Someone left a note for you, Miss Malloy."

"Thanks." Aden took the paper, but Scotty quickly took it from her fingers.

He read the small note, wadded it up, and stuck it in his pocket. "The writer said he saw you on TV this morning and didn't like it."

Aden was quiet for a moment. She had to know. "Did he make any threats?"

"A ratty little man like that guy? Don't worry about it. I'll let you read it after you've eaten. Any snot-nosed bully like him should never be listened to before you enjoy your meal."

Aden laughed. It felt good to have power over fear. "We'll have to take the note to Detective Alverez. Angela may want to see if there are any fingerprints on it."

Leaning back, he scrunched his eyes. "I wadded it up."

"We'll let Angela's experts unfold it." Aden's beautiful salad looked good. Even her appetite was back. She chose a piece of multigrain bread from the basket and then answered the question that still hung in the air. "Of course, you can stay … for as long as you want."

Scotty focused his gaze on his steak. When he looked up, he grinned like the tease he always was. "You don't know how long I want to stay."

CHAPTER FORTY

The next morning, Aden and Scotty stormed into the police station. It was crowded with those in uniforms, suits, and every kind of clothing one could imagine. One young man with dyed green hair spiked four inches above his head like a stegosaurus was slumped in a chair and tried not to be interviewed by other detectives on duty. That corner of the room smelled like the pine and lavender goo that held his hair up mixed with … stink.

Aden slapped the newest threat, tucked in a small plastic bag, on the detective's desk. "Angela, I need this stuff to stop."

"We had just sat down in a restaurant," Scotty explained with an edge to his voice. "The guy must have followed us. In fact, we may have been followed all morning." Scotty tapped the note in the small bag with his fingertips. "I took the note when the server handed it to Aden and wadded it up. Now, my fingerprints are on the paper, too. Sorry," Scotty apologized.

"And you are—"

"Oh," Aden forgot Angela hadn't met Scotty. "This is Scott Russell, my friend from Ohio."

Detective Alverez looked at Scott calmly yet forcefully. "Where were you the night Aden was attacked?"

"Me?" Scotty nearly jumped. "I came to the performance and sat in the back. I left after the final curtain call."

The detective pursued the questioning. "Why did you leave so early? Didn't you want Aden to know you were there?"

Scotty's expression grew stiff and anxious. "Sure, I wanted to see her, but it looked like she was all wrapped up in Caleb Johansson." He looked at Aden with pleading eyes.

"You were jealous," Alverez concluded.

"Of course, I was jealous—"

"Angela," Aden interrupted, "Scotty is not a suspect. He has been my friend since we were children."

"Sometimes, it's hard to recognize an assailant when we care about them." Alverez closed her notepad and stood up.

Aden was confident yet firm. "And it's easy to recognize a friend when we care about them." She balanced herself on the fancy cane. "I knew it was important for you to get the evidence as soon as possible. If there's nothing else, just let me know if you get any information on this guy."

"You're free to go," the detective told Scott. "But stick around New York while I sort this out."

"I'll be staying through Thanksgiving." He smiled at Aden.

Detective Alverez looked at Aden and sighed. "Let me know if you decide to leave the city. Aden, keep your eyes open."

The two friends were silent as they walked toward the stairs. Not a hostile silence, a warm silence.

Aden had to know. "Why didn't you stick around on opening night? You could have shared in my success?"

"I was jealous, Skeeter. I felt like I wasn't part of the wonderful things happening to you. I didn't sing with you or hold you in my arms. Someone else did."

"But I always wished it was you."

"You didn't say anything," Scotty whispered as they passed patrolmen in the hall on the way out.

Aden had to admit her silence. "No, I didn't." As they stepped out into the Monday morning, sunshine-gold and orange colors were everywhere, from the Thanksgiving decorations to the last of the leaves that clung to a few fading trees in Central Park. "Scotty … when I visited you on campus that time, I knew it was right for you. But I didn't fit in. I was living in the largest city in the country, going to class every day, and dancing in a chorus line every evening."

"I didn't know you felt that way, Skeeter." Scotty put his arm around Aden's shoulder. "And now?"

"It's different. Everything is different in my life now." Aden searched for the words that could describe her experience with her friend. "You're the same Scotty, but you stepped through my door as an adult. I think you would belong anywhere."

"And you would, too," Scotty added.

"Well, I'd belong anywhere people will let me be me." She was quiet for a moment as Scotty patiently listened. "If they'll let me be Aden Malloy from Ohio and Aden Malloy from New York. I don't want to have to choose. If I get the starring role in a Broadway musical, only a few know how exciting that would be for me. Others think I'm claiming to be better than they. I have no desire to be better than anyone, but I will not be less than others, either. If a nomination for a Tony Award comes my way, there are very few, except strangers, I can tell. No one but my parents join in the joy of my success. It can be very lonely, sometimes."

"I'll cheer you on and praise your accomplishments, Aden." Scotty wrapped his arms around her and drew her close. "I know Aden from Dayton, from the top of your curly chestnut hair to the taps on the bottom of your shoes. I know I'm proud of Aden Malloy, the newest star on Broadway, who carries the Aden of Dayton with her wherever she goes."

"Scotty Russell—" She didn't know if she dared express how much she appreciated that Scotty saw her for herself. She couldn't allow herself to use words buried deep inside. Not yet. Maybe never.

CHAPTER FORTY-ONE

Gretchen Carpenter's photography studio was about ten blocks north of the police station. They would have to hurry. With Aden's slow pace, another cab would be necessary.

"You look great for your picture, Skeeter. Sorry, I forgot to tell you earlier," Scotty apologized.

"You are always saying the right thing, Scotty." Aden wondered what Caleb would have said if anything.

The traffic was smooth. The cabbie only yelled out the window one time. And the driver chose his words carefully.

"Get out on the curbside, ma'am," the cab driver warned. "You're not fast enough to dodge the traffic, Miss Malloy."

Aden was amazed. "You recognize me?"

The cab driver shook his head and laughed. "With that beautiful face of yours shining down from billboards and the sides of buses? Everyone knows who you are."

The two got out of the cab and entered the building on Broadway, north of the theater district. Aden was quiet as they rode up on the elevator. The doors opened on the third floor into a small waiting room with a large photo studio beyond.

"Aden, thank you for coming," Gretchen sang out. "I didn't know if we could take the pictures at your apartment.

The lighting might be a problem. I can control the shoot more easily here."

"I'm glad it worked out." Aden gave her a little hug and then took the duffle bag from Scotty. "You asked me to bring my Waist Knots."

"Yes." Gretchen moved over to an area set up for the picture. There was a trifold screen with a scene from the *Honeysuckle* production as a backdrop. Aden recognized it as a pre-production promotional piece.

"This will be perfect," Aden said as she took it all in.

"The wardrobe department loaned me the costume you'll wear in the Macy's Parade. You can go into that dressing room and change." Gretchen pointed to a small room off to the side.

Aden opened the door and was thrilled with what she saw. The long dress with the sweeping, ankle-length skirt was both familiar and terrifying when she pulled it over her head. Her hand trembled, and her leg refused to hold her up. "Scotty," she whispered through a slightly opened door, her voice cracking.

Scotty jumped up and hurried to the door. "Skeeter, what's wrong?"

Aden laughed with embarrassment. "I have a mechanical problem and an emotional one." She turned slightly, presenting a half-zipped zipper.

"I can solve that," he said, his voice warm like hot chocolate. Slowly, he pulled up the zipper tab. "And emotional?" he asked as Aden fell into his arms.

"Scotty, this costume is the last thing I wore before I changed into my street clothes and walked out into that alley. As colorful as it is, that costume makes me relive that terror all over again."

He put his arms around Aden and pulled her toward him. Softly caressing her back, he said, "I'm sorry it brings back all those bad memories. Will you be able to wear it for the *People Magazine* cover photo Gretchen is going to take?"

"Oh, Scotty," she started to sob.

"Don't smear your makeup, Skeeter. Just try to think of the excitement of winning the most coveted part on Broadway, getting to know the cast, the fun of singing and dancing again on stage." He took a handkerchief from his jacket pocket and blotted her eyes.

Staring into the dressing room's full-length mirror, Aden frowned. Quickly, she applied a little foundation, powder, and a touch of lipstick. It made her feel normal.

"You look wonderful, Aden," Gretchen assured her when she came out into the studio. "I can touch up any puffiness. Let's make a magazine cover."

Aden handed her cane to Scotty before following Gretchen's posing instructions. Trying to find new and interesting positions with her stiff and painful leg, she wiggled and turned left and right. Each shot included her wearing one of the Waist Knots. In her familiar costume, in front of the promotional screen, she felt warm, like she was home.

"That's it, Aden. You were beautiful," Gretchen said with a broad sweep of her hands as she placed the camera on a table.

With his arms outstretched, Scotty gathered Aden in his embrace. "The shots looked beautiful, Skeeter. I wish I could swing you around like I used to. But I don't want you to get hurt."

"It won't be long before you can turn me every which way," Aden said as she hurried into the dressing room. Stopping, she added, "I'm not a glass doll. If I'm dropped, I'm repairable." She whispered with her back turned to the door, "Scott, zipper, please."

When Scotty laughed and moved closer, Aden could feel him there like a magnetic field encircled him. She glanced at Gretchen, who smiled sheepishly. "I'll be ready in a minute."

Everything took Aden longer than before the attack, but she tried to hurry. She had her finger around the last button when she heard a commotion in the studio.

Dressed and ready to leave, Aden came out to find Caleb pacing back and forth. "Caleb, what are you doing here?"

The deep baritone voice was gruff as Caleb walked around in circles. "The better question is, why are you here posing for a magazine cover, and I wasn't contacted?"

Gretchen shot a glance at Johansson. "Why would I have contacted you?"

"I'm the star of the show," Caleb bellowed.

"But you're not the star of Aden's new life and adjustment." Gretchen folded her arms in front of her.

Scotty walked a fine line between assertion and confrontation. "Aden will be on *People Magazine's* cover because of her ability to rise above her attacker's attempt to bring her down. What have you done to help her?"

"Come on, Aden," Caleb insisted. "I'll take you home. I'd like to talk to you some more."

"You mean, talk *at* her some more," Scott corrected.

Caleb stiffened. "Mind your own business, Russell."

"Thank you for your offer of a ride," Aden said, ignoring Caleb's rudeness, trying to be polite yet positive. "Scott and I have some work to do. He'll take me home."

Aden swung wide around Caleb, took Scott's hand, and walked to the door. "Thanks, Gretchen."

"I'll email the photos from today, Aden. We'll narrow down the choices."

"Sounds good," Aden sang out. To Caleb, she added, "Thanks for the offer, Caleb. See you later."

CHAPTER FORTY-TWO

"One last task," Aden said as she took a deep breath. "The interview with the *People Magazine* writer." She carried a cup of coffee to the living room couch. "At least the writer agreed to come to the condo."

Scotty watched how slowly she sat down. "Are you sure you're up to this?"

As Aden got up to answer the doorbell, she responded. "I'll be sitting most of the time. The condo isn't large enough to wander around." She checked through the peephole. "Show me your ID, please."

The lady on the other side lifted her credentials up to the door. "My name is Paulette Mitchell. I'm with *People Magazine*."

Aden released the deadbolts and let her in. "Welcome, Paulette," Aden greeted as she took the reporter's coat. "This is my friend, Scott Russell."

"Nice to meet you," she said as she looked at Aden, then Scott, and back again. "Are you—?"

Aden did not want to explain her relationship with Scotty for the whole world to read. She immediately cut in, "Scott just finished his law degree. He's a lawyer," as if an occupation would adequately explain a relationship.

Wiggles danced around them and wedged her way between Aden's legs. Aden snatched the opportunity to shift the discomfort she experienced to the cutest dog in the room. "This young lady is my new dog, Wiggles." Turning to Scotty, she added, "Will you hold the fluffy one or put her in her crate?

"Sure," Scotty agreed and scooped up the fluffy one.

"I'm happy to meet you, Wiggles." Paulette studied Scott, then looked at the little dog and back at Scott. She seemed to mask a wealth of presuppositions, but she asked no more. "I am glad you invited me to your condo for the written part of the article. There is so much to see here." After taking pictures of Aden in the terrace garden and the dance studio, they settled in the living room for a deeper interview.

"Would Scott like to join us?" Paulette asked.

"No," Scotty started for a chair, placing him out of the interview circle. "I'll just sit over here. This is Aden's time to shine."

"That's very caring," Paulette said and smiled again. "Did you go to opening night, Scott?"

"Well—" Aden answered for him.

Scotty came over and sat down beside Aden but looked at Paulette. "Yes, of course, I was there. But I couldn't stay. I had to get back to Ohio." Scotty stroked Aden's hand and looked into her eyes. "I also went to the hospital." To Aden, he added, "You were still in recovery."

Aden forgot Paulette was there and whispered. "Like I said, I knew you were there, Scott." She tried to put the pieces of that night together. "Why did you have to go back to Ohio on that one special night?"

"Aden, I took the Multistate Bar Exam that Monday," Scotty whispered. "I had to get back to find out the score, follow up on job possibilities, … and, well, everything."

Aden squeezed Scotty's hand and met his eyes with hers but said no more.

Scotty stood up. "I'm going to get a cup of coffee and then sit right over there." He pointed to the chair he was headed for before the questions became uncomfortable.

"Thank you, Scott," Paulette said with a smile that looked like she knew a secret. "This is certainly starting out to be an interesting interview."

CHAPTER FORTY-THREE

On Tuesday and Wednesday, Aden planned to dance and exercise. She was still stiff. But she knew the only way to loosen up was to move.

"Come here, Skeeter," Scotty said with a jar in his hand.

"What is that stuff?" Aden asked when he opened the container. Surprisingly, no aroma escaped.

Wiggles twisted and tried to wedge her way between the attention Scotty was giving and Aden's magical touch. She would have put her little nose in the jar, but Scotty was too fast for her. Scotty waved the jar around like an orchestra conductor directing the William Tell Overture.

"Wiggles," Aden called with a laugh, "come here for your lovin'. Janna will be here in a minute for your walk."

Aden patted her lap to encourage the fluffy pup to jump up. With one grand leap, the cockapoo landed in her lap and licked her face. Aden scratched behind the little dog's ears and across her nose until the doorbell rang.

"I'll let her in," Scotty volunteered. With ample caution, he checked through the peephole and opened the door. "Janna, come in. I'll get Wiggle's harness and leash, and she'll be ready to go."

Janna inched into the condo and waited. "Hi, Miss Malloy. How are you doing today?"

"Janna, call me Aden. I'm only a few years older than you."

"Yes, ma'am … Aden."

"My grandmother is ma'am, Janna," Aden said with laughing blue eyes as Janna wrapped the leash around her hand. "Bye," Aden called after them.

Scotty put his arm around Aden's shoulder. "Let me rub this pretty blue stuff into your legs. It should help." Scotty scooped out a little dab and rubbed the cool cream into Aden's muscles. His touch was both strong and gentle.

Tears again threatened her eyes as Scotty's massage reached all the way to her memories. It was the December they were both fifteen. She was to dance the Sugar Plum fairy part of the Nutcracker on that Sunday afternoon.

"Scotty, let's go ice skating," she remembered coaxing. And that's where the problem began. Aden was good on skates, but the ten-year-old boy in the red stocking cap who darted in front of them wasn't. She winched when she remembered how hard the ice felt when she landed on the rink.

"Are you okay?" Scotty looked up as he rubbed in the blue stuff.

"I was remembering," she whispered.

"Is your throat sore?" Scoot looked at Aden intently. "You were whispering again."

"It's okay." She touched Scotty's hand. "I was thinking of the time that kid knocked us down on the ice rink, and the blade of his skating boot cut my leg just two days before I was to dance the Nutcracker."

"But you did dance that performance, Skeeter."

Aden ran her fingertips over the faint scar just above her right ankle. "That's because you bandaged it expertly. There's hardly a mark." She had nearly forgotten about it.

"It looks like your ortho surgeon didn't leave much of a seam this time, either." Scotty patted her leg, then put the lid back on the jar.

They danced and exercised in Aden's apartment studio for hours that day. Aden continued rehearsing the words to *Honeysuckle Rose*, lip-syncing every lyric. While she danced, Scotty sat in the garden, transposing some music to a lower key.

When the phone rang, Aden jumped. "Hi, Bobbie."

"Just a heads up, Aden," Bobbette began with a giggle. "The Waist Knots are selling fast. There is a little hitch. It's hard to get grommets for the cinch style."

"That's a problem but maybe a good problem." Aden's mind scattered in many directions, from worries about the business growing too fast to the thrill of it growing at all. "It's great that the belts are selling. Do you have any idea why there are no grommets?"

"Supply line failure?" Bobbie guessed. "Never mind that. I can work super-strong buttonhole stitches if I can't get the grommets. You should know in case someone asks you about it in one of your interviews. It's solvable … different, but solvable."

"Thanks, Bobbie." Aden hung up. *That's life, different but solvable.* As Aden tried to understand why there were so many detours in her road, Scotty came in from her garden.

"What do you think, Aden?" Scotty walked over to her digital piano and sat down. His playing of the Clavinova was masterful, with full chords and expansive runs.

"That's beautiful, Scotty. Let me try out the range." Aden put her hand on his shoulder and hummed the beginning bars of the song she knew so well. *"When first I met you, my Honeysuckle rose."* Her voice was deep and soft, but the underlying breath and tone were stronger than she expected. It was hard for her to believe she could sing a little that she felt giddy. At a louder volume, she sang out, *"Why you chose me, only heaven knows."*

Scotty leaped up and swung her around the room. "Skeeter, it sounds amazing."

"Scotty, that's perfect. Email it to Randolph today." Aden was thrilled and insistent at the same time.

"I will. I promise." Scotty sat back down at the piano. "I know you'll have to be careful and not overdo. But do you think you could try *Like the Rose*? I'll sing it with you if you want."

"Would you? Yes."

Scotty played a short introduction while Aden looked over his shoulder at the words and music, he had scratched out on staff paper.

Aden melted into the melody that stuck in her heart and lifted her above her sore back and strained throat. Yes, God had found a way.

Like the Rose

Honeysuckle Rose

CHAPTER FORTY-FOUR

Carl Fritz called earlier in the week. "Aden, would you join me on my radio program? I am impressed with your positive attitude and know my listeners would benefit from your story."

"I'm not always positive, Carl," Aden confessed, even though it stung a little to admit it.

Carl was insistent. "When you and I talk in the building, I hear a young woman who nearly died and had her dream interrupted. Aden, you had more adjustments to deal with than most of us have in a lifetime. My listeners would like to hear how you do it."

Aden was silent. She didn't believe she was someone to emulate. And she didn't speak positively about her injuries and limitations all the time. "Carl, I will go on your show if I can be totally honest."

Carl's voice had a little chuckle in it. "I wouldn't want it any other way."

"Thanks." She asserted, "I would like to bring some soft, back support belts with me. Your radio audience won't see them, but I can describe the belts better if they're right in front of me."

"Aden, if you can come and tape a segment to be aired later, you can bring your piano, your barbells, and your pet dog."

"You've met Wiggles?" she asked as the little fur-baby jumped up and nuzzled under Aden's arm.

"I sure did. Your dog walker, Janna Russo, on the fifth floor, introduced me to your pile of curly hair the other day."

"Then, I'll be there," she added. "But I won't bring Wiggles. She would try to take over the interview."

"Okay, great." Carl's voice sounded energized. "You are lucky there's a college student living with her parents in our building who wants to earn extra money. For the interview, I would like you to meet me at the WBKR studio on Forty-Second Street at 1 p.m. tomorrow. Please come get there a little before one."

"I'll be there." As soon as she hung up, she wondered if she had made the right decision.

####

The next day, Aden and Scotty had lunch at Lindy's. With it right around the corner, Aden thought it felt safe.

Scotty loved the food they delivered to Aden's condo the night he arrived. And Aden always enjoyed each entre. She could eat from their menu every day and not tire of it.

As Aden struggled to sit down and find a comfortable position, the server took her cane and parked it in the corner near her table.

"I'll get this out of your way, Aden," the server offered but didn't wait for Aden to agree. "The walking stick is beautiful."

Moving the cane made Aden feel helpless. Having it out of her reach allowed someone else to determine when she could move around the room.

Aden ordered a quiche with a tossed green salad. Scotty chose corned beef and Swiss cheese on pumpernickel, with sauerkraut and Russian dressing. It was topped with delicious-smelling French fries.

"How can you eat all that?" Aden asked with a laugh.

Scotty shrugged. "I don't have to stay svelte and gorgeous like you do, my beauty."

"Ah," she chuckled, "you can get fat and soft."

"If I keep dancing with you for hours each day," he sipped on his coffee, "I may need more food than I ordered."

"I guess you're right. You don't nibble on my carrot sticks or rice cakes throughout the day." Aden sat back when their food was brought to the table. The food looked good, but Aden was anxious.

"What's wrong, Skeeter?"

"Scotty," Aden sighed deeply, "I don't know what I'm going to say on Carl's program. It will be a longer interview than the two TV spots. Direct questions sometimes stump me."

Scotty placed his silverware beside his plate. "I never noticed you hesitating before speaking."

"I've thought about it," Aden said with a distant whisper. "Do you remember, Mrs. Henry, our sixth-grade teacher?"

"Sure," Scotty agreed.

"The principal, Mrs. Barber, asked me to help in her office after lunch, doing some filing. I was thrilled. Of course, I said, yes. I didn't think to tell Mrs. Henry. I assumed, if the principal needed me in the office, she took precedence over the teacher."

Scotty nodded. "I would have thought the same thing."

"When I got back to class, Mrs. Henry yelled at me the moment I got into the classroom. 'Who do you think you are?' Scotty, I was eleven. All I knew was that I was Aden Malloy. But I made up my mind, I'd figure out who I was. The next time someone asked, I wouldn't be speechless. I'd have an answer."

Scotty reached across the table and took her hand. "Just relax while Carl is interviewing you. When he asks a question, re-word it in a way you are comfortable and answer your newly created question."

"I can do that," Aden said as she dug into her hot quiche. The eggs with cheese and the accompanying green salad with romaine lettuce and nuts were delicious. As to the interview, suddenly, she had a plan.

CHAPTER FORTY-FIVE

After their meal, they walked over to the radio studio. Walking that far was still hard for Aden, but it was a beautiful day. She felt herself move a little faster, and that was good. Clinging to Scotty's arm, she moved in closer to him. "Being able to walk around before the snow begins to fly in a month or two is quite a privilege."

Pigeons swooped down to the sidewalk to snap up any crumbles people dropped as they hurried on their way. A bike-riding delivery boy rode by with his hands and eyes on his cell phone. Aden smiled as she watched him operate his two-wheeler as if he had a radar beacon in his hat.

The radio station was housed within the large building complex of a local television studio. Scotty held the door as Aden entered. Inside, the walls in the entry were covered with shelves, displaying a multitude of radios in various sizes, styles, and eras. Everything from wireless crystal set radios to 1930s and 1940s red and yellow Bakelite models.

"Aden Malloy," a tall lady in blue slacks and a white top greeted her. "I'm happy to meet you. I was there on opening night. You were amazing. I'm Trisha."

"Thank you, Trisha." Aden shook her hand. "This is my friend, Scott Russell."

"Mr. Russell, you can sit outside the studio and see the broadcast through the soundproof glass," Trisha offered.

"Thanks." Scotty followed Aden to two chairs just outside the studio. Leaning down to her, he whispered, "Just remember what we talked about. You will do fine."

"Carl is finishing up a phone call," Trisha said. "You two can sit on this side of the glass until Carl is ready for you." She smiled and excused herself.

After they sat down, Scotty took Aden's hand but said nothing. His only message was that he was nearby as he massaged her hand with his thumb.

"Aden," Carl greeted as he burst out of the soundproof studio. "Come on in. Let's make good radio."

"This is my friend, Scott Russell," Aden introduced them. "He'll wait out here and cheer me on, silently."

"Nice meeting you." Carl extended his hand. "I've seen you around the condo building."

"I've been there a couple of days." Scotty reluctantly let go of Aden's fingers to shake Carl's hand. Sitting down, he leaned his elbows on his knees.

Carl led Aden into the studio and made sure she was comfortably placed behind the second microphone. "I have a real treat," Carl announced to his audience when the timer on his desk began. "My guest is Aden Malloy, the star of the Broadway hit, *Honeysuckle Rose*. Welcome."

"Thank you, Carl." She took a deep breath and prepared for Carl to begin.

Carl leaned into his microphone. "Tell me how this Ohio girl got to New York City."

Aden hesitated a second and thought about what Scotty had said. "How I got to New York? That is a many-pronged question, Carl. I imagine there are many Buckeyes here in the city. I'll answer it with a little history. I took dance lessons as a child and voice training in high school. In school, we presented a musical every year. I sang in each one, graduating from the chorus to the lead. I knew what I wanted to do, sing on Broadway. My mom's college roommate lived in the city, so I stayed with her and her husband when I first came to New York." Aden paused again and added, "Thank you, Valery and Herb," then she continued. "After I finished acting classes and a few commercials, I auditioned for *Honeysuckle*."

Carl nodded a knowing smile. "So, being in a musical comedy on Broadway has been your dream since you were a child."

"For as long as I can remember." Aden smiled and looked for Scotty through the glass.

Carl paused and asked, "After the final curtain call on opening night, tell us what happened."

To Aden, it felt like her heart had stopped. What could she say? "You want to know what I don't know. I can't tell you very much because I don't remember. I do know that everyone had left the theater ahead of me except some of the cleaning crew." She thought for a moment and slowly tried to explain the details of her lost memory. "I went out the stage door into the alley, and … I was told … someone attacked me. I don't know who it was because I don't remember the attack. I only know about my injuries from what the doctors told me. The attacker cut my throat, nicking my vocal cords. My right calf was slashed, and he flipped me over a railing, injuring my back."

Carl reached his hand across the table, making a connection. "I know all of us feel awful that this terrible thing happened to you, Aden. Since it did, how have all those injuries affected you?"

Aden wanted to scream. Inside, she seethed. Affected me? I couldn't talk above a whisper for many days. The throat specialist said I shouldn't try to talk. I lost the entire top octave of my singing voice. The injuries to my leg and back made walking difficult, and I couldn't dance. I had to use a cane and a back brace. Everything I had worked for since I was a young child was stripped from me within a few minutes.

"Aden, we are all sorry for your pain and losses. You, and my wife and I live in the same building. I have watched you grapple with your life and find ways to overcome your limitations. Tell us about your Waist Knots."

"I have one on, Carl," she said as her voice lilted positively. "My orthopedic doctor said my belts could replace a moderate back brace. But they won't provide the support needed for someone following surgery. They are intended to help support a tired and aching lower back while you enjoy your normal day. I drew the designs, and Bobbette Carpenter, a gifted costume designer, made them. Olivet Department Store has ordered several thousand to sell on its website. They are also available on my website, www.waistknots.com."

Carl sounded amazed. "What a great idea."

Aden smoothed the belt and smiled. "The one I'm wearing is a cinch, peasant-style belt. It's wide enough to protect the injured, painful area of my back and strong enough to tighten it to meet my needs. The grommets for threading the cord are sailboat strength, and the fabric is strong enough to suspend Peter Pan from the rafters. I can wear it anywhere and feel fashionable, not feeble. There are several styles."

Carl shook his head in amazement. "You had a limitation and designed a way to handle it that put you in charge of yourself."

"I will not be a 'can't do it' whiner. There are many things that some people can do that others cannot. There are also many things we could do at one time that we can no longer do, at least not in the same way. Do we feel helpless? Or do we get ourselves up and find out what we were created to do. Our creation is continuous, not a onetime event with nothing but death that follows. Think of a severe handicap. If you were an injured quadriplegic, you could still dictate emails of encouragement to others using voice-activated computer software. You can do something."

Pointing to the cane Aden brought in, Carl asked, "Now tell me about that wonderful cane you carried in here?"

Aden smiled with satisfaction. "Exactly. I brought the cane in. It didn't bring me. In my mirror, I looked like the actress, Rebecca Portman, in her wonderful film costume that included a cane. The cane she held was part of her elegant style, not an aluminum stick to hold her up."

"That is amazing, and you designed the cane yourself?"

Beaming with pride, she pointed to the cane. "I told Bobbette Carpenter what I wanted, and she brought this beauty over."

"It is stunning, like it's part of a theater costume." Carl folded his hands in front of him. "Aden, you have found a way to overcome your injuries. I'm sure our listeners would like to know how you convinced yourself you could do it."

"I will try to explain how I made peace with my body." Aden slowed a little, hoping to be helpful without being vulnerable. "When I feel depressed or grieving over my losses, I tell myself, 'Stop it.' Then, I think of something creative to replace the negative thoughts and fill myself with creativity. For me, it's belts and canes. For others, it might be crazy-quilt patterns or the next-best birdhouse design. Creativity is the basic building block of healthy thinking. For my back, I created Waist Knots. I asked for fancy walking sticks to conquer my hatred of the cane I needed after my leg was slashed. The loss of my singing voice has been the hardest for me to accept. An old friend is rewriting my music in a lower key. He'll also arrange the harmonies differently."

"Amazing, Aden. Thank you. We are all looking forward to your return to *Honeysuckle Rose*. And I am sure our listeners appreciate your honesty in our time together."

"Thanks, Carl." Aden looked through the window to see Scotty's face. "I have found the only way to handle life is, to be honest with yourself and others."

CHAPTER FORTY-SIX

Carl gave Aden a little side hug when they finished recording the show. "Thank you so much for coming in to pre-record this segment of my program. I know the usual *late-night* hour might not be safe for you to be out. A live show at that late hour could also be hard on you physically. Rest is needed for healing."

"Thank you, Carl. This was my opportunity to pass on some things I've learned." Aden paused and looked at Scotty, "And practice speaking about it."

The sudden sound of the studio phone ringing filled the soundproof space. "Odd." Carl stopped and stared at the telephone. "Since the show isn't live, there should be no call-ins."

Carl's producer spoke through the connecting microphone. "Carl, Caleb Johansson is on the line.

"Caleb?" Aden blurted out and motioned for Scotty to come into the studio.

Carl picked up the receiver and pushed a button on the control panel. "Caleb, how did you know we were in Studio B?"

"There was a rumor around the cast. I couldn't believe it. If Aden was on your program to plug the show, why wasn't I contacted?"

"This is Aden here, Caleb. Carl contacted me. I didn't reach out to him."

Caleb sputtered. "Aden, I know Fritz lives in your building."

"Many people live in our building," Carl answered, his lip curled in sarcasm.

Caleb sounded arrogant. "Aden, I have been a Broadway star for many years. *Honeysuckle Rose* is my show. I should have been in the radio studio to record the spot. We've had this conversation before."

Scotty's neck veins bulged. "The show belongs to the entire cast. And this interview had nothing to do with *Honeysuckle Rose*. Carl wanted his listening audience to hear about Aden's wonderful success in overcoming the limitations of her injuries. She has a right to talk about her personal circumstances and how to stay positive through it all. Unless," he paused, "you have some ulterior motive for controlling what Aden says."

"Who's talking?" Caleb snapped.

Scotty straightened his shoulders as his jaw tightened. "This is Scott Russell, Aden's friend and attorney. Freedom of speech is not a state law. It's one of our constitutional rights."

"Well, she can't sing, Scott Russell." Caleb's tone was mocking. "Advertising a show where she cannot sing because some of the notes are too high is a waste of her time."

"Thank you for your concern," Aden whispered sadly.

"Johansson," Carl snapped back, "as we all told you. Aden was not here to talk about the show."

Aden began to understand that Caleb didn't want to hear what anyone else had to say. It was easy for her to see his entire focus was on himself. "I am finding a way to overcome that vicious attack." Then she added a masked sting. "Scott is here to help me through other vicious attacks."

Caleb finally lowered his tone. "Sorry, Aden. A deserved that jab. But as the male lead, I should have been in the interview. Please remember that."

Aden sighed deeply. "If I am offered an opportunity to plug the show, I will remember your desire to be a part of it." Aden stopped talking. Caleb wasn't interested in what she was saying.

Scotty put his arm around her shoulder and spoke with comforting authority. "The place you should have been, Caleb, was in that empty alley outside the stage door. She was alone. Please remember that."

####

On the way back to the condo, they stopped at the theater. It was between performances, so no one was around.

"Hi, Chandler." Aden waved at the box office attendant. "Is anyone here."

"Aden, hi. How are you doing?"

"I'm improving," was all she could answer. She would be brought down to her knees if she talked about everything that hurt and didn't work right. "I wanted to get into my dressing room for a few minutes. I was taking my time in there before the attack. When I came out, everyone was gone. Maybe that will take some of the fear out of that space."

"No, Honey," Chandler answered. "They are all gone. I was going to leave here in a minute myself." He patted the smooth marble surface of the ticket booth. "Hailey would have locked the door."

"Okay." She started to leave with her arm through Scotty's.

Chandler closed the shutter behind the bared ticket window. "Wait, Aden. Someone left an envelope for you." Chandler slipped a note-size, powder blue envelope under the cage bars and locked the ticket office.

"Another note?" Scotty asked as he watched her open the envelope. He quickly asked Chandler, "Did you see who left the note?"

"No," Chandler shrugged.

Aden wondered what she should do. Was the message from a fan who may have seen her on *America Today* or *Morning Brunch*? Or was the writer her attacker? The paper looked different. With trembling hands, she handed the note to Scotty.

He pulled out a tissue from his pocket and wrapped it around the bottom corner of the envelope. "Hopefully, this will protect any fingerprints that might be on it." With another tissue, he pulled the note from inside the envelope and began to read. "You haven't learned. You thought I wasn't serious. I warn you, do not perform in the Thanksgiving Day Parade. This time you might not live through the attack."

Aden felt weak. Her injured leg buckled. Grabbing Scotty's arm, she hung on as tightly as she could.

"Skeeter," Scotty threw his arms around Aden as her body went limp.

"Scotty," she grabbed his shirt and buried her head in his shoulder. "He won't stop."

CHAPTER FORTY-SEVEN

Aden always jumped when her doorbell rang. Her stomach flipped over as she squirmed uneasily. Peering through the security peephole, Aden's fear turned to—*What?* Who could be at the door?

"Mimi!" Aden was so excited when she opened the door that she grabbed her grandmother's hand and pulled her into the condo. "I didn't know you were coming. Grandpa, it's good to see you, too," she added as she hugged her quiet grandfather. With her arms around his neck, she smiled. He smelled like the peppermint he always kept in his shirt pocket.

Her grandparents put their suitcases on the floor just inside the door. Grandma Malloy smiled as Aden's eyes popped. Mimi shrugged, "Well, we couldn't leave the luggage in the taxi, to ride all over Manhattan, from the Flatiron Building to Battery Park."

Aden smiled hesitantly, "I do believe you are right." She stepped back and invited her grandparents in.

"Your garden still looks beautiful. It adds color and hope to your condo." Mimi pointed to the terrace and smiled approvingly.

"Hope? I'm trying, Grandma." The color of the flowers filled Aden's heart.

Rosemary Malloy put her hands on Aden's shoulders. "Aden Rose, our family always spends Thanksgiving together. You live over six hundred and fifty miles away. But I wouldn't miss sharing the wishbone with you this year because of the distance. I could smell the bird roasting in the crock pot from Ohio. Last year, you came home. This year is different. Still, there is much to be thankful for." She started out to the small kitchen. "How about some coffee, Dear?" she asked her husband. "I'm sorry, Aden, you, too. You want coffee?" She shouted from the kitchen to the living room. "Now, don't get excited. We're not staying with you. Your parents have reserved a room for us in a very nice hotel."

"There's coffee in the carafe," Aden said as she started to get up. "Should be enough."

Her grandmother peered around the corner of the kitchen. "Now, sit still, Aden. I can get the coffee." When she returned with three mugs of steamy brew, Rosemary looked around quickly. "Your mom said Scott is staying here with you. Where is he?"

Aden placed the mug on an end table next to the couch. "He had a meeting this morning and will tell me about it later. He had to settle some stuff. Some sort of a surprise."

"A surprise?" Rosemary asked with raised eyebrows. "You seem excited about it."

"Maybe. But I don't really know what excites me anymore," Aden mumbled but couldn't help letting a little smile escape.

"Aden?" her grandmother asked as she and Grandpa Malloy sat down. "Is something wrong? I mean, of course, besides everything else that's wrong."

"Oh, Grandma, I feel like I'm going around in circles. Scotty is back in my life, and it feels right. I step out on the stage, and that felt right, too. I don't know where I belong." She rubbed her fingers across her forehead.

"That's easy," her grandmother said with a relaxed smile. "I don't want you to be all bound up in a love-fluffle. Comparing the love of the theater with a person's love is a false comparison. You belong where you were intended to grow."

"But, alone, Grandma? Scotty will soon go back to Ohio. I'm seeing Caleb with fresh eyes, and I don't like what I see." Aden looked at the playbill for *Honeysuckle Rose* she had framed and hung on the wall.

"Sweetheart," her grandfather began warmly, "you are our rose. You belong wherever you put down roots."

"Look at the cover of your program," Grandma Malloy began as she pointed to the framed playbill. "That rose has no thorns. A thornless rose means love at first sight. The honeysuckle is a symbol of pure happiness." She reached out and took Aden's hand. "One time, when you were about thirteen, you told me you were starting to have a funny feeling every time you looked at your friend, Scotty."

Aden was amazed. "You remember that?" She ran her fingertips over her grandmother's hand. "I know. I remember that feeling because it's never gone away. I feel at home when I'm with Scotty. But I don't know if I'm supposed to be at home in Ohio or New York."

"You just told me, Sweetie. Home is where Scotty is."

"But the blessing of achieving a lead in a Broadway play is not in Ohio." Aden rolled her eyes. "There I go around in the circle again."

CHAPTER FORTY-EIGHT

Scotty propped his computer on his lap that evening. After some planning, he began an email to Randolph Primmer while Aden worked out in her studio. Scotty added several attachments.

"I want you to know that I am not attempting to infringe on your copyright," he wrote in an accompanying note. "As a newly elected Ohio bar member, I understand your rightful ownership of the music. I am Aden Malloy's longtime friend and a lover of music. I've arranged Aden's music in a lower key. The doctor hasn't been able to tell her how long it will be before her higher register returns, if ever. However, pitching the melody in the lower register will make wonderful close harmony in some songs and a new sound in others. It is a wonderful arrangement for her. If you think you might like this new placement, I am sending you some music I arranged for your consideration. I've chosen one of the shorter songs from the musical as an example. Consider it a gift to Aden. In addition to one of the show tunes, I am sending a song I wrote recently for her. You will be able to see my musical interests go beyond the arrangements of other composers' songs. I look forward to hearing from you."

Scott Russell, JD.

Mornin' Mr. Sun

When prepared to send the documents, he thought he may never hear from the composer. Certainly, the turnaround time could be weeks. Some people never get around to reading their email. While Aden rehearsed in her studio, Scotty uploaded the music to *Mornin' Mr. Sun* for Mr. Primmer. For an example of his own work, he added, *Like the Rose* to the attachments.

Before Aden even finished rehearsing, Scotty checked his email. Primmer had gotten back to him already. *Bum. Primmer didn't give the idea much thought. Bet he's telling me off.*

"Hi, Scott," Randolph's email began, "Love your idea with the music. That will get Aden back in the show earlier than she may have been able to return. It will also give a whole new sound to an American musical. Thanks. Glad to hear you've finished your degree. I have another idea for you."

Scotty couldn't believe the next paragraph. Primmer had formed a question Scotty had never even thought about. Should he tell Aden what Primmer had asked? How should Scotty respond to Randolph Primmer? He decided to do the telling after Thanksgiving. Randolph Primmer's question, especially Scotty's answer, could change everything.

CHAPTER FORTY-NINE

Aden woke up before 5:30 a.m. on Thanksgiving morning. It would be nearly an hour and a half before sunrise. While the parade would begin promptly at 9 a.m. at West 77th Street and Central Park West, those from *Honeysuckle Rose* would meet near the platform in front of Macy's Department Store at 8 a.m. The cast would not be on a float. Their performance wouldn't be until about 9:45, following the high school marching band from Aden's school in Ohio. The Parade committee thought it would be an apt tribute to Ohio's newest exported daughter.

Aden was surprised. When she came out into the living room in blue plaid sleeping pants and a long-sleeve T-shirt, Scotty was already dressed. "You're up early. Did you come in and shower while I was asleep?" she asked him while rubbing her eyes. "I didn't hear a thing." Wiggles pranced beside her, her toenails clicking on the floor like a tap dancer.

"Good morning, Skeeter." Scotty looked up from his computer. "You were asleep, and I was quiet." He studied Aden in her choice of sleepwear. "Wow, you look great in the morning."

"Thank you, kind sir." She gave a little curtsey. When their eyes met again, Aden could feel a warm blush and stammered, "You stay right there, and I'll start the coffee. I picked up Danish last evening. Do you want yours nuked?"

Scotty followed her with his eyes and smiled. "I made the coffee. It's ready. And yes, I'd like my sweet breakfast nuked."

Four dings of the microwave later, Aden put the coffee mugs and small plates of Danish on the tree-slab-turned coffee table her dad had made. Aden called out from the kitchen, "Do you want some cream cheese with your pastry?" She laughed when she added, "How did you manage to get up so early? That's not the Scotty I remember."

Scotty chuckled. "New habits, right? Since I'm going with you to the performance, there is no way I will make you late, nor do I plan to be hungry."

"I hate to make you hang around Herald Square all morning," she apologized as she bit into the pastry.

Scotty stopped abruptly. "You don't want me to come? You know, for a guy from Ohio, the idea of hanging around a place like Harold Square, which I know only from movies, isn't a bad thing." He waited. "Do you want me to come with you, Aden, or not?"

She fell into his arms and buried her head in his chest. "What's happening? All of a sudden, we seem to be tiptoeing around each other."

Stroking Aden's hair, Scotty asked, "Does it have anything to do with this being Thanksgiving? Can we talk about whatever is bothering you?"

"I love Thanksgiving … at home. Except for Mimi and Grandpa, family isn't here, and you're leaving."

"You need a little positive emoji." Wrapping his arms around her, they snuggled down on the couch. "You danced every day this week, Skeeter. Since you're getting stronger all the time, you deserve a reward."

Aden looked up at Scotty. "Performing at Macy's is my emoji. Having you here is my reward. That's two."

Scotty gently kissed the top of her hair. "Remember, I'm staying until after Thanksgiving. And … what if Miles and Pat came with your grandparents for Thanksgiving dinner after the parade? I made reservations at Tavern on the Green for ten of us."

Aden couldn't believe what she had heard. "Ten?"

Scotty moved a little closer to face Aden squarely. "My little sister Marta will play her flute in the high school band. Of course, my parents came from Ohio to see her march to Macy's. And they are really excited to see the cast from *Honeysuckle* perform. With you and me and several others, that makes ten."

Aden sat straight up. "Scotty … are you kidding me? I couldn't take a tease that wasn't even true. Are they really coming? I just talked to Mom the other day. She didn't say they would be here."

Scotty wagged a pleading finger at Aden. "It's supposed to be a surprise. Aden, please be completely flabbergasted when you see them at dinner."

He pulled her close again. "They are all coming. My parents, Marta, and her best friend, Gale, who plays clarinet. Those are the extras that make ten. They got in late last night and hoped to surprise you. I decided you need something positive with all those threatening notes you've received. That will make your day brighter. I know you'll need something special to look forward to after the performance, or you will fold up like a lawn chair when the adrenaline stops flowing."

Aden popped him on the shoulder with a couch pillow. "Wait. Scotty, you said Tavern on the Green. For ten people, that will be way over $600. How are we going to pay for that?"

"We aren't. I am." Scotty rubbed her shoulder reassuringly. "I worked as a paralegal for an attorney during my last year of law school and saved all my money."

Aden sat up and stared at him. "Scotty, if you have been working, how were you able to take time off when you came here? You seem to have a very flexible schedule."

"You bounce up and down a lot, Skeeter. Come here." Folding her in his arms again, he began humming *Like the Rose*. "I finished my JD degree, passed the bar, and quit my job before coming to New York."

Aden wanted to sit up again, but Scotty's strong, soothing arms calmed her. She asked, "Why? Why did you cut all your professional ties in Ohio?"

Scotty didn't look at her and whispered. "I had to know. If I had nothing keeping me in Ohio—"

Aden's cell phone rang so loudly they were both startled. Or they were both caught up in a world of maybes where cell phones didn't play a part. While she reached for her phone, Scotty rubbed her back. His fingers touching her felt wonderful. It felt warm and comfortable. She wanted to stay connected to him.

"Hello?" she answered reluctantly. When she heard the voice, she looked away and spoke even more softly. "Yes, Caleb, we're up."

"Of course, *we*," she said impatiently. "I told you. Scott is staying here."

Aden sighed, "I'm sorry, Caleb. We're having Thanksgiving dinner with my parents and grandparents. Scott said they got here last evening. I haven't seen them yet."

"A party with the cast tonight?" Her brow knitted. "Please, tell everyone I'm sorry I can't be there. I didn't know about it."

She shook her head even though Caleb was on the receiving end of the phone and couldn't see it. "No. Hailey was here to practice on Tuesday but didn't say anything."

"That sounds nice." Aden's smile was faint, but it was growing. "I'm glad all the kids who don't have family in the city can get together. Um-hum. I miss everyone, too."

"Of course, you are part of *everyone*." Aden looked at Scotty, who couldn't help but hear her side of the conversation. "Why do I have to say it? Caleb, you know how much I've appreciated all the help you've given me. From day one, you were right there. I'm going to need your continued support. The music will be re-scored with the range lowered, making a new sound. I'm sure it will be great." She listened and nodded.

"Thanks. I don't think I'll be able to stop by tonight since my family is here." Aden felt Scotty get up and walk out into the kitchen. She wondered if there was meaning in his walking away.

Aden started rolling her eyes and raking her hand through her hair. "Caleb, I need to get ready. I'd better—"

She listened as Caleb added something interesting. "That's nice of you, but Scott is paying for it all. I couldn't ask him to add another guest."

Caleb would not let her off the phone. He kept talking, and Aden decided to let him rattle on.

She shook her head vigorously. "Of course, I'd love to see everyone, Caleb. The cast has become my New York family, and I miss them all. Mostly, I have been alone here for a long time. … Yes, everyone has meant a lot to me."

"You mean that tall, muscular singer in the chorus I had dated for a while when the musical was first cast?" Aden asked while Caleb went on about the singer's improvement.

Aden added impatiently. "Yes, he's a nice guy, but I found out right away that we had very little in common."

Scotty peered around the corner of the kitchen. With Aden still on the phone, he heard only Aden's side of the conversation. It can be dangerous to get only half of the available information. Scotty's expression changed from sparkling eyes and a smile to a dullness that overtook everything. Only hurt remained.

Aden started feeling uncomfortable as Caleb droned on. Wanting to get off the phone, she prattled on and said, "I know, Caleb. Thanks. You know I do. I'll see you at Macy's at eight." When she looked up, Scotty wasn't still in the room.

CHAPTER FIFTY

"Scotty," Aden called out toward the bedroom. "We'd better leave."

Scotty came out into the entry hall, buttoning his blue blazer. "Are you sure you want me to go along?" It was obvious he wasn't teasing in his usual Scotty style.

Aden's smile faded. That same uncomfortable feeling she had before overwhelmed her. Her voice couldn't hide her feelings when she asked, "You said you wanted to come." Pulling her coat out of the closet, she whispered, "Of course, you don't have to come to the performance if you'd rather not."

"It isn't that so much. I just don't want to get in your way." Scotty's voice was low. "I've invaded your space for several days now. Maybe you need to get some stuff done or talk to a friend without a shadow behind you. You have quite a job to do at Macy's today."

Aden didn't know why, but Scotty sounded defeated, sad. "Well, at least ride with me over there. Then you can leave if you want to." She struggled to clear her throat.

"Well," Scotty said slowly, "Marta will play in the band. Mom and Dad will be there. I should go and watch her."

"But … Scotty, are we all right?"

"Remember, Skeeter," he said, touching her hair, "I'm a nice guy, and I can't miss my sister's performance."

Aden's heart sank as she checked her watch. "We don't have time to get into this now. I have to leave."

"Like you left before?" Scotty asked as he opened the door for her.

Aden was so confused. What was he talking about? It was all so tangled, the disappointment, the loneliness, the pain. "Scotty, you left for Ohio State before I went to New York. You left me." She couldn't get to the bottom of years of wondering "what-if" in the next few minutes. They'd have to talk later.

Neither of them said anymore as they waited for the elevator. It was odd … and awkward. But it wasn't because Aden was angry with Scotty. It was because they had never fought before, except in play as children. She wished she could take his hand, but she didn't. Her mind flooded and swirled with song, dance, and a lifetime of living. From the song Scotty wrote for her, she thought their relationship was beginning to straighten out. But then it wasn't.

If You Were Mine

CHAPTER FIFTY-ONE

The snap in the morning air felt like autumn had nearly passed, and the cold weather would soon completely overtake the city. The trees had already taken on that boney look of winter. Most of the foliage stopped displaying brilliant colors when the leaves peaked in mid-October, nearly a month before. Aden felt blessed that a few of the colors of fall were willing to stay around while she went through her recovery. The crimson and golds that remained in recent days were like nature's colorful decorations for the Thanksgiving holidays. The evergreens proudly clung to their minty-green fragrance to add interest to Central Park. Paths and friendly benches beckoned Aden to stroll through the oasis of peace and forget Scotty would leave soon. Added to missing Scotty before he left, Caleb's push to get their relationship back to where it had been before it all changed was annoying.

Aden and Scotty didn't say much in the taxi. She enjoyed the passing excitement as people walked toward Herald Square. The colors outside tried to hold her together as her heart broke all over again.

Scotty looked at the growing throng and finally spoke. "Many of the roads are blocked. This is far enough. We'll walk from here. Can you make it, Skeeter?"

"Sure." It didn't look like a four-wheeled vehicle of any kind could get closer to Macy's.

It was decided. With the streets near Macy's Department Store blocked off for the parade, Aden and Scotty would have to walk the few blocks from where their taxi stopped. With two-and-a-half miles of public viewing along the parade route, there would be a lot of closed streets. The parade would kick off soon. They might have to tack their way like a sailboat over to the platform in front of the store.

Aden was glad her costume included long white tights under her ankle-length red skirt and white peasant blouse. The tights would help keep her legs warm. She wore the cinch Waist Knot, a perfect addition to the costume.

Scotty got out of the taxi and helped Aden with her shoe bag. "Thank goodness there's no ice on the sidewalks. It would be too dangerous for you to walk to the stage."

Aden took a few steps in the low boots she bought to keep from slipping. "I sure hope my high-heeled Capezio dance shoes will grab the stage. I'd hate to land on my face, my first time back in tap shoes."

"The guys who set up Macy's stage will make sure the surface is safe. You won't have to worry about that." Scotty paid the driver and wrapped Aden's hand around his arm. "I'll help you walk. You better not fall now, or we will both go down."

But things were different. Holding on to Scotty's arm felt stiff.

At the corner, they waited for the light. It was the 300 block of West 34th Street, a major east/west city corridor. The sidewalk was packed with pedestrians all flowing toward the parade. When the light changed, everyone started across the street. The light was definitely green.

Aden saw the traffic light clearly, and Scotty had checked it, too. Although they still didn't talk much, there was no need to discuss the obvious. When the throng of parade watchers started into the intersection, it was evident Aden wasn't the only holiday stroller who saw the traffic light give the signal to walk.

Suddenly, a man in a pickup truck flew around the corner on 8th Avenue into the middle of the intersection and headed north. Families with children, and young couples holding hands, all laughing and hurrying across, were stuck in the middle of the street. There was no sound of breaks squealing or skid marks on the pavement. The truck driver didn't slow down. Everyone heard the engine revving as the driver aimed his truck at Aden as she crossed the street. The driver didn't look back.

"Skeeter," Scotty yelled, pulling Aden out of the path of the erratic driver, who jerked and swerved directly at her. The truck had brushed close enough for Aden to smell whatever was in the truck bed.

Together, Aden and Scotty quickly cleared the intersection and curb. At the nearest skyscraper, he steadied her against the brick wall in the inset of a doorway. "Are you okay? Did he brush against you at all? Was my jerking you around a strain on any of your muscles?"

"No, I'm fine." She moved her neck in a circular motion, shook each leg, and twisted a little, checking for pain. "But, Scotty, what was that odor? Something in the back of the truck smelled awful."

Scotty looked in the direction of the speeding truck. "He's long gone, but the stink lingers, doesn't it?" Several people stopped to make sure Aden was all right. Most of them recognized her and called her by name.

"Are you okay, Aden?" a slim, middle-aged blond woman asked. "We were afraid he would hit you." A few others also slowed in their hurried walk.

Scotty looked from one to another. "Did anyone get the license plate number?"

"It was a New York plate," the man with the blond woman stated. "I was watching Aden and didn't see anything else." He blushed and looked away.

A twelve-year-old boy wearing a New York Knicks sweatshirt stayed around for a second. "I didn't get the license number," the boy apologized. "But I got a picture of a funny bumper sticker." He turned his cell phone around so Aden and Scotty could see it. "Give me your email address, and I'll send you the picture."

Aden pulled out Detective Alverez's business card and scribbled her own name and email address on the back. "Here." She pointed to the last line on the card. "Send it right here." Turning the card over, she added, "And send it to me, too, please. Thank you. In your email, give the detective any other information you might think of later, and she'll let me know. I will send your family tickets to *Honeysuckle Rose*."

"Gee, thanks. Got it," the boy said as he hurried to catch up with his family. Walking backward, he called out, "I'm Trevor."

Aden remembered the smell the truck had left behind as he walked away. "It's … I don't know." She started walking again toward Macy's, then stopped. "Turkeys. Scotty, it smelled like the mountains of turkeys Grandpa would deliver to families as a Thanksgiving gift from the church. I'll never forget the gamey, ammonia, or … rotten eggs smell of one of them one year. There was a spoiled turkey in the bed of his truck."

"You're right." Scotty put his arm around Aden's shoulder. When he saw Aden stumble, he said, "Skeeter, you have been through a lot. Should Hailey fill in for you today? Do you want me to take you back home?"

"No, absolutely not." Aden wiped her eyes with her gloves and set her jaw. "I will not be struck down or threatened." She pulled her phone from her pocket. "Just wait, Scott Russell. You have supported me almost every minute since you got here. Why, suddenly, have you tried to get me to drop out of the live Thanksgiving Day performance?"

"Aden, I am not trying to convince you to drop out. But someone did try to run you down a few minutes ago. It's just that … I wasn't there to protect you when someone flew out of the darkness in that alley. When someone tried to run you down today, I was here, but still, I couldn't protect you."

"Yes, you were here." Aden ran her fingers over the dark wool of his coat. "And you pulled me out of the driver's path. You can't stop someone before they strike out." She tried to think of some way to tell him but not scare him off. "Scotty, I can take care of myself to the degree anyone can. I have a keen sense of danger and avoid situations that don't feel safe. I don't need you to protect me from living my life, walking ahead to check all corners. But, Scotty," she hugged him so close she could feel his heart beating, "I—" What could she say? Things had changed.

CHAPTER FIFTY-TWO

Music from a full-instrument marching band filtered through the clear air. The beat was strong, inviting everyone to join in the march. Aden wanted to walk to the band's tempo, but would she be able to keep up?

"Scotty, the parade," Aden inhaled with an excited gasp. She put her phone to her ear. "We may have to run, but first, I have to call the police." She punched in Angela Alverez's number, her hand still trembling. "Detective, this is Aden Malloy. Someone tried running me down a few blocks from Herald Square."

Aden explained the speeding truck, the near-miss, and the terror she felt. Even while determined to live her life, she still could not hide the fear that hung over her like a shroud.

Detective Alverez leaped into action. "Where will you be? I'll be right over."

Aden swallowed hard. "I'll be on the stage in front of Macy's for thousands to see in person and millions to watch on television. The performance is in an hour. The cast is supposed to meet soon for any last-minute changes. The number had to be re-blocked. We got here early to make sure it fits on the stage."

"You will be quite a target at center stage, Aden. I can be there in five minutes. I was following a lead on another case a few blocks from you." Aden could hear the detective open her car door.

Aden looked east and west into the growing crowd. "Angela, you'll probably have to walk the last few blocks, depending on what direction you'll come from. Herald Square and the blocks near here are on the parade route and are closed."

"Aden," the detective said positively, "you take care of your return to show business. I will find you."

Aden and Scotty hurried another block over to Herald Square. Pressing through the crowd, Aden stopped, frozen in fear. In a fedora hat like a gangster of old, Harry Metzger sat on the second row of the grandstands erected for the best view of the performance. As Aden passed, Metzger touched his hat with two fingers and nodded. She was positive she recognized him. She had seen him through the peephole in her front door and felt enough fear to imprint his face in her memory for many years to come.

Scotty saw him, too. "Focus on the production, Skeeter."

In front of Macy's, the world's largest department store, Aden found the cast gathered around Floyd Blackstone and the director, Brad Rumskeller. Everyone listened intently for any details that remained unsaid. "Five minutes, kids." Brad waved. "Swallow your coffee, doughnut, or whatever."

When Hailey looked in Aden's direction, she bounced lightly over to her. "Before we begin, I have another note for you. Someone left it at the box office, the same as the other one."

"Thank you." Aden felt weak again, and she didn't like it. She didn't open the envelope but handed it directly to Scotty. "When Detective Alverez gets here, please, make sure she gets this."

"Will do," Scotty said. Studying Hailey, Scotty said nothing but dialed the detective.

"Hailey," Aden called after the dancer as she started to walk away, "why does Chandler give you the stuff left at the box office for me?"

Hailey turned with a semi-pirouette. "I thought you knew. Chandler Daniels is my father. Also, I've had a stepfather for many years."

Aden was shocked but had no time to process it. Floyd was talking again.

"You all know your places," Floyd bellowed out as if he had the use of a megaphone. "Any new steps were blocked out the other week. Aden, the new positions are just added fluff around you. Don't worry. Your steps are the same as we discussed during our original re-working of the number." He stopped and banged his hands together. "That's it. I have no more for you than … thank you for being the best cast in recent years." Finally, Floyd gave a dismissive wave of his hand. "If our director, the great and original Bradley, has no additional words of wisdom, relax, stretch out, limber up, and enjoy the parade until it's our turn."

"I couldn't have given better instructions." Brad put his arm on Aden's shoulder and gave her a side hug. "Our fantastic star is back. You all can practice with Aden a few times, like a soft-shoe rehearsal. Most of you have the same part, position, and placement. Basically, it's Hailey's additional steps that we added. The music is the same. As you know, it's the recording from opening night. When Aden is back, we'll flip the solo parts. I should say, Randy Primmer and Aden's friend, Scott Russell, are rewriting the arrangements."

Aden beamed as she watched Scotty's face turn red and light up with joy. When she reached over to Scotty, wrapping herself in his arms, she saw Caleb scowling at them. Scotty held her close as if nothing were wrong. She wondered what their time together meant to him.

Brad's tone became serious. "A quick word of thanks again to Hailey Daniels. She was willing to step up, step in, and step down, all for the good of the company." He put his arm around her. "Hailey has become the greatest Broadway dancer since Gwen Verdon. And I say, *Whatever Hailey Wants, Hailey Gets* … sorry for the play on a famous musical comedy song." The cast laughed and relaxed. "While Hailey didn't ask for recognition, Randy will write an additional dance routine for her. And we'll add her name to the posters out front, including her with Aden and Caleb in the star listings."

Everyone cheered, threw kisses, and joined in Hailey's joy.

Aden looked at Scotty and motioned toward the envelope. "You might as well hand it over. I should see what's in it this time. The writer isn't very creative. All the notes sound the same." She stared at the envelope and set her jaw. But she had to admit, that note was different. The color of the paper was white, not blue. And there was a stamp in the corner and a return address. Even Aden's address was complete, not just her name. "I will not be intimidated," she said firmly. She opened the envelope slowly, careful not to smudge any fingerprints. Pulling the note paper out with the tip of her fingernails, she read—

Dear Miss Malloy,

Police tell me I am a suspect in your recent attack. I assure you; I had nothing to do with it. I came to your apartment by mistake. Sorry if I frightened you. Today, I wish you well in your performance. Let me know if any of my associates bother you. I will set them straight.

Harry Metzger

"The police have nearly ruled him out as your possible attacker," Scotty soothed her fears. "It seems he may have told the truth about looking for another couple. But he was on the wrong floor."

"Can you imagine," Aden shook her head in disbelief "Harry Metzger was probably telling the truth. Scotty, what a relief." She handed him the note. "I believe Metzger for some reason. He seems too dishonest to lie."

Scotty's eyebrows raised. "Now, that is an interesting conclusion. I'll wait nearby." He put the paper in Aden's coat pocket and folded the outer wrap over his arm.

CHAPTER FIFTY-THREE

Aden turned when she heard the music grow louder as the band approached. It had a better sound than some school bands heavy on clarinet and snare drums. A high school mascot was painted across the bass drum. "Scotty," Aden shouted with joy. "there's Marta, second row, second flutist from the end."

"Yeah," Scotty shouted, whistling loudly with his thumb and first finger in his mouth. He put his hands together and clapped enthusiastically.

Marta didn't take her eyes off the drum major who maintained the beat. With the huge crowd cheering and talking, Scotty's sister would have heard nothing except the music the band played.

"Aden?" Chandler came up from behind her. "Are you sure you're okay out here in the crowd? I don't want you to re-injure yourself."

"Chandler? You came, too. How nice." Aden studied the ticket manager. It seemed strange to see him out of the theater. He was one of those people you never expected to see except in his own little corner of the world.

Chandler smiled but looked away and watched Hailey as she limbered up on the stage. "I feel like I'm part of the production, too," Chandler mumbled.

His expression changed to something Aden couldn't read. "Chandler," she laid her hand on his shoulder. "I hope

I didn't insult you. Of course, you're part of the team. The cast could practice and perform all day, but the actors wouldn't get paid if no one was there to sell tickets."

"Hailey really worked hard filling in for you," he said with an edge to his voice. It seemed that he had lost the celebration mood. "You could thank her."

Aden's jaw dropped. "Chandler, what's wrong? I've thanked her many times." Aden felt embarrassed for the faithful box office manager. Why was he misreading the entire situation?

"She said you did." He took a step closer to Aden.

Aden stepped back. She felt crowded. Why was Chandler acting so strangely?

"Two more parade units, then it's our turn," Brad called out a ten-minute warning, like when the lobby lights dim, warning that the intermission will soon be over.

When Aden turned back from Brad's announcement, Caleb stood there, his arms folded across his chest. "Did they roll you in bubble wrap, so I don't break you when we dance?"

"That's not very encouraging, Caleb." Aden's brow knitted as her jaw drooped in a rigid scowl. Caleb was certainly an inconsistent friend. In fact, he had been her boyfriend. Now, he seemed cold, taunting her.

"Sorry," Caleb's eyes fell, and his tone softened. "It's just that I had gotten used to Hailey in the lead."

"Since you adjust fast, I'm sure you'll get used to me again." Aden shuddered when she thought how close they came to being a "star power couple."

A little smile began to warm her face. *How strange life can be.* Major events in a person's life can change more quickly than the immediate circumstances. She might have continued to think that Caleb Johansson was wonderful if the attack hadn't happened. And Scotty would not have come to New York, and life would have followed a path that only made her shudder now.

Aden patted Caleb on the chest. "You'll be fine. I'm sure you'll reconnect with Hailey sometime." Then she gave him a narrow-eyed smirk. "I imagine you already have."

Caleb smiled sheepishly. "Maybe you know me too well." He gave her a quick hug. "You will be great, Baby Girl."

"Thanks." Aden watched Caleb rejoin the cast as he slipped his arm around Hailey. Inside, Aden thought, *Baby Boy.*

Aden felt someone close behind her. Not a stranger. But someone who could get close enough that she could feel his breath on her neck. It made her feel uneasy. It wasn't Scotty. With her peripheral vision, she saw Chandler crowding in behind her, near her face. He grabbed her elbow and squeezed. "Come with me," Chandler snarled.

It was only then that Aden felt the sharp point of a blade against her back. Her heart raced, and her breath stopped as panic overtook her. She looked around for Scotty. He was joking with Randy in a noisy group just a few yards away. *Scotty thinks I'm safe because I'm with my friends. I thought I was, too.* "Come where?" she asked Chandler. "Why?"

"Stay close to me, Aden." Chandler didn't sound like himself. With the knife in her ribs and his hand gripping her shoulder, he guided her away from the rest of the cast.

"That's her," a teenager whispered to the woman she was with. "Aden Malloy. I know it's her."

Aden smiled weakly and tried to signal to the girl that she was in danger. The teen jumped up and down, giggling. But she was only excited about seeing her favorite star.

Chandler moved in toward her ear. "There's an alley up there about half a block."

Aden could see the opening to the back street up ahead. The thought of being alone with an attacker in the dark, narrow space between the brick buildings sent another wave of panic, causing nauseous dizziness. "Why? I don't understand." Terrifying scenes flashed through her mind, resurrecting memories she was trying to bury. Blazing pain-memory in her neck nearly threw her to the ground, even though Chandler hadn't cut her this time. She choked on phantom blood dripping down her neck, not that there was any, but horribly remembered. When she was attacked, the agony in her back was nearly as excruciating as her throat and leg. She could not go through that painfully frightening experience again.

"Hailey worked longer and harder than you did." Chandler hissed. "You just flew into town and stole her chance for a starring role on Broadway."

Aden began to add it all up. Chandler was taking revenge for Hailey's loss of the part in *Honeysuckle Rose*. How could Aden settle him down? "You and Hailey are really close? She said you're her father."

He jabbed the blade into the back of Aden's costume. "Hailey told you that? We don't talk about it. I was a choreographer with a growing reputation as the magic feet behind some Tony Award-winning plays. Her mom and I divorced when she was little, and I moved back to Baltimore. I came back to New York about fifteen years ago. Hailey was playing the part of one of the children in a remake of *Annie*. I hadn't seen her in years. Wanting to be near her, I got a job at the theater. We talked and got close again. But she seemed embarrassed to tell anyone I was her father, the ticket guy, not the choreographer. You are making me relive my years apart from my daughter, which I don't want to think about. Watch what you say. This time, my knife only nicked your belt. The next time, the cut will be through your skin. I don't want to hurt you some more, Aden. But you have to stay away from Macy's until after the performance, so Hailey can have the part she was destined to play. She will be seen by millions."

"But—" As Aden began to panic, breathing deeply, the turkey smell returned. Chandler had to be the one who tried to run her down. "I smell turkeys." Aden tried to get him to admit to his second attempt to kill or injure her.

"Turkeys?" Chandler stammered.

Aden tried not to lose control of herself. "Did you bring your daughter a Thanksgiving turkey?"

"No. I delivered a truckload to the Mission near the theater. Mr. Rumskeller is always doing something grand for the little people. But I'm the one who has to schlep it around for him."

"But none for your daughter," Aden tried to empathize.

"Never. None for Hailey, my daughter. When her mother and I divorced, I never celebrated one more holiday with my only child." He was silent for a few seconds as they neared the alleyway. "Keep going."

Aden took one step into the alley. The same black truck that nearly ran her down stood parked along the side of the adjoining building. On the back bumper was a sticker decorated with a picture of Donald O'Conner dancing up the side of a wall from the movie, *Singin' in the Rain*. The words were, "Dance 'til you climb the walls." That was proof sitting right there in the alley. Aden froze and refused to take another step. "Chandler—"

From the multitude around them, a shadowy figure leaped through the air in the dim alley. The unidentified shape landed hard on Chandler, causing Aden to fall forward into something hard, yet cushioned, or … someone.

The stranger in the alley caught Aden as she fell into him. "I've got ya," the man said.

"Thank you," Aden gasped. She braced herself on the man's outstretched arm and turned. When Aden saw who had tackled her assailant and rescued her, she jumped into his warm and loving arms. "Scotty," she stammered. "You came. Be careful. Chandler has a knife."

With strong and jerking movements, another man pulled Aden away from the tangle of arms and feet. "A knife?" To Scotty, the man in blue offered, "Buddy, I'll get the knife."

"Thanks, officer," Aden gasped as she dissolved in Scotty's arms.

Suddenly, they were surrounded by more uniformed police and a few in plain clothes. "We'll take Aden's attacker," Detective Alverez snapped as one of the many police in the alley read Chandler his rights. A tall patrolman spun Chandler around and cuffed him. "Are you okay, Aden? The ambulance is on its way."

"No." Aden clutched at Scotty's lapels. "Not again. Not the hospital. I'm not cut or broken in any way." With her head buried in Scotty's shoulder, she pleaded, "How did you know where he had taken me?"

Scotty smoothed Aden's hair and kissed her forehead. "I turned around, and you weren't there. I knew you wouldn't walk away from the cast on your own. Then I saw your auburn hair bobbing up and down. When I caught up to you, I saw something shiny in the guy's hand."

From the streets behind them, Aden heard the piercing shriek of the approaching ambulance. "No, Angela. I am not going to the hospital. His knife didn't even nick me. We're about ready to perform."

Detective Alverez studied Aden's face. "I can see you're determined. Okay. I'll have to have your statement. I know it's Thanksgiving Day. Can you come to the station after your performance?"

Scotty nodded. "Our dinner reservations aren't until later. It should work."

The detective relaxed. "I plan to stay right here and watch all of you perform. I can only assure myself that you are all right by not taking my eyes off you." Angela offered Aden her hand. "Now, break a leg."

Aden pulled Metzger's note out of her coat pocket and handed it to Angela. "You might need this for the file. This time, it's not from my attacker. It's from Harry Metzger. He wished me well on our performance today. Oh, and you'll receive some pictures soon."

Scotty pulled out his phone and took another picture of the black truck. "Just for good measure," he said as he slipped the cell back into his pocket. Taking Aden's hand, they hurried back to the stage area.

"Where were you?" Brad threw both hands up in a surrendering sigh.

"She was kidnapped," Scotty announced with very little patience.

"What?" Brad gave Aden a hug. "Are you all right? Do you need to go to the ER?"

"No," Aden demanded, clinching her fists. She hurried to take her place in front of the chorus. *Gotta relax. My whole body feels stiff and sore.* Aden bent low, from the waste, like a dangling marionette whose strings have been cut, as her body responded to her familiar relaxation technique.

The cast struck a pose and remained motionless. Aden was front and center. When the introductory bars of the music began, the talented actors danced into their routine, singing to the music of *Honeysuckle Rose*. Unaware they had arrested her father or that he caused Aden's terror and pain, Hailey danced as the gifted professional she was.

Rather than grieving over her losses, or the aches and pains that remained, Aden focused outside herself, on the cast, the music, and Scotty. Gracefully interpreting the emotions in each word of the song, her arms floated weightlessly in the air. Even her dancing feet surprised her as they softly kissing the stage floor with sweeping dance steps. Finally, after recovering from her injuries, Aden was able to dance again, in her style, at her pace.

Few people would recognize that the movements were not tapped out as vigorously or as expansively as originally choreographed. The dance was more gentle, more graceful, different, yet better. While the entire cast danced and sang, Aden's heart reached out to the one who had always been there for her. When she opened her mouth to sing, the sweet melody streaming out was directed only to Scotty.

Honeysuckle Rose

CHAPTER FIFTY-FOUR

Aden was still electrified with energy from the exciting performance at Macy's. She felt like she was back where she belonged. Amazingly, her leg felt strong, and her Waist Knot helped support her back. When the music stopped, and the audience in the stands applauded, it would take a few deep breaths before Aden moved another muscle. She bounced down off the stage with a second wind, melted into Scotty's arms, and clung to him. She could feel her heart pounding as she pressed against his chest. It was all amazing to her.

"You were fabulous, Skeeter," Scotty whispered softly, making sure his words were only for her. Thousands of parade-goers were clapping, laughing, shouting, and enjoying the morning at the ninety-ninth Macy's Parade.

Still panting after the dance, Aden grabbed Scotty's lapels and whispered, "It was more than fun, Scotty. It was like life energy healing my body, patching the cracks in my jar of hope and my spirit."

Scotty laughed and snuggled her close. "You are home, Sweety. God gave you a talent, and you found a way to continue singing, even after someone tried to stop you. You created a way."

With her head on Scotty's chest, Aden savored the moment she triumphantly returned to the amazing world of song. "Oh, Scotty," she pleaded quietly, "don't let my life be stolen from me again."

At the same moment, they both knew that Scotty wouldn't be able to protect her from nearly seven hundred miles away in Ohio. Maybe Scotty would be staying, like Aden thought she heard him say.

Later that morning, after the Macy's performance, Aden and Scotty went down to the Midtown North Precinct on West 54th Street. Aden had been in the police station so many times that it was all beginning to feel comfortable. The smell of holster leather and burned coffee under the glass carafe filled the space. She stepped up to the Desk Sergeant and explained, "I'm here to give my statement to Detective Alverez."

"Aden," Angela greeted as she came out of her office. "Your performance was wonderful. Now, it's Thanksgiving. Come in here, and let's get your statement, so you can catch up to your turkey." The detective led the two into a room with a recorder. Nodding for the assistant to turn on the machine, she asked, "Okay, Aden, please tell us what happened this morning near Herald Square."

Aden briefly described the entire frightening incident. "On the way to Herald Square, a black truck tried to run me down." She knew she would have to talk about it even though reliving the experience succeeded in bringing her spirits down. Still, she told Angela about Trevor and the truck with the identifying sticker on it. "The boy is sending the picture to your inbox." But the near hit by the truck wasn't the only incident that morning. The thought of having to explain all that happened turned Aden's stomach. "When we got to Macy's, Chandler, the ticket office manager, stopped me and insisted I go with him. He had a knife and told me to go into an alley. Chandler's truck, with the bumper sticker the boy described, was parked in the narrow side street, so I refused. I thought I was safer out in the open with all those people around. Scotty took a picture of the truck, too. He's also sending you the picture he took. It will be another piece of evidence to convict the man who attacked me."

Angela opened a folder and took out two pictures. "I've already received and printed Trevor's two pictures. The second one was of a bumper sticker with the words, *Our Honeysuckle Rose* is back! A bold line was drawn through the name Rose, and *Hailey* was written above it."

Pointing to the second picture, Aden studied it and frowned, her brow knitted. "I've never seen any other stickers like that one."

Angela shook her head slowly, with her jaw clenched. "He must have been so sure no one would ever catch him that he had the sticker made and proudly advertised his guilt all over Manhattan."

Aden gathered up her coat. "Angela, I cannot thank you enough." She started to shake the detective's hand but chose a small hug instead.

"You kept your head and gave us more information than we would have been able to gather," Angela assured her. "Now, you two go and enjoy your Thanksgiving Day."

Outside, Aden hopped down the three steps at the entrance to the precinct, from the door to the sidewalk. She surprised herself with her agility. With her hands in the air, she twirled around in a giant circle, squealing, "It's over. It is really, finally over!"

"I see your leg has healed quite nicely. One would think you were just released from prison." Scotty had to jog a little to keep up with her.

"Yep. My leg is getting better. And parole? Yes, released." Aden laughed, clutched Scotty's necktie, and pretended to pull him down the sidewalk. "Tavern on the Green is in Central Park, about twelve blocks from here. Let's get going."

"Sure," Scotty agreed.

Even though her attacker had been caught, the chaos in Aden's life, from the damage Chandler inflicted, remained. And it would be there in many ways for a long time. Scotty watched her carefully. "Skeeter, you've had an exhausting day, from the highest highs to the lowest lows. A twelve-block walk would be too much any time."

Every taxi seemed to pass by on the street in front of them as they stood at the curb. Tire screeches, a few horn-blasts, and cabbies leaning out of their cab window yelling at the driver in the next car filled the city with the music of the street. Aden stuck her hand toward the traffic buzzing by and flagged down the first taxi that would stop. Once settled in the cab's back seat, she relaxed, took Scotty's hand, and watched the passing scenes of Manhattan. Regardless of the confusion in their relationship that she felt earlier, there was no place else she would rather be than close to Scotty Russell.

CHAPTER FIFTY-FIVE

Aden felt her body relax further as she and Scotty sat back on that Thanksgiving Day. The cabbie slowed as she approached an intersection, and Aden opened her eyes. Off to the right, Aden saw one of the many alleys in the city. Suddenly, she felt her breathing increase, pounding on her ribs. Instantly, she felt lightheaded and faint. There were tingling sensations around her mouth and fingertips.

"Skeeter, you're hyperventilating," Scotty said as he quickly reached for Aden's big tap-shoe bag. "You should breathe into a paper sack, but we don't have one. How about breathing into your bag?"

Aden tried to smile, then stuck her head into her tote. She closed her eyes and felt Scotty gently rubbing her back. When the anxiety passed, she lay her head on his shoulder. "Thank the Lord you were here, Scotty. I wouldn't have known what to do. The hyperventilating caused by anxiety would have caused more anxiety. I would have continued hyperventilating."

"Skeeter, I understand," Scotty said as he rubbed her shoulder and helped her relax. "Your anxiety will be there for a while, but I'll help you work through it."

Aden's anger mounted. "That man robbed me of weeks out of my life, the joy of doing the first few weeks of performances, and my singing voice." She sat up and pounded her fist on Scotty's leg. "I will not let him take one more precious moment away from me."

Scotty pulled her close. "Tell me what you want me to do. I'll do anything to give you some peace of mind. Remember when you came out of the police station a few minutes ago? You seemed to feel set free."

"That's it, Scotty," she said as her eyes glistened with excitement. "I want you to walk with me down every alley in New York City. I'll conquer my fear by facing it head-on." She laughed a little. "But not today. We're busy celebrating."

Aden's thoughts went to all the dark alleyways in the city. With Scotty accompanying her in the dark passageways, she visualized herself as an avenging angel, conquering the demons that lurk in the darkness. With a wide sweep of her golden sword, she cleaned out every sinister corner of the cavernous space.

"You're quiet, Skeeter," Scotty's touch was soft and comforting.

Aden traced the line of Scotty's fingers where they intertwined with hers. "Just thinking, I guess."

Scotty's voice cracked as he asked, "About things … or people."

"Oh, just everything. Conquering all the alleys of New York, singing with the cast again, seeing everyone." Aden's voice trailed off, following her thoughts around the city.

Scotty was quiet as they rode through the sparkling streets. Most stores had already lit their windows with the reds and greens of the holidays. "Was it hard to sing with Johannsson again?"

"Caleb?" Aden straightened and looked squarely into Scotty's eyes. "No. Isn't Caleb a jerk?" She smiled as she thought about all the times Caleb had shown his true personality. "Before I was … temporarily out of the show, I thought Caleb was the king of Broadway. Sure, he was arrogant and self-centered. But I thought all musical theater stars were supposed to put on an act of superiority. Oh, brother, did I ever get tired of him when I saw the real Caleb beneath all that phony shine. But I always respected his talent."

The corner of Scotty's mouth turned up slightly. "You two aren't a couple, not anymore?"

"Scotty." Aden gasped and socked Scotty on the shoulder. "I thought—"

"You thought what, Aden?" Scotty asked, then pleadingly added. "Say it." He grabbed her in his arms and pulled her close. "Talk to me, Skeeter. I just can't—"

Aden didn't ask him what he … *couldn't*. That might have made their relationship even more awkward. They had grown closer with every year that passed. That is, while they were still at home and even when he came to visit. Then something changed. "Um, okay. I thought … that we, you and I, were a couple." Aden looked away as she began to wring her hands.

"I had to hear that," Scotty admitted. "I have thought about you every day of my life. You are the sunshine that lights my path, and the rain that lets me grow. We have always been a couple. I love you, Skeeter."

"Scotty, I love you. You are my everything." Aden leaned up to her friend, the love of her life, and kissed him passionately.

The cab driver pulled onto a winding road into Central Park, where autumn foliage had passed its red and yellow phase, and light snow had begun to fall. The brilliant crystals of the tiny snowflakes seemed to cleanse away all the fear surrounding Aden. When they arrived at Tavern on the Green, Scotty paid the driver. The red brick façade of the beautiful Victorian Gothic architecture welcomed them as soon as they stepped out of the cab.

Inside the restaurant, the aroma was intoxicating. The amazing fragrance of richly browned turkey and the Tavern's own yeasty dinner rolls greeted them as they entered. Scotty had made reservations for a table in the glittering Crystal Room, decorated in sparkling gold and chocolate-brown accents. Deep orange pumpkins were arranged in pleasing clusters to celebrate the joys of Thanksgiving and harvest. Aden's parents and grandparents had already arrived. Mr. and Mrs. Russell, Marta, and her friend walked into the sparkling room, and the holiday perfume of savory food, right behind Aden and Scotty.

"Dad, Mom," Aden sang and rushed to embrace them. "Everyone, it is so good to see all of you."

"Aden Rose!" Mimi jumped up from the table and pulled out the chair beside her. "Come, sit by me. Your performance was wonderful."

Aden clung to Scotty's arm. Her eyes flashed with excitement. "Is there room for all of us? Does the staff need to find more chairs?"

"They have arranged ten chairs around the table," her mother assured her. "We will all be comfortable."

"Scott Russell?" Grandma Malloy thrust out her hand. "It is good to see you again. We missed you when we stopped at Aden's condo."

Grandpa Malloy popped Scotty on the back with strong, hardworking hands. "Good to see you, young man."

"And Marta Russell," Miles Malloy threw out both hands in welcome, "the flute player. You were great today." He turned to Marta's parents. "You two are doing a great job raising her. She is a talented young lady."

"A high school band is not the same as a Broadway play," Marta protested, embarrassed.

Aden laughed and hugged Marta with her hand on the teenager's shoulder. "Marta, you did a wonderful job. Just like a college degree is not a pedigree, all music is a blessing. Singing is what I do, not who I am. You don't need an agent's contract to validate that."

"This place is beautiful." Aden looked through the floor-to-ceiling glass wall and the courtyard beyond the dining room. By then, the snow had dusted every sidewalk surface, bush, and swaying branch. "The table is a good choice. We wouldn't fit into one of the parallel banquettes."

Thankful that the chairs faced the large windows, Aden knew she would be better able to see who was coming. That would be something else she would have to work on, not turning her back to a door for fear of who was creeping up behind her. The list of things to overcome was growing.

"What took you two so long to get here?" Grandpa Malloy asked as he picked up his coffee cup.

Aden didn't say anything. She looked at Scotty with a knowing expression.

"Aden has had quite a day." Scotty took her hand and kissed her fingers. "On the way to Herald Square, the attacker tried to run her down in the middle of an intersection. Then, her attacker abducted her when he failed to harm Aden with his truck. I saw the direction he was forcing her to walk, caught up to them, and jumped him. I held him for a moment until the police came. After all that mayhem, she performed in the cast presentation of the theme song to *Honeysuckle Rose*, a performance in which she did a magnificent job, as you all know since you were in the stands. After the Macy's performance, we had to make two incident reports at the police station, one on Chandler's attempt to run Aden down, and the one about the abduction." He took a deep breath, "And then she hyperventilated on the way over here."

"Just a normal day in New York City," Aden added with a laugh. Still, she wondered how her family would take the horrendous news. They always worried that Aden wouldn't be safe alone in New York. Years ago, she had convinced her parents that she would be safe in the big city. And she was. Now it seemed like her safety network was falling apart.

"Aden …" her father started in, his face stern and concerned.

"No, Daddy. Don't worry about me. Scotty and I have a treatment plan in mind. He's going to help me with exposure therapy. We're going to visit every alley in New York City."

"Every alley?" Her mother burst out. "Won't that take a long time?"

"Scotty promised," Aden pledged. "Every alley, regardless of how many or how long."

"I'll be here," Scotty announced. "We'll take a few alley-walks every week until we hit them all."

"Scott, thank you for being there for Aden this morning," Miles and Pat said in unison. Pat tried to hide her tears. "This time, it could have been a lot worse."

"She's my girl," Scotty said as he helped Aden remove her coat. "I'll be there for her."

Aden still wondered. *But how long would Scotty be here?* Aden had to put her mind in a happy mood. It was a holiday, and the danger had passed. "This is a wonderful place." She looked around the Central Park Room. "The earth tones and off-white colors of the woodwork are beautiful."

Mimi lifted her water glass in a toast to Aden's many talents. "Aden, you are an artist with many gifts: music, art, and design."

"You saw me on TV?" Aden nearly leaped off her chair the moment Mimi mentioned design. She appreciated that her grandmother had seen the shows.

"I love the belts, Sweetheart," her mother joined in. "I ordered one of the leather ones from your website. I saw you on both shows."

"Yes?" Aden stomped her feet on the floor in excitement and stood up. "This," she pointed to the belt she had on, "is a Waist Knot, too." Like a runway model, she showed off the belt made of gold elastic fabric, with a rhinestone-studded front and double gold buckles and closure. "Audrey Hepburn, eat your heart out."

"Rebecca Portman," Scotty agreed. "I like the sound of that."

A tall man with a dancer's strong physique crossed the room. "Aden," he greeted her with a hug. "I didn't get a chance to tell you how happy I am that you are back with the cast."

"Kevin, thank you. It is amazing. I am thrilled to be back. Returning to the show will even help me mend faster." Aden started to turn and looked back at the table where Kevin and others had gathered. "Are you here with your family?"

"Friends," Kevin pointed to the smiling group. "I'd better hurry back. My date doesn't like my table-hopping. See you next week."

"Make that two weeks," Aden said with a smile and gestured to Scotty. "Scott will re-pitch the lead soprano parts a little lower for me. Good to see you, Kevin."

As Kevin walked away, Scotty followed him with his eyes. "Someone you're close to?"

"I've been close to all of the cast members," Aden said with a shrug. "I dated Kevin a few times when we were just reading through our parts. He's a nice guy, but we have very little in common."

Scotty swept Aden off her feet. "Oh! *He* is the nice guy," he laughed. "Skeeter, I love you. I thought—" He kissed Aden tenderly with all the years of promises of things to come behind their embrace.

Aden was confused. "You thought what?"

"Okay," Scotty's face turned pink with embarrassment. "I overheard your side of the conversation when you were talking to Caleb on the phone. I … jumped to a conclusion.

I … thought you meant me when you said, 'He's a nice guy, but we have nothing in common.' I'm sorry, Skeeter."

Now, it was Aden who grew hot and red. She turned away from the family sitting around the table and spoke low. "But, Scotty, I thought we had talked. I thought … maybe … your plans had changed."

Scotty threw back his head, smiled broadly, and whispered tenderly in Aden's ear. "Skeeter, I've changed every future plan I have ever had in the last few days." He held her close. "I have a better name for you than Aden Portman. What do you think about a reprise of *Skeeter-and-Scotty?*"

The light from Scotty's eyes shone like moonlight on the snow and melted Aden's heart. She felt warm from the inside out as she allowed Scotty's arms to envelope her in love. She was finally home again. "Scotty, I know who 'I think I am,'" she whispered. "I've learned so much since the attack. And it all began when I accepted Mimi's garden. I know myself to be a child of the living God, and He walked with me through this nightmare. And, Scotty Russell, I am Skeeter to your Scotty." She fell into his arms.

"Wow!" Marta gasped. "Scotty, look at you two."

"Aden," her mom gulped on her coffee. "Has something changed?

"Looks to me like it has," Scott's father added as he jumped up and gave his son a hearty shoulder squeeze.

All the family members in the dining room cheered Aden and Scotty's embrace. With everyone around, Aden smiled but said no more. It was just his touch as Scotty took her hand that spoke the unfinished words. But that was all Aden needed.

"Wait a minute," Pat stopped. "What did you just say about wrestling with the alley ghosts? Scott, you're going to be living in New York?"

"He hasn't decided," Aden put her arm through Scotty's.

Scotty cupped his fingers under her chin and kissed her sweetly. "You won't feel smothered if Randolph Primmer gives me an amazing job in his music business? He offered me Junior Vice President, in charge of legal issues and music acquisition."

"Here in New York?" Aden leaped into his arms again. The excitement made her giddy inside.

"You bet ya." Scotty laughed, lifting her off her feet.

"Music acquisition?" Miles asked.

Aden squeezed Scotty's arm in pride. "Scotty re-pitched *Honeysuckle Rose* a little lower at Randolph Primmer's request. And … he wrote a song just for me."

Aden looped her arm around Scotty's. A cappella, Aden began singing, and Scotty joined in. Together, they sang out a new future.

Like the Rose

Honeysuckle Rose

Life Lessons Learned While Overcoming Crisis

1. Trusting God is the first and the last answer—the alpha and the omega.
2. In a crisis, there are two speeds, slow and hysterical. Slow down in order to speed up.
3. Welcome the prayers of family, friends, and church friends.
4. Accept the kindness of others. Their kindness to you fulfills their ministry to God.
5. Anger is a normal reaction to a destroyed dream crisis. Linger in the prison of anger briefly until you are willing to give the anger to God as a sacrifice to his love. Anger eats at your health, your energy, and your hope, like a rat in the corner of your anger prison cell. You have a right to be angry. But whose book of rights are you following.
6. Healing takes belief, belief takes trust, trust takes looking at life with hope.

7. Make peace with your body and circumstances. Replace your focus on pain, either physical or emotional, with a focus on others.

8. Help from others is not control. Help gives you the strength and new ideas to control yourself. Rewrite orders from others in your own words as directions for success. Then follow your own outline.

9. Don't wallow in darkness. Allow His light to shine on you. Light heals. Darkness steals.

10. Make peace with your limitations. As you overcome and/or replace your injuries or disappointments with alternative healing, you glorify God.

11. Do not entertain negative thinking or fear. Use thought stopping. Say, "Stop it." Replace those negative thoughts with positive ones. Sing along to music. Listen to audiobooks. Fill your mind and hands with doing something positive.

12. You don't need others to validate your ideas. Don't waste energy arguing with someone. Quietly go about being right until you hear another.

13. Deliberately do what you do not naturally do. Example: If you don't remember to go to the "Y" to continue strength building, put it in your appointment book, tell "Alexia" to remind you, and ask a friend to meet you there.

14. Accept painful therapy as a gift that will return you to yourself.

15. Refocusing through creativity can turn resistance into triumph. Doing vs. complaining. Creativity helps you focus outside yourself, drawing on God's creative energy. Since talents aren't who you are, they aren't your pedigree. They are what you do. A few talents are: good at explaining things, encouraging others, artistic works, speaking, singing, writing, including everyone, can make other comfortable. Those unable to get out, can pray for others. They can call young mothers, isolated at home, to energize their day. And a world of other talents.

16. Enjoy your successes. They are an outward testimony of God's blessings.

ABOUT THE AUTHOR

Doris Gaines Rapp, Ph.D., author, psychologist, educator, speaker, has written over a dozen novels and several non-fiction books. Her books are loved by all those who read them. Doris enjoys painting and drawing, including the covers of three of her books and the interior pages of one. She has spoken before many groups and has led continuing education programs for psychologists. Rapp has sung frequently and has written songs she shares with others. Readers continue to ask for additional books in her series, *Tucker McBride*. They love the characters, the history, the tales of adventure and Tucker's antics. While still a full-time psychologist, Doris directed the counseling centers at Taylor University and Bethel University. She has taught undergraduate and graduate courses in psychology at local universities. Twenty years after she and her husband raised their first family, they adopted two little girls. Now that all six children have filled the world around them, the Rapps enjoy their small-town life. Doris loves the stories that burst forth from her computer, and Bill still serves as a pastor and Chaplin. Her desire for all of you—"I hope you live all of your life."

REFERENCES

[1] *In the Garden* by Charles Austin Miles in 1913. (1912). In the public domain.

Music: *Like the Rose* Copyright © 2022 Doris Gaines Rapp. All rights reserved. Use by permission only.